Country Clubbed

A Piper O'Donnell Social Lite Mystery

by

Jennifer Vido

Copyright © 2013 by Jennifer Vido

For information, email **Cozy Cat Press**, cozycatpress@aol.com or visit our website at: www.cozycatpress.com

COZY CAT
P R E S S

ISBN: 978-1-939816-02-3
Printed in the United States of America

Cover design by Covershot Creations
www.covershotcreations.com

1 2 3 4 5 6 7 8 9 10

Dedication

This book is dedicated to my niece, Morgan Rose
Plisky. You mean the world to me.

Acknowledgments

During the process of writing this book, my father
passed away. For a long time, it was difficult for me to
find my voice again. If it weren't for the encouragement
of my mother, family, and friends, Piper O'Donnell
would have remained just a figment of my imagination.
To the Pliskys, Vidos, Bakers, and DeMaries, thank you
for your continued love and support. To my arthritis
class, thank you for making my mornings brighter. To
my plot sisters Liz Murphy and Denise Holcomb, thank
you just isn't enough. To my Jen's Jewels authors,
especially Jane Cleland, Elaine Viets, and Karen White,
thank you for your support of my site. For all of my
friends who read early drafts of this book, thank you for
the precious gift of your time. To Sally LeSage, thank
you for sharing life's ups and downs. To my husband
Durbin and sons Henry and Sam, you will forever hold
the key to my heart. Finally, to my dad...you're always
with me. I love you.

Hole 1

"It shouldn't be this hard to select an outfit," insisted the curvaceous blonde while surveying the mound of clothes accumulated on her king-size bed. Every inch of the flowery comforter was covered with bright colored articles of sportswear in various sizes. It was the first Tuesday morning in April, opening day for the ladies' golf season at the Woodlawn Golf & Country Club. Piper O'Donnell had spent the majority of the night tossing and turning in anticipation of the annual kick-off event. Now if only she could find something to wear.

It was hard to believe that a year had passed since the untimely demise of her wealthy older husband Charles. It seemed just yesterday she was contemplating which designer handbag to buy or which pair of pricey stilettos would best complement her outfit. These days, her go-to designer of choice was whoever she could find at the local discount fashion store. Much had changed in a short amount of time, especially within her social circle. Piper was no longer the doormat for her country-clubber friends.

Piper's fashion emergency was temporarily suspended by the ringing of the cell phone securely tucked in the pocket of her pink bathrobe. There was no need to check the caller ID. She knew exactly who was calling and why. "Hello, Tanya. And no, I'm not ready yet."

Tanya Vance was the best friend every woman wished she could have. A pleasant- looking Ohio farm girl turned country-clubber, Tanya had proven to have Piper's back. Though oil and water had more in common than these two, their friendship was securely anchored on pure trust and respect. Nothing could come between this unusual pair. Unless, of course, fashion was involved.

"I thought you said you'd decided to wear your yellow Lilly? What happened since last night that made you change your mind?" The petite brunette Tanya never could understand what all the fuss was about when it came to Piper's wardrobe emergencies. In her opinion, a white collared shirt and a blue skort were just fine. Yet by now Tanya knew better than to suggest that simple combination for Piper. Each respected the other's sense of fashion, or lack thereof.

"Five pounds. That's what happened. It doesn't fit," Piper replied as she patted her bloated stomach. "Evidently, I've been snacking way too much while watching reality television. I need to be more careful about what I eat and drink. Summertime is right around the corner. From now on, it's skinny margaritas, sangrias, and whatever else my favorite ex-housewife is bottling. Maybe I should start eating protein bars or something."

"Okay, we can discuss your eating, drinking, and shopping habits later. For now, we need to get you dressed and out the door. Go put on your aqua Lilly shirt and matching neon capris with those hideous stars. I'll be in front of your house in about five minutes. Don't make me wait. I need some time to warm up before we start playing," insisted Tanya. "By the way, it wouldn't hurt if you took a few swings as well." A not so subtle hint from the woman who prided herself on having the lowest handicap of the group.

"No, thanks. We each have a job to do and mine is to look good. And, don't think I didn't hear what you said about my pants. For your information, neon colors and stars are really in right now."

"Whatev!" Tanya couldn't help but laugh.

Piper giggled. "Look who's up on the latest lingo! You go, girl!"

And with that, the day had officially begun.

By the time the ladies arrived at the club, all the preferred parking spots in the shade were taken. Gone were the days of valet parking for Piper. Just being a social member of the club put a strain on her budget. Rather than bemoaning the fact that it was a long walk to the clubhouse, since it was technically her fault for being late, Piper took the opportunity to fill Tanya in on the latest gossip rocking the tiny suburb of Woodlawn, Ohio. Stuck in between corn fields right outside of Cincinnati, this quaint community was the hubbub of the area. A place where few secrets were kept and gossip spread like wildfire; no topic was too scandalous to report. Outsiders were always welcome, although not especially liked.

"Tanya, did you hear we have a new member joining the Ladies Nine Hole?"

"No!" The news apparently caught Tanya by surprise. She adjusted her worn handbag on her left shoulder as the pair continued to walk. "But...I'll bet Janie and Carolyn do. Fresh meat for them to devour. Who is the poor soul?"

"Her name is Danielle Barnes." Piper was delighted being privy to some inside scoop.

"As in State Representative Barnes's wife?" Tanya asked with wide eyes. It was obvious Piper had piqued her interest.

"Whoa! I'm impressed that you're so up to speed on the latest political players. Yes, the one and only." It was so much more fun for Piper when Tanya expressed a sincere interest in the day's fodder.

"Aren't there some shady doings or something sketchy going on with his cousin Jack Conway?" inquired Tanya as they headed towards the row of golf carts. They needed to find theirs and fast. All the ladies were expected to be warmed up and ready to go before the squirrely golf pro Jay Baker sounded the horn. It was quite obvious that Piper and Tanya were already behind. It wouldn't be long before Jay announced their tee time.

"Well, yes. As a matter of fact, there is a bit of a stain on his record due to his connection to Jack. From what the twins have told me, Representative Barnes may have helped smooth the way for his cousin. Rumor has it those zoning variances for the strip club were pushed through without any objections from the county. The newspaper didn't even know it was happening until after the deal was done."

"What?" Tanya shouted a little too emphatically.

"What do you mean 'what?' as in, no way could he be involved with a strip club? Or, is it more like 'what!' as in, what am I doing listening to the twins again?" Piper was confused.

Before Tanya had a chance to reply, they were interrupted by the sound of a familiar voice. "Hello, ladies!"

"Carolyn," they sang in unison. Carolyn DeWitt, a bleached-blonde woman with too many surgical enhancements to count, considered herself the queen bee of Woodlawn. Fake and flirty, she acted as if she owned the club. Dripping with an array of sparkling baubles, it was a wonder how she even managed to swing the golf club with all that extra weight.

"Oui, c'est moi! Back again for another go-around. My, the winter just flew by, didn't it?" Miss Snooty announced.

"Flew by?" questioned Piper. "I don't think so. More like dragged on. Don't you remember that horrific snowstorm, or shall I say snowpocalypse, we had? Hello! I was trapped in my house for an entire week. Where have you been?"

"So glad you asked. Florida. Isn't that where everyone who can, goes during the harsh winter months?" Carolyn never missed an opportunity to flaunt her worth.

"Not really, unless you're a retired New Yorker and the words 'early bird special' have significant meaning in your life." Piper couldn't help but needle Carolyn. The woman's self-righteous attitude constantly grated on her nerves.

"Carolyn," interrupted Tanya. "What's this I hear about a new member joining the group?"

Thankful for the reprieve, Miss Know-It-All replied, "Yes, as a matter of fact we do have a new player. Her name is Danielle Barnes, and she happens to be a good friend of mine. We've known each other since grade school."

"Why am I not surprised?" mumbled Piper. "Well if that's so, then maybe you can fill us in on her husband's business affairs? From what I understand, he …"

"Piper," scolded Tanya. "I'm sure there will be plenty of time for that later. By the way, have you seen Janie? It's getting late."

"Oh, sorry I didn't mention this sooner. I spoke with her earlier this morning," Carolyn reported. "She sends her regrets to the group. She's suffering from a wicked spring cold that just won't go away. But, no worries! I asked Danielle to join our foursome. And, she even volunteered to keep score. You don't mind do you, Piper? I figured it would be a welcome relief. I know how stressful it can be for you, having to add up all those numbers under watchful eyes."

"How thoughtful of you," Piper answered with just a hint of sarcasm. It was no secret that there was no love lost between these two women. From Piper's very first day in Woodlawn, Carolyn had made it quite clear that the two would never be friends. "Of course, I don't mind. That'll give me more time to text between holes."

"Piper," said Tanya disapprovingly. Texting was a definite no-no on the greens.

"I was just kidding. Oh, isn't that Jay over there? I bet he's about to announce the line-up," said Piper hoping to avert a lecture from her best friend. Tanya followed the rules all the time, every day, no matter what. Piper? Well...not so much.

"It's about time he showed up," said Tanya. "I've been trying to schedule a lesson with him for weeks, but he never returns my calls. He's the hardest man to pin down."

"That's not what I heard," quipped Carolyn with a devilish look in her eye.

"I'm sure that's not from experience." Piper couldn't resist. Her not-so-innocent smirk was duly noted by her so-called friend.

Just then, a tall, gorgeous model-like woman with bouncy red hair approached the group. From head to toe, signs of wealth and importance oozed from her pores. *This has to be the infamous Danielle,* thought Piper.

"Hello, ladies!" Danielle said with an air of authority.

"Dani," Carolyn said affectionately. "I'm so glad that you were able to join us today." The women embraced and then exchanged the obligatory air kisses. "Let me introduce you to our foursome."

"No introductions needed," interjected Danielle. It was quite obvious that she was used to being the center of attention. "Their reputations speak for themselves. You must be Piper O'Donnell." She reached out and grasped Piper's hand with both of her own. "Carolyn often speaks of your beauty and charm. And you must be Tanya Vance," she continued while doing the same. "From what I understand, you are the team's ringer. It's truly a pleasure." The woman's presence radiated warmth and kindness.

"The pleasure is all ours," said Tanya as if she were under a spell.

Tanya may have been hypnotized by this woman's penetrating stare, but not Piper. Something was off kilter. Piper could feel it in her bones.

"I have to say, we've heard so much about you, too. Isn't your husband..." began Piper.

"Representative Barnes," Tanya added hoping to stop Piper in her tracks.

Pleased the ladies realized the clout she carried, Danielle said, "Yes, it's true. I'm one of the lucky ones. My husband is an important man."

"That he is," Piper assured her. Piper could relate to a woman who knew how to use flattery to get what she wanted. "I hear he's busy these days with some new..."

"Bills to pass," finished Tanya. This game of cat and mouse was getting harder to play.

"From health care to welfare, my husband has his hands in quite a few pies." Danielle surveyed the room as if she were in search of some familiar faces.

"Isn't that the truth?" said Piper. Before she could corner the woman concerning the supposed opening of the strip club, Jay's sexy voice came over the loudspeaker. Out of the corner of her eye, she could see Carolyn sigh with relief. Evidently, Carolyn, too, wanted the conversation to cease.

"Ladies! Welcome to the Woodlawn Golf & Country Club Ladies Nine Hole season. It's wonderful to see so many familiar faces out here today as well as some new ones. If you all would kindly make it over to your carts, we'll get started." Jay gently nudged the ladies in the right direction.

Piper couldn't help but smile at her golf pro friend. If it weren't for his quick thinking, Piper might not be alive today. Who could have predicted that he would become the town's hero overnight, all due to his stopping Piper from meeting the same fate as her murdered husband? Of course, his much-deserved fame was now just a distant memory. Most viewed Jay Baker as just the hired help. Piper knew differently. He'd proven his loyalty, and for that, she'd always be grateful. Furthermore, it was no easy chore keeping the housewives of Woodlawn happy. That was for sure. Lucky for Piper, she had a confidante right under her wing. It never hurt to have reinforcements, especially when dealing with the women at the club.

As Jay went about describing the format for the day's play, Piper took a moment to contemplate the fanfare surrounding Danielle's arrival. Sure, she was the newbie to the Ladies Nine Hole group. And yes, she was a Representative's wife. But, something just didn't sit right with Piper. First of all, what kind of woman would allow her husband to condone the opening of a strip club? Secondly, how come Carolyn had never mentioned Danielle's name before? Carolyn DeWitt was the type of woman who relished the fact that her pedigree was superior to all those in Woodlawn. Being privy to the inner circle of a politician's wife would most certainly be a feather in her cap. Why then had she chosen to keep it quiet? What else were these two bosom buddies hiding?

"Let's go, Piper!" shouted Tanya while turning on the golf cart. "Stop daydreaming and get in."

"Oops!" replied Piper. "Sorry about that!" Piper jumped in just as the twins whizzed by. "I guess you can say the season has officially begun. The twins are raring to go, as usual."

"You know I'm not one to gossip…" said Tanya.

"But…." coaxed Piper. The mere mentioning of news fired her up.

"Well, the other day I just happened to be in the grocery store and I bumped into Carolyn's younger sister, Candace Bailey." Tanya made a point of lowering her voice.

"Candy is always in the loop on the latest dirt. If she's not dishing it up, she's somehow involved. Do tell." Piper was excited about the thought of a tantalizing scoop, especially when it didn't involve herself.

"Did you realize that Janie Vanhorst had hired a nanny?" Even Tanya seemed to find this to be a bit strange.

"No," replied Piper. "Why would she need a nanny? She doesn't work and her kids are in grade school. Although every time I see them on the soccer fields they look like a bunch of orphans on Red Bull. Are you sure she didn't say housekeeper?"

"Quite sure. Candy just happened to mention it in passing. Her scoop du jour had something to do with Carolyn's Member-Member pre-party. Supposedly, she's gotten her hands on some flavored vodka. I'm not much into those frou frou drinks, as you well know, but this one has my name all over it. I can't wait to taste it." Tanya licked her lips.

"Okay, I'm happy for you. It's about time you give up on beer and try something more girly. Now, what's up with the nanny?" Piper wanted details.

"Oh," said Tanya. "Janie claims that she needs an extra set of hands for when the kids get home from school. And from what I understand, the girl is drop-dead gorgeous."

"Wow! That's some news. I never pegged Janie as a cheater, cheater pumpkin eater." Piper rearranged the golf tees in the holder.

"What?" asked Tanya. "Are you listening to what I'm saying?" Tanya was struggling trying to navigate the cart while deciphering what Piper was really trying to say.

"Of course, I am. Don't you see what's going on? The only reason any sane woman would have hired a sex kitten to watch her children would be if she herself were on the prowl. Diversion, my dear. Janie's husband Ed won't have time to keep tabs on her because he'll be too busy chasing after the hired help," Piper said matter-of-factly.

The blank stare on Tanya's face made Piper feel as if she had just announced the secret to finding world peace.

Unfortunately, their conversation had to be tabled until later as the ladies arrived at their starting hole. Danielle and Carolyn were already there and ready to begin. They didn't look too pleased to have been kept waiting.

"Nice of you two to join us. We were starting to think we'd been stood up," said Carolyn.

"Reminiscent of your high school days?" asked Piper.

Danielle stifled a laugh which did not please Carolyn. Gauging Danielle's reaction, Piper's gut instincts went on high alert. This woman could not be trusted.

"Okay, I think we better get started," stated Tanya. "Why don't you tee off first, Danielle, since you are the newest member of our foursome?"

"Splendid, idea!" she exclaimed, thrilled to get the ball rolling. "I hope I can measure up to your team's high expectations," said Danielle.

"No pressure, Dani!" replied Carolyn. "Piper is here. Our expectations are minimal at best."

Before the bickering had a chance to take flight, Tanya took the unusual turn of engaging in some senseless chatter to smooth things over.

"So, Danielle. Has your return from Columbus been a smooth transition?" Tanya's blatant interest in Danielle's business caused Carolyn to make childish faces behind her back.

Danielle stepped up to the tee box and firmly planted her tee into the ground. Next, she planted a neon yellow ball gently on top. "As a matter of fact it has, despite the constant chatter from Gus's constituents. Just when one crisis appears to be resolved, the next one pops up. My poor husband. He's completely stripped of all his free time."

"From what I understand, he's not the only one losing his…"

"Piper!" shushed Tanya. "Let's be quiet now. Danielle needs to concentrate."

Piper couldn't help but roll her eyes. If nothing else, Tanya had a knack for keeping her friend in line. For just once, Piper wished she'd loosen the noose.

Danielle hit a very respectable shot which quite honestly surprised not only Piper, but also the other ladies. From appearances, Danielle Barnes looked more like a reality show housewife type. Who knew she could swing a club like a man?

"That's some swing," commented Carolyn as she approached the tee box ready to take a turn.

"With all the extra time on my hands, I decided to take up martial arts. It's surprising how strong and disciplined I've become. Sometimes, I don't even know my own strength."

Martial arts and a killer body? thought Piper. *This lady was full of surprises.* As if she were a foxhound setting out on the hunt, the thought of catching an artful dodger sent chills down Piper's spine.

Before they knew it, the ladies were approaching the final hole. An appropriate segue on the strip club topic never presented itself during the round which greatly disappointed Piper. She really wanted to get to the bottom of this salacious rumor that was swirling around the club. However, Piper did discover some interesting clues about Carolyn's relationship with her supposed dear, childhood friend. First of all, despite her claim of a common bond, there was a definite underlying schism between these two chums. If Piper were a gambler, she would have bet that some past transgression on Carolyn's part had landed her in the unenviable position of having to cater to Danielle's every whim. Something was just not right.

Secondly, it became quite apparent as the morning unfolded that Carolyn was on edge whenever Danielle spoke. It seemed as if she were afraid that Danielle was going to spill the beans. But, what could she possibly be privy to that would cause Carolyn such angst? Would Danielle risk betraying Carolyn's trust in order to score some points with her new friends? That would be highly unlikely, or would it? Before Piper could dissect the morning any further, she was interrupted by Carolyn's grating voice.

"Piper, dear. It's your turn. Would you mind saying good-bye to the little friends in your head so that we can finish this game before sundown?" Carolyn snickered.

Snapping out of it, Piper replied, "Only if you promise to share with us the secret for a lasting friendship like yours and Danielle's. I can only imagine the skeletons you have hidden in your closets, Carolyn. Right, Danielle?"

Taking the bait, Danielle said, "Oh, the stories I could tell. The Carolyn I know is nothing like the woman you two have the privilege of knowing today. We all have secrets that are better off forgotten. Wouldn't you agree, darling? "

If looks could kill, Danielle would have been six feet under. Carolyn was not pleased by her friend's willingness to give in to Piper's insinuation. It was obvious that allowing Danielle to join the group was not a good idea after all. Although as far as Piper was concerned, the party was just getting started.

After successfully sinking the final putt, the ladies headed to the locker room to primp for the après-golf luncheon. Danielle proved to be a very respectable golfer making Piper a tad bit self-conscious due to her own lack of skill. Since the sun was especially hot that morning, they were all looking a little drained. Nothing a little powder and fresh lipstick couldn't fix. After freshening up, the foursome continued on to the dining room. Of course, Piper's top priority was to secure a place next to Danielle at the table. She was not going to let this golden opportunity for virgin scoop pass her by. As if Tanya had read her friend's mind, she bee-lined it to the table in order to serve as a buffer. Not surprisingly, Piper was oblivious to Tanya's need to run interference.

"Why don't you sit next to me?" Tanya suggested to Piper. "You'd have a much better view of the ballroom from here." Tanya knew Piper's priorities. To see and be seen were high on the list.

"If you insist." Piper nonchalantly sat down relishing her unobstructed view of the ballroom. Scoring a prime seat made her happy, happy even if it meant being separated from Danielle.

As expected, Danielle sat to Tanya's right and Carolyn took the empty seat between her and Piper. The tables were covered in white, crisp tablecloths accented by daffodil yellow napkins. A modest sprig of flowers arranged in dainty glass vases were set in the middle.

As the waitress took their drink orders, Piper decided to jump in feet first.

"So, Danielle. Now that you're back in Woodlawn, any new or exciting projects on your plate?" From the corner of her eye, Piper watched as the others filed into the room in search of an unoccupied seat.

"Actually, I am thinking about resurrecting my old book club. We had a fabulous group of smart, savvy women. We met once a month with each member taking a turn to host as well as pick the selection. It was a fantastic opportunity to catch a glimpse of what was going on behind closed doors. Good books and lots of wine. What's not to like?" Danielle spotted a familiar face and waved hello.

"Was it a requirement to read every selection, or could you just come and socialize?" Piper was piqued by the prospect of testing her intellectual chops, but she knew her literary limitations.

"Piper, dear," said Carolyn quite condescendingly. "I don't think Dr. Seuss's *Green Eggs and Ham* is the type of book she's talking about."

"Well, of course not," Danielle butted in. "But if that's your speed, Carolyn, I'm sure I could make some adjustments."

Before Piper could make heads or tails of what had just transpired between the two so-called friends, Jay started the program. As was necessary for the beginning of the season, Jay reviewed the rules of play including scoring tips and procedures. After every round, the score needed to be entered into the computer which was used to calculate each player's handicap. The lower the score, the lower the handicap. This helped even the playing field to make the competition fair. Of course, this was done all under the assumption that the ladies accurately kept track of their scores. For some, like Piper for instance, that was a challenge. Too many distractions. From gossip to texting, there was always a lot happening. With a handicap of thirty, there wasn't any chance that she would be vying for the best overall golfer award anyway. As long as Piper had a good time in the process, she was content.

Before leaving the podium, Jay took the opportunity to remind the ladies of his availability for private golf lessons. As expected, this self-serving plug was followed by a few choice comments made by those who had benefited from his services. Not surprisingly, he appeared relieved when it was announced that lunch was served. Typical of these affairs, the ladies were given only two menu choices, a type of frou-frou salad or a crab cake platter, which made it much easier on the kitchen. Since the club was known for its scrumptious crab cakes, Piper always chose the latter. In her mind, allowing herself this simple indulgence was a well-deserved reward for tolerating her so-called friends on a weekly basis. The need to constantly prove her worth was no longer on her to-do list. As far as Piper was concerned, she had every right to be among the who's who of Woodlawn. Truth be told, she had earned a spot at the top of the list.

The ladies spent the rest of their time together entertaining one another with idle chit-chat. Danielle highlighted the congressman's latest accolades which seemed less than impressive to the ladies. Not to be outdone, Tanya recapped the *Dancing With The Stars* results show which was as important in her opinion, while Carolyn rolled her eyes with disgust. Evidently, reality shows were beneath her, although Piper wouldn't have been the least surprised if Carolyn sneaked a peek from time to time. Still, she reconsidered bringing up the strip club. That bit of juicy gossip needed the benefit of alcohol to really loosen lips. With nothing else on her agenda, she decided instead to broach the topic of the Member-Member Social.

At the beginning of every season, the men paired up for a three-day tournament which would determine the best golfer in the club. Like the Masters, the men vied for the coveted green jacket to be worn throughout the season as a badge of honor. Of course, this year's tourney would be a somber reminder for Piper of the demise of her deceased husband, Charles O'Donnell. Despite her loss, though, she wouldn't be hindered from attending the social event of the season. Where else could she get caught up on the latest adulterous acts being committed by her fellow club members? Who needed reality television when she had the real McCoy right here in Woodlawn? Better yet, who knew what would be divulged by Danielle with the help of wine or liquor? Piper, for one, was more than eager to find out.

"Carolyn, will you be attending the Member-Member party on Friday night? I hear the tables are almost filled up." Piper placed her fork and knife on her plate. She had eaten every last morsel of her scrumptious lunch.

"Yes, Don and I will be here. We wouldn't miss it for the world. Actually, he's playing in the tournament with Ed Vanhorst, Janie's husband. Mark my words, ladies. The two of them together will be unstoppable." Carolyn was known to brag about her husband's prowess on the greens.

"I wouldn't go celebrating quite just yet, my dear friend," warned Danielle. "I hear we've inherited quite a few good golfers due to the membership drive. Better wait and see what the competition looks like before you place any bets. Just a suggestion."

"Speaking of the "new" members, I realize the club had no choice but to lower its standards due to the tough economic times. I get it. Bottom line…the extra cash flow is needed, but for heaven's sakes, did we need to open the floodgates for every Tom, Dick, and Harry to walk in through the front door?" Carolyn was not used to rubbing elbows with the local riff-raff. This sudden influx of questionable individuals, according to her set of high standards, bothered her to no end. What she failed to acknowledge was that her disdain merely reflected her fear of financial insecurity. If truth be told, her own bank account had seen better days. Even some of her closest friends found themselves unemployed with mortgages going unpaid and daily living expenses mounting to unbearable limits. Despite the dire circumstances of many, Carolyn firmly believed the club needed to uphold its high standards. The *Members Only* sign affixed to the door was not an open invitation for anyone to walk in unannounced.

"Carolyn," said Tanya, "I'm not sure it's as grave as you suggest. Perhaps hob-knobbing with people from the other side of the tracks might do you some good." Tanya wiped her mouth with her napkin.

"You're right, Tanya. If nothing else, it'll give her an opportunity to screen potential hired help," suggested Danielle. She winked at Carolyn as she raised her glass in a pretend toast.

"I have all the help I need, thank you very much. Fine, make a joke about it. We'll see how funny you think it is when the pool opens and our 'new members' arrive adorned with tattoos and thong bikinis. From what I hear, even Piper's creepy neighbor who only comes out at night has joined. Mark my words, this is just the beginning," insisted Carolyn.

"Really, Carolyn. I think you're being a bit melodramatic. C'mon. How bad can it possibly be?" questioned Danielle. She took a sip of water and then placed her glass down.

Just then the conversation ceased as all eyes turned towards the door. "Speaking of riff-raff," said Carolyn, "look what the cat just dragged in!"

Hole 2

One of the club's newest members was the owner of the local liquor store, Rusty O'Brien, who was heading right towards the group's table. It was true, the club had seen better times, but the members had to face the reality of its present situation. Full golf privileges were few and far between. Companies no longer included country club memberships on the list of acceptable expenses. Every nickel and dime had to be accounted for in order to prevent Uncle Sam from knocking on their door. If the club wanted to continue being the beacon of the social scene in Woodlawn, it had to make some changes. And unfortunately, those included lowering its standards just a smidge. For some, the new membership additions were embraced wholeheartedly. For others, they were the kiss of death. Like it or not, they were here to stay. The alternative of having the course turned into an over fifty-five community kept most members in line.

It was no secret around town that Rusty was courting the recently widowed Piper. As a matter of fact, if it weren't for his keen detective skills, she might have spent the rest of her life behind bars. Like many couples, their relationship started off on an innocent note, as friends rather than lovers. Not by mutual choice, mind you. According to Piper, Rusty was her rock of Gibraltar, the friend on whom she could rely. As for Rusty, Piper epitomized his fantasy pole dancer. Her vibrant personality coupled with her quirky sense of humor sealed the deal. To each his own.

Their relationship had been moving along at a snail's pace, so Rusty decided to join the club in an effort to speed things along. Despite Piper's Barbie-doll appearance, she was a woman of high standards. Having been burned once, she now had a take-no-prisoners type of attitude towards dating. As long as she was happy in the moment, all was well. No need to take the relationship to the next level. That was how the two differed. Rusty was at the point in his life where he was looking for a long-term commitment. Of course, the sex was downright amazing. No surprise on that front. Piper knew how to please her man as well as herself for that matter. He'd never look at whipped cream the same way again, but now he wanted more than just her body. He wanted all of her. The question was …would Piper be willing to take the next step?

Rusty knew Piper would be dining at the club with her highfalutin' group of friends that day, so he deliberately planned to stop by to gauge her reaction. Was her reluctance to commit due to the aftermath of Charles' torrid affair, or was it simply the fact that Rusty could not measure up to her country clubber standards?

"Hey, Rusty!" shouted Piper while getting up from her seat. Turning back to her tablemates she continued, "I'll be right back. Please excuse me." She fluttered away ignoring brief hellos from fellow golfers seated at neighboring tables.

"I wonder what he's doing here?" asked Danielle as she lifted her glass of iced tea and then took a sip. Her raised eyebrows were directed at Carolyn.

"Scouting for Piper's replacement," mumbled Carolyn under her breath.

"Too bad I'm already spoken for or else I might volunteer for the position," quipped Danielle while admiring Rusty's godly assets as he headed towards the bar with Piper in tow.

"I thought you were done with that chapter in your life," said Carolyn. Disapproval was written all over her face. "Or is there truth to that old adage…it's possible to teach an old bitch new tricks?"

"Look who's talking, my dear. I'd be careful whom you cross. You never know what might slip off my tongue," Danielle challenged her.

"I'm not the one who married a man twice my age, darling," rebuked Carolyn. "We both know your courtship wasn't exactly the fairytale come true as you claim it to be. I'd hate for the ladies to know the true Hollywood story behind your relationship."

Piper hadn't been gone but a minute when a surprise guest sat down in her place…Representative August Barnes.

"Hello, ladies," said the tall, dark-haired man while surveying the room. Being a politician, he was always on the lookout for the next hand to shake. "Carolyn DeWitt. My goodness. You haven't changed a bit." Gus leaned over and gave her a quick peck on the cheek. "My buddy Don must be treating you well. Speaking of which, I've been meaning to give him a call. I need to get myself back on the greens. Too much time spent behind closed doors. "

"Gus, you've always been a charmer," giggled Carolyn. "It's so good to see you. I'm sure Don would love an excuse to skip out of work early. Do give him a call. You all have a lot of catching up to do." She made direct eye contact with Danielle.

"What a nice surprise, dear!" Danielle butted right in. It was obvious from the look on her face she was concerned about what he might have overheard. "I didn't realize you were going to be here today."

"Does a man need a reason to stop by and see his wife?" The pair exchanged an icy stare. Both sat rigidly in their seats as if they were complete strangers.

Just then, Piper returned to the table. Not missing a beat, Representative Barnes quickly offered up his chair, allowing Piper to resume her seat among the ladies. Of course, his casual once-over of her near-perfect body did not go unnoticed by his wife.

"That was fast," observed Carolyn.

"Sorry about that. Rusty just stopped by to confirm his tee time for the tournament. He and Johnny Vance are playing together this year. He just wanted to say a quick hello before heading back to work." Turning towards the newcomer she continued, "Representative Barnes, I presume," as she extended her hand in his direction. "It's a pleasure to finally meet you." His presence was too good to be true as far as Piper was concerned. Who better than the man himself to get to the bottom of the strip club mess? Full steam ahead, Piper was ready to blow.

"The one and only. I hope to have your vote in the upcoming election in November."

Feeling left out, Tanya chimed right in by saying, "You certainly have ours. My husband Johnny and I have followed your career quite closely. We admire the way in which you go head to head with the big dogs."

"I try to do my best for my fellow Buckeyes. If only I had more time to get things done. There are never enough hours in the day. Quite frankly, I seem to do my best work at night." Gus glanced over at his wife.

"Funny, that's exactly what I heard," added Piper as Tanya gave her a little nudge. Ignoring the obvious warning to tread lightly she continued on, "So tell us what you know about Peeps & Petals. That club just popped up overnight. Literally! Is it true that the owner Chad Freedom has some big time financial partners? Honestly, he must. Where else could he have come up with that kind of money?"

Not liking the sudden change of topic, Representative Barnes did his best to steer it in another direction. "I'm not one to get involved with other's finances." And with that, he gently prodded his wife to get up.

Like a pit bull, Piper dug in, "And how 'bout the zoning variance? I'm surprised the board so willingly allowed the opening of a strip club in the county. I also hear they've applied to the Liquor Board for a license. Really, is this the kind of message we want to send our youth? Next thing you know, we'll have drug dealers on every corner. Perhaps you can look into it for us. As our representative, it's the least you can do." Piper could tell by their body language she had struck a nerve.

"I hate to cut our day short, ladies, but my husband and I have another engagement to attend this afternoon. I'm sure you understand." Danielle was used to coming to the Representative's aid. Just another part of her never-ending job description.

Hoping to score some points with her friend, Carolyn added, "No worries, dear. We all understand the demands on your time. Thanks for being a part of a truly lovely morning."

With that, the power couple scooted out the door. They'd been gone less than thirty seconds went Carolyn let loose on Piper.

"What the hell were you thinking? Since when did you become the Glenn Beck of the club? For goodness sakes, Piper. We want Danielle to feel welcome among the group. Backing her husband into a corner surely isn't the way in which to do it. Right, Tanya?" Carolyn forced Tanya to address the issue at hand.

Feeling the need to play both sides of the fence, she simply replied, "Piper just said what everyone else was thinking. Perhaps her timing was off just a tad, but sooner or later someone was going to put him on the spot."

Carolyn just shrugged in response and took off towards the exit. It was obvious she was done discussing this unfortunate social faux pas. Damage control was her top priority. Having Danielle lash-out at her in retaliation was a foremost concern. God only knew what would come spewing out of her lips.

Realizing it was time to call it a day, Tanya and Piper headed towards the parking lot. The warm spring air caused their hair to gently blow in the breeze. On the way, they noticed a familiar face, the one and only Laura Wagner, getting out of her car with a tennis racket dangling from her hand. Hoping to avoid detection, Piper sped up, but to no avail. She'd been spotted. Of course, Piper had every reason not to want to engage in idle chit-chat with the woman. Laura was no more than just a passing fancy who had danced between the sheets with Piper's beloved, deceased husband. Sure, bygones were bygones. But honestly, what woman in her right mind would forgive another woman for crossing the line? Not to mention that horrid image conjured up in Piper's head of their illicit love affair was impossible to erase. Hopefully, with the passing of time, she'd make peace with her husband's indiscretion. Until then, she would keep the tramp at arm's length to prevent a possible mercy killing.

"Piper! Tanya! Over here!" Laura was stumbling across the parking lot in hopes of catching up with the ladies.

"Must we deal with this today?" asked Piper. She quickened her pace. "I think I have had about enough drama for one morning."

"Let's just say our hellos and be done with it." Tanya took hold of Piper's arm. "If you avoid her then she'll just keep on bugging you. It takes two to tango, Piper. She wasn't the only one to blame for your husband's affair."

"Yes, but she's the only one still breathing, so unfortunately for her, she's it."

Laura could see Piper's reluctance, even from a distance, but she was hell-bent on mending fences with the woman. If she and her husband Jim planned to make Woodlawn their permanent home, she needed to establish a social circle. Like it or not, Rusty was Jim's closest confidant. Their friendship took a major beating when Rusty accused her of murdering Charles. Once her innocence was proven, things settled down; however, their relationship was still on somewhat shaky ground. So unless she wanted to live under a rock for the rest of her adult years, she was going to have to do some major ass-kissing to make up for her past stupidity.

As soon as Laura caught up to them she said, "Hi, ladies. How was your golf game?" Neutral ground. It was the best way to engage Piper in a conversation.

"It was eventful," conceded Piper. Despite her feelings of resentment, she secretly kind of liked Laura. If it weren't for her philandering husband, she might have even chosen to call her a friend.

"We had a respectable start to the season," bragged Tanya. "And, *we* also had the pleasure of meeting Danielle Barnes. She was in our foursome. What an athlete." Tanya tried her best involve Piper in the conversation.

"Really?" said Laura. "Gus and Danielle are back in town? I thought they preferred to stay in Columbus away from us commoners."

"Do you know them?" Piper's curiosity was piqued.

"As a matter of fact, Danielle and I go way back." Laura volunteered.

"Why am I not surprised?" muttered Piper under her breath. *They're probably charter members of the hussy international club.*

Representative Barnes was no spring chicken. A ladies' man at heart, he had walked down the aisle a time or two or three. News of his scandal rocked the town when he divorced his last wife despite her heroic bout with terminal cancer. When she finally passed, Representative Barnes wasted no time in marrying wife number three, Danielle Keeler. Theirs was a whirlwind affair romanticized by the press in order to clean up his less than stellar reputation.

Tanya had had just about enough gossip for one day, so she decided to cut Piper and Laura off to avoid the inevitable who's who discussion that was bound to begin.

"Ladies, I hate to be a party pooper, but I need to get going." She glanced at her watch. "Johnny was expecting me back at the house around twenty minutes ago. I'd hate to keep him waiting any longer."

"Understood," said Laura. "I was on my way to the courts anyway. I have a lesson with Mike, the head tennis pro. He is trying his hardest to perfect my backhand. He says my game needs a little fine-tuning." She took a few pretend swings.

"That's not what I heard," Piper whispered to Tanya. Old habits were hard to break.

"Well then, I guess I will catch up with you later," said Laura. She searched their eyes for any hint of a possible get-together, but none was given.

Thankful for the reprieve, Piper began to walk away; however, the conversation was not quite over as far as Laura was concerned.

As a last-ditch effort she blurted, "Ladies, Jim and I look forward to seeing you at the Member-Member party on Friday." She headed towards the courts without waiting for a response.

Piper was disappointed to hear that they were going to attend, but she was not totally surprised. The entire membership was invited. And, it was the kick-off to the social season. Being newbies, Piper realized Laura and Jim needed to establish their place in the pack. She just wished it was with a different herd.

By the time Piper arrived home, she was beat. It had been a long morning emotionally as well as physically. Golf was not her favorite sport, but it served its purpose twofold. Not only was she able to get in some much-needed exercise, but also, it allowed her to keep tabs on her fellow club members on a regular basis. Today, for example, there was a windfall of information that came her way. This Danielle woman was certainly full of surprises. Connected was an understatement. Who knew she had some sort of relationship with both Carolyn and Laura? Twisted was more like it. If she knew Carolyn as well as she led them to believe, then she was privy to some hot, hot Woodlawn scoop. And if she had some history with Laura, then perhaps Danielle knew Rusty from his New York City days, too. The way things were heating up, it looked as though this golf season would be one to remember.

As if on cue, Piper's doorbell rang. Ever since her husband Charles had passed away, she'd been tempted to pack everything up and head back home. The only thing keeping her anchored in Woodlawn was the man at her front door, Rusty O'Brien.

"Coming!" she shouted while checking her make-up and hair in the hall mirror. Now that she was single, she needed to be on her game 24/7.

"Well, hello," she purred while opening the heavy wooden door. "Twice in one day." She couldn't help but smile. Rusty brought out the best in her.

"Well, hello to you," he replied while pulling her into his arms for a quick embrace. The two lovebirds quickly entered the house to prevent the neighbors from getting a free show. "How did you make out with the ladies? When I stopped by earlier, it looked as though the club was packed to the gills. Has the new season started off with a bang?"

"You could say that. Do you want something to eat?" She led him into the bright, white kitchen area.

"No, thanks. I already ate, but I would love a Diet Pepsi if you have one." He picked up a magazine on the counter and flipped through a few pages.

"No problem. Go ahead and sit down at the table while I get you one. I think I'd like some sweet tea." She opened the door of the stainless steel refrigerator in search of their beverages and rummaged around until she found them. With one in each hand, she walked over to the table and joined him.

"Thanks." He cracked open the Diet Pepsi. "So tell me, what did you learn from the ladies?" Rusty seemed to like being in the know.

"Well first off, Janie Vanhorst was sick, so we had a substitute player." Piper twisted off the bottle top.

"Really? Anyone I know?" He took a swig of his soda. It was just what he needed on this warm spring day.

"You tell me. Does the name Danielle Barnes mean anything to you?" She took a sip of her tea.

Caught off-guard, he choked on his drink and replied rather quickly, "No. I mean yes."

Piper raised her eyebrows. "Well, which is it?"

Rusty was quite hesitant with his response. It was as if he were calculating exactly what he should or should not say. "Isn't she the state representative's wife?"

"Indeed she is," Piper confirmed.

"Well then yes, I know who she is. Doesn't everybody?" he shrugged in agreement.

"Evidently, yes. Tanya and I bumped into Laura on our way out of the club and according to her, she and Danielle go way back. Did you happen to run in the same circles with them when you lived in the city?"

"No," he said rather adamantly. "If you remember correctly, I met Jim Wagner at a bar way before they hooked up. We both were single and living the good life."

"Oh, that explains why you've never mentioned Danielle before." Piper's radar went up. There was something not quite right about their exchange.

"Anyway, so what else did you find out?" Rusty was trying to move the conversation in another direction.

"Nothing really. I was hoping to get to the bottom of the opening of the strip club. I think good ol' Representative Barnes is behind it, but I have no proof." Piper narrowed her gaze.

"Why the sudden interest in politics?" Rusty looked at his watch. It was the second time he did it within the last couple of minutes.

Noticing his distracted demeanor, Piper blurted out, "Am I keeping you from something?" Piper despised playing second fiddle to anyone, let alone the man who occupied her bed.

"No," he replied, rather blasé. "I just need to keep an eye on the time. Did I mention that I'm training a new guy at the store this week?"

"Is business picking up?" Piper knew last year had been very hard for Rusty. Even the liquor stores had been hit by the recession. Customers still needed their wine and spirits, though they were cutting back big time on pricier items. Everyone was looking for a bargain these days.

"Sort of. It has its ebbs and flows. Actually, I was thinking of moving on." Rusty was hesitant to broach the subject with Piper. Better to get it over with sooner rather than later.

"What exactly do you plan on doing?" Rusty had piqued her curiosity. She leaned in closer.

"Well, I'm thinking of opening up my own private investigation firm."

"Really? Are you serious?" Piper didn't look pleased.

"I take it you don't like my idea?" Rusty was insulted by her attitude.

"Big man, it's not that I don't think you wouldn't make a hot P.I. It's just not what I would have pictured for you. What about the liquor store? That's your bread and butter."

"I know," he insisted. "That's why I'm bringing in a new guy to run things while I pursue this new venture."

"You trust him with running your store? Who knows? While you're climbing ladders playing peeping Tom, this guy could steal you blind." She threw her hands up in the air.

"I doubt that very highly," Rusty answered.

"How can you be so sure?" Piper was not letting him off easily. She stood there with her arms crossed.

"Well, for one thing, he's my brother."

Hole 3

For the past year, Piper had been spending her time trying to piece her life back together. Soul searching was not an easy task, especially for someone like her who was afraid of what the mirror might reveal. Rusty had been a constant in the aftermath of her husband's death, gently prodding her to move forward and erase the painful memories of her tarnished marriage. Along the way, he'd offered words of encouragement solely for the purpose of closure. Not once had he shed any light onto his own familial relationships as a means in which to help her heal. And quite frankly, it never dawned on her to ask.

To say Rusty's childhood was less than ordinary would be an understatement. His early years were spent in Columbus among his father's family until the break-up of his parents' marriage. The next few years were spent in various places from New York to New Jersey, and finally back home to Ohio. His mother Helen moved Rusty and his younger brother Thomas to Woodlawn when Rusty entered the fourth grade and Tom kindergarten. For as long as Rusty could remember, Woodlawn was the place he called home.

His relationship with his father was non-existent. He truly believed his dad's departure was the catalyst that caused his mother's spirit to slowly die. When a freak car accident left her paralyzed, Tom took off for parts unknown, and Rusty escaped to New York City where he eventually met his good friend Jim Wagner. Much had happened from then until now. The brothers had grown from boys to men without each other for support. Tom's entry back into Rusty's life had been a long time coming. None could be happier about it than Rusty himself.

By the time he'd explained the ins and outs of his relationship with his brother to Piper, it was time to call it a day. Though he'd barely skimmed the surface, the abbreviated version sufficed for now. Piper had mentioned something about Chad Freedom, the owner of Peeps & Petals, but Rusty was too tired to concentrate on exactly what she was saying. Most likely it had something to do with her crusade to close the strip club's doors. Since Piper had plans for dinner with her sister, Penelope, she needed to cut their rendezvous short. The couple said their good-byes and promised to hook up on Wednesday when they'd have ample time to discuss this recent development.

Piper was in the midst of walking out the door when her cell phone beeped. She had a text message from Penelope informing her that she was running late. Shocker! Honestly, it wouldn't surprise her in the least if Penelope managed to figure out a way to be late to her own funeral. The words *punctual* and *Penelope* most certainly did not go hand in hand.

So, rather than waste her time standing around, Piper decided to make a quick pit stop at the club. It had been a while since she'd had a tête-à-tête with her favorite confidante, Jay Baker. After his heroic deed in which he saved Piper and her friends from despair, he'd become somewhat of a big shot around town. Rumor had it that the showering of attention had made him cocky, as if that were even possible. His ego already had a hard time fitting into the pro shop. Piper felt it was her duty to set him straight.

Upon her arrival, Piper found him nestled in the corner with her least favorite person, Laura. *Why am I not surprised?* she thought. *Everyone knows that it's impossible for tigers to change their stripes.*

"Uh....hum," she coughed.

Bumping his head on the display shelf, Jay tried his best to quickly straighten himself up. From the looks of things, he was up to no good.

"Piper," he shouted. "I didn't expect to see you back here today." He quickly adjusted his green polo shirt.

"No kidding," she retorted eyeing up the guilty party.

"Jay was just sizing me up for..." Laura began. Her hair looked rather tousled.

"No need to finish the sentence. I know exactly what he was doing. Been there, done that. By the way, the tennis courts are outside to your left. I assume you must be lost."

"Oh, it's not what you think, Piper. I'm in need..."

"Of some direction," Piper stated. "I think it's time for you to go." Piper was clearly not amused.

Realizing it was best to part ways, Laura promptly exited.

The door had barely swung shut before Piper let Jay have it. "Explain to me why you'd be caught dead with that woman. Have you no common sense? May I remind you how much angst she's caused?" Piper was mere inches away from him in total disregard for his personal space.

"Now, now, Piper. Calm down. I was simply fitting her for new golf shoes. She wants to take up the game." Jay headed towards the counter. He knew darn well that he was in for a lecture of sorts.

"Whatever. You know what I think of her. The least you could do is respect my feelings. The wound is still fresh." Piper nonchalantly backed away a few steps.

"Fine. Next time she comes in here, I'll get Gabe to wait on her." Jay hoped that was enough to mollify the anticipated rant. "By the way, what's up?"

Piper's visit was by far not solely a humanitarian mission. She was bound and determined to get to the bottom of Peeps & Petals. "Tell me what you know about the strip club that just opened."

"For goodness sakes, Gabe just can't keep his mouth shut, can he? I told him I'd take him next time. He can forget it now. He's on his own. And, I hope his wife finds out, too." He moved some papers from one stack to another.

"You've been there?" Piper was not entirely surprised. Jay was a mover and a shaker. No doubt, he'd been one of the first to check out the new hot spot.

"Yes, I've been there. The older gentlemen of the club were curious, so they threw me some dough and asked me to check it out. Perfect location for an all guys' night out, if you ask me." He opened a drawer and took out a bunch of scorecards.

"Since when have you become a social planner?" Piper couldn't help but chide him.

"Ha, Ha! Real funny! Since when did you care about strip clubs?" Jay gave the impression that he was offended by her patronizing tone.

Piper needed Jay's help, so she decided it was time to cool her jets. "Well, normally I wouldn't, but I have a hunch that something fishy is going on there."

"What do you mean?" Jay was hooked. He listened while arranging the scorecards into two neat piles on the counter.

"Rumor has it that Representative Barnes may have used his political influence to help his cousin Jack Conway get all the necessary permits and whatnot through so quickly. Don't you think it's rather strange how quickly it popped up? There was no mention of it in the paper. I'd think some people might have objected to its opening. Not everyone is keen on stripper poles being erected in town," Piper said.

Jay's interest was piqued. "I'm sure that's not the only thing being erected. C'mon, Piper. Spill it. Where did you hear that?" He seemed doubtful.

"Doesn't matter. I just need to get to the bottom of it. Can you help me?" She moved closer to the counter.

Jay stalled for a moment savoring the taste of adventure. "Of course! Count me in."

Piper was thrilled she'd sealed the deal. Looking at her watch, she knew she was cutting it close. "Fabulous! I will be in touch." She clapped her hands in delight and then turned to walk away.

"What do you mean? That's it? Where are you going?" Jay was deflated. He was ready to take the case, not sit around and wonder what the next step would be.

Heading towards the door, she said, "I'm meeting my sister for dinner and I'm probably going to be late. Keep your eyes and ears open. I'll text you later with more details. Thanks, Jay. Ciao!"

And with that, she disappeared leaving Jay completely befuddled.

Arriving at The Corner Bistro, the chic nouvelle cuisine hotspot in town, Piper found her sister waiting impatiently at a table. By the looks of it, Penelope had bided her time well. The two empty wine glasses sitting on the table attested to that. On the plus side, Piper knew that Penelope would be much more amenable with Chardonnay running through her veins. Perhaps being tardy wasn't a bad move after all. Piper couldn't wait to sit down. She was so looking forward to ordering her own elixir just to calm her rattled nerves.

"Finally!" Penelope knew she held the upper hand. She loved watching her sister squirm.

Squeezing into the booth, Piper said, "Sorry, sis. I had to run by the club and see Jay. And, guess who I ran into while I was there?" She tossed her purse on the seat.

Penelope just raised her eyebrows in a questioning glance. She knew Piper was just winding up for the pitch.

"Laura," Piper seethed. She removed the napkin from the table and placed it gently across her lap.

"Oh, please. Were you harassing her again? You need to move on, Piper. She's not worth your time nor energy." Being nonjudgmental was not Penelope's strong suit.

"That's what Jay said, too. I wasn't really harassing her. I just made sure she knew who was in charge. And, why are you both so quick to defend her?" It was obvious to everyone including Piper herself that she still hadn't come to terms with her husband's deception, despite him being six feet under.

"Not tonight, Piper. Let's just move on. You look like you have more on your mind than just Laura. What's up with you and Jay? The two of you together equals trouble. Spill it."

Within twenty minutes, Piper had filled her sister in on all of her recent discoveries including the startling revelation of Rusty's new found brother. Fortunately, Penelope had had the foresight to anticipate what was coming. Ordering a light dinner of red snapper and sautéed spinach complemented with a savory sweet white wine prior to Piper's arrival had been a genius idea. Had she not, the two would have still been sitting there waiting to place their order. Interrupting Piper was a definite no-no for which Penelope gave the utmost respect.

"Is he cute?" It was no secret. Penelope was available and on the prowl.

Piper hadn't even thought of asking Rusty what Tom looked like. Taking a bite of her fish she replied, "Well, I assume so. I mean look at Rusty. If Tom is half as good looking as him, well, then I guess the answer would be yes."

Pleased with the news, Penelope added, "Well, then. You have your work cut out for you, sis. Set me up on a date. I've been here for exactly one year and I have yet to find a suitable catch. I'm about ready to pack my bags and head home, but now I just might have a reason to stay."

Piper knew her sister had issues with the lack of potential suitors in Woodlawn; however, the thought of Tom and Penelope together was a little unsettling.

"Hey!" Penelope continued. "I have an idea! Why don't you invite him to be my escort for the Member-Member on Friday night? Oh, that would be the perfect way to check him out without having to go through that uncomfortable first date. There will be plenty of booze and lots of diversions. No pressure for either of us to make it work. What do you think?" She picked up her wine glass and savored a generous taste of vino while waiting for Piper to respond.

As if she had a choice, Piper agreed, with the caveat that if Penelope felt there was no chance of a relationship, she'd end things as quickly and painlessly as possible.

Penelope was thrilled.

The next topic on Piper's agenda was Representative Barnes. Dessert was in order for this delicate conversation. Piper knew she'd need all the help she could get in order to convince Penelope to march in this parade. Her kid sister was by no means a pushover. Now was not the time for drama or emotional baggage.

Lucky for Piper, about six months ago Penelope had landed a part-time job at the notorious Dr. King's office. For a dermatologist, he had quite the reputation. Single and fancy-free, his yearly mole exam was quite the talk of the town. Ladies were known to book their appointments a year in advance just to guarantee their spot.

Not only was the doctor himself scrumptious, but also the office staff's penchant for gossip was just as tasty. His ladies knew more about what was going on in town, as well as behind closed doors, than the local newspaper reporter. If it was happening in Woodlawn, they were talking about it.

Since uncovering Representative Barnes's involvement was Piper's main objective, she needed to get familiar with someone in his inner circle. His political status made that task a tad bit difficult. That's exactly where Penelope would come in handy. If anyone could find the cherry cordial in a box of chocolates, it would be her smart, savvy sister.

"You know, I haven't heard you talk about work lately. How's your job going with the hot Dr. King?"

Before Penelope had a chance to answer, the waiter discreetly walked over and subtly suggested the chocolate molten cake. The sisters wholeheartedly agreed. One piece of cake, two forks.

"Business as usual. The amount of scandalous fodder that circulates in that office never ceases to amaze me."

Piper knew this was the opening she was waiting for. "Ever hear anything about the political powerhouses?" The dessert arrived just in time. Piper took a big bite in anticipation of a sweet tidbit of scoop.

"Don't insult my intelligence, sis. I know you're digging. What do you want to know?" Penelope savored her own sweet morsel while waiting for Piper to fold.

Realizing she'd been beaten at her own game, Piper unloaded. "See, here's the thing. Peeps & Petals has opened up and rumor has it that Representative Barnes helped pave the way. I don't know about you, but having a bona fide strip club in Woodlawn repulses me. I want that place closed down and I think I know a way of getting it done."

"Whoa, sis! That's some accusation you've got rattling around your head. Who's your source? And, I don't want to hear it's the twins." Their reputation spoke for themselves. Penelope's dislike for them was ever-present.

"I can't reveal my source at this time, but believe me. It's a reliable one." Piper nodded her head.

Penelope was in no mood for playing detective; however, Piper's reputation for engaging in hare-brained schemes outweighed the possibility of just taking her word for it. "If you want my help, then you'll have to fill me in. Remember the time you said Mrs. Hartwell had a boob job when really the poor woman was just trying out a new push-up bra?" Penelope knew she had her beat.

Rolling her eyes, Piper replied, "Well, Jill Brock told me she'd had some work done. How was I to know that Mrs. Hartwell was that flat to begin with? Anyone could have made that mistake."

"Well, sure, but announcing it on the playground was where you went wrong. Sometimes it's better to keep things to yourself." Penelope couldn't help but chuckle. Her sister's escapades always seemed to bring a smile to her face.

"Fine. So that means if I tell you, you'll help me?" Piper had no choice but to give in to her demands.

"Why not? If it means keeping you out of trouble again, well, then, yes. Count me in. We all have a role to play. Mine just happens to be your life coach or better yet…social advisor. Call it what you will."

By the time Piper had filled Penelope in with all of who was who and what was what, it was late. The two sisters hurriedly paid the check and said their good-byes in the parking lot. With the member-member event just days away, they had a lot of work ahead of them in order to be fully prepared for the evening. Having the opportunity to corner the representative on their own turf was crucial. The sisters both realized this fact; however, it came as no surprise to either that beauty sleep won out over whatever lay ahead. Despite the seriousness of the situation, the girls always managed to keep their priorities straight. That was for damn sure.

As Piper waited for her sister to pull out of the parking spot, she searched for her phone at the bottom of her Tory Burch purse. Having been knee-deep in strategizing, Piper had neglected to check her texts. As usual, there were quite a few. One was from her mom reminding her of a department store sale. Of course, it was marked urgent. The Davenport women always put fashion first. Another came from the vet confirming her pussy cat Ralph Lauren's vaccination appointment. Good thing. Piper had completely forgotten about it. She'd have to figure out how to squeeze these necessities in with her already filled agenda. The third text was from Jay. Curious as to what was up, she texted him right back.

Watup?

Got news. R u free?

On way home. Had dinner w/ sis.

Call me ASAP. GB at club 2nite. Big pow-pow in card room.

With??

U'll never guess who.

As Piper meandered her way back home, the wheels in her head were spinning. If Representative Barnes was truly involved in the opening of Peeps & Petals as she thought, her exposing him would surely be the death of his political career. Perhaps he was more than just pushing through some paperwork. Without a doubt, the people of Woodlawn would revolt. But, what price was she willing to pay to bring this man down? More importantly, who among her friends might also have played a part in this devious plan?

Hole 4

Waking up bright and early on Wednesday morning, Piper was ready to tackle the day. First on her agenda was a quick game of tennis at the club. Unlike golf, Piper excelled in the sport. It was a simple game which required minimal smarts. Hit the ball over the net and keep it between the white lines. Even a chimpanzee could do it. Plus, the scoring system was a piece of cake. How could you not like a game which used the words *love* and *ace*?

Drop-in doubles was held only once a week, so Piper tried her hardest to get there on time. The resident tennis pro Mike ran the program with verve and vigor. Participation among a mixed-bag of attendees kept the level of play interesting. Piper prayed Danielle would be there today. What better time than between sets to pry into her business? Danielle's supposed connections with many of Piper's inner circle made her wary of this new mystery woman. And, why their paths had never crossed before, really hit a nerve with Piper.

By the time Piper made it to the courts, a somewhat sizeable group had gathered by the tennis shack. It appeared Mike was running behind, due to a previous lesson. Piper was thankful for his lateness. It would give her some extra time to cozy up to Danielle. As she made her way over to the ladies, she was crestfallen to see that Danielle was nowhere to be seen. Her plan to kill two birds with one stone had backfired. Piper did a quick scan of the small crowd to find a suitable partner. Her options were limited due to the influx of new members. There weren't many familiar faces to choose from except for one. Second choice would have to be Janie Vanhorst.

Despite her initial gut reaction of displeasure, Piper was actually okay with Janie. She had wanted to be the first to congratulate Janie on the brilliance of hiring a nanny in order to hide her sexual indiscretion anyway. Others may have been fooled by Janie's supposed C.E.O. of the household decision to hire an extra set of hands. Not Piper. If anyone could snoop out an adulterous affair in the making it would be Piper. Thanks to Charles, she was well-schooled in that subject matter. Even though their relationship had never been more than perfunctory, Piper was fond of Janie. Engaging in a dirty little secret was not what she had wished for her friend, but to each her own. Then again, who knew what was going on behind closed doors in the Vanhorst house? Piper, for one, could attest to that. If truth be told, she believed Janie deserved better, but it was not her place to say so. Piper was well aware of the boundaries set up in terms of their friendship. Stepping over the line was not in the foreseeable future even if she did have Janie's best interests in mind.

"Good morning, Janie," Piper said. "Do you want to be partners?"

Fiddling with her strings, Janie looked up and nodded slightly in agreement. Piper blamed Janie's sluggishness on her recent illness and made a mental note to use hand sanitizer after the match. Pleased she had secured a mate, Piper took a seat near Janie on the bench. No need to get too cozy for fear of getting sick. As she unzipped the protective cover of her tennis racket, a car came roaring up to the fence, coming within inches of barreling right into it. A red-headed woman tumbled out of the passenger's side screaming at the top of her lungs a long list of expletives that would make even the crudest truck driver blush. Barely believing her eyes, Piper announced loud enough for everyone to hear "Isn't that Danielle Barnes?" All heads whipped around in their direction anticipating a scene that would surely make headlines in tomorrow's daily paper.

Not surprisingly, Janie perked up rather quickly. Her previous state of numbness took a sudden backseat given the scent of salacious gossip permeating the air. Piper counted to three and like clockwork, Janie's cell phone flipped open. The speed with which she texted guaranteed that Carolyn was now in the know. With bated breath, all the ladies gawked at the irate couple in the car as if they were watching a train wreck about to take place.

"Thanks for nothing," screamed Danielle. "After all I've done for you and this is how you treat me. Why don't you go screw one of those pole dancers instead? Oh, yeah. That's right. You screwed her mother instead. I hope you drop dead." Danielle slammed the car door. With her tennis racket in hand, she twisted her body around and looked straight at the group of women gathered. "Hello, ladies." Her calm voice was enough to send shivers down their spines. "Ready to play?"

Piper's steady voice replied, "Of course. Let's go girls." The group hustled onto the courts dutifully obeying Piper's command while Representative Barnes, the driver of the car, made a hasty exit. The squealing of his tires said it all. He was not a happy camper.

The intensity of play challenged the group and the morning breezed by. Danielle paired up with some new member and that suited Piper perfectly. No use trying to squeeze any information out of her today. The woman seemed spent. However, Danielle's fierce swing must have worked wonders in getting the aggression out of her system. By the time they were done, she was downright pleasant.

Walking towards the water cooler which was perched by the side of the net, Danielle spoke to Piper. "What's on tap for you today? Care to join me for brunch?" Sensing her stars aligning Piper replied, "Sure. Where do you want to go?"

Danielle gingerly wiped the sweat from her brow, "The diner if that's okay with you. I love their eggs Benedict and the coffee there is bold and bitter. Just how I like it."

The expression on Janie's face was priceless. How Piper had snagged an invitation and not her was beyond imaginable. Not one to be outdone she chimed in, "Mind if I join you?"

Taken aback, Danielle hissed, "If you must."

Seeing that was as good an offer as she could get Janie said, "Terrific. Shall I meet you both there say in about fifteen minutes? Does that work for everyone?"

"How about in a half hour?" asked Danielle. "I have an errand to run first. Piper, is that okay with you?" Fifteen minutes, thirty minutes, two hours. It didn't matter to Piper. Just being Danielle's first choice…that was the icing on the cake.

With an agreed upon time, the ladies dispersed each with her own agenda. Knowing Janie as well as she did, Piper anticipated that Janie would arrive early in order to scout out the diner's prime table. Being seen by her fellow country-clubbers with the representative's wife would be a feather in her cap. Hopefully, Janie wouldn't feel the need to bring her side-kick Carolyn along for the ride.

With thirty minutes to spare, Piper chose to swing by the liquor store to spy on Rusty's brother Tom. This revelation of a long-lost sibling had been at the forefront of her mind. First on the list…check out his looks for her sister. Second...evaluate his loyalty factor. Piper could spot a phony a mile away, especially when it came to men. Once a snake, always a snake. And since he'd not had the pleasure of meeting her yet, it would be easy to test the waters without Rusty's disapproving eye.

From the look of the parking lot, the store was doing a tremendous amount of business. Piper took this as a favorable sign. The windows were covered with numerous advertisements which was a new look for the place. The one highlighting skinny margaritas especially caught her eye. *Might as well stock up while I'm here*, she thought.

Piper breezed right in as if she owned the place. Technically, she did. In the world according to Piper, dating the owner put her in that category. Standing tall behind the counter lounged a luscious blond-haired man. Dressed in an Abercrombie henley shirt paired with torn jeans, he oozed sensuality. His eyes appeared to be a sort of crystallized blue and his crooked grin made his come hither look downright tempting. Before she got too carried away, Piper averted her eyes to the wine display. No sense in getting herself all worked up. Rusty was nowhere to be found.

As if he could sense her lustful attraction, the man moved in Piper's direction bypassing a customer who was trying her hardest to grab his attention. "May I help you?" he offered.

Taking this as an open invitation to play, Piper slowly turned her gaze to him and said, "Quite a crowd you have in here today. Is it always this busy?"

Sizing her up, he replied, "Lately, yes. Looking for anything in particular?"

"Just something to keep me warm tonight. Have any suggestions?" On cue, Piper gave him her best sexy pose.

Taking a step closer, he leaned over and whispered, "It all depends on what needs warming." He stared deep into her blue eyes.

Tantalized by this man's ability to make her weak in the knees but cognizant of exactly with whom she was toying, Piper decided to squelch their little tête-à-tête before it got out of control. "Tom, I presume."

Not missing a beat, "Piper," he replied. "It's nice to finally meet you."

Flabbergasted, Piper just openly stared at the man not knowing what to say next.

With a smile in his eye, he continued, "Rusty told me to be on the look-out for you. After all these years, he still hasn't changed much. He always had a soft spot for blondes, although there was a redhead at one time. I didn't care for her much."

Caught at her own game, Piper acquiesced. "Nice to meet you, Tom. I thought it my duty to come check up on you. I'm just looking out for your brother. His leaving the store in your hands is so out of character for him. And, opening a detective agency? I'm not sure how he came up with that idea in the first place. I have my doubts about this whole thing."

Walking towards the front counter, he said, "Well, if you ask me, it has something to do with a pretty little blonde who happened to have found herself in a heap of trouble once. It was definitely the spark that ignited this fire. Know anyone who fits that bill?"

Piper shrugged her shoulders as she followed close behind him.

"No use in fighting him. If he's made up his mind, it's a done deal. I'd love to shoot the breeze with you, but like you said, we're really busy in here. I gotta get to back to work. Enough fraternizing with the so-called customers." Tom winked at her and then said, "Next in line."

Satisfied that Rusty's younger brother appeared to be on the up and up, Piper exited the store without saying good-bye. Looking at her watch, it dawned on her where she needed to be. Twenty minutes had flown by. To make matters worse, she realized that she'd left her Tory Burch clutch in her locker at the club. Making a swift turn out of the parking lot, she gunned it. The club was a mere five miles away. With her driving, she'd be there in minutes.

Pulling up to the member entrance, Piper slammed her car in park and made a mad dash for the door. The valet boy gave her a nasty glare she chose to ignore. No time for manners. There was gossip to be had at the diner. Rounding the corner, she grabbed hold of the banister and began her descent to the lower floor. Just as she reached the locker room door, a hand grabbed her from behind. "I knew I'd find you here."

"Ah!' screamed Piper. Turning around she came nose to nose with Jay. "You scared the living daylights out of me, Jay. Haven't you ever heard of just saying hello?" Clearly shaken, Piper slowly inhaled and then exhaled.

"Yeah, sorry about that. We need to talk." Jay anxiously looked around as if he were being followed.

"You looked spooked. What's up? I really don't have time for this now. I'm supposed to meet Danielle and Janie at the diner. Isn't that exciting? Did you hear what I said? Danielle! This could be our big break." She hugged Jay in triumph.

Jay was not in the least impressed. "Well, I have better news than that. Representative Barnes was here last night for a big pow-wow, and he looked like he'd been through the wringer. Jim Wagner was also in attendance."

"Really? That's interesting," said Piper. She never really trusted Rusty's friend Jim. Being involved with an unscrupulous man would be right up his alley.

"Yeah, and the representative was back here this morning, too. He seemed worse off than he did last night." Jay took a quick glance around to make sure no one overheard them.

"Oh, he and Danielle had a fight," Piper informed him. "An ugly one, witnessed by the ladies of the courts. I'm sure you'll hear all about the nitty-gritty details in the bar this afternoon. I hate to rush out on you, but I really need to split." Piper tried to leave.

"Hold on. There's more. He was supposed to pick something up." Jay could hardly contain himself.

"Spit it out, Jay. I really need to go." Piper had had about as much as she could take. No more Ms. Nice Gal. Time was of the essence.

"Fine. I don't know exactly what, but he was really angry that it wasn't here."

"That's all you've got? C'mon Jay. You're killing me." Piper shook her head.

"What I can tell you is that he asked Beth the barmaid if anyone had dropped off a package for him. When she said no, he stormed out of there. Practically knocked me over on his way out."

"Well, is he still here?" Slightly intrigued by the news, Piper continued, "Is his car still parked in the lot?"

"I don't know. Do you think I should go look?" Jay paused.

"Knock yourself out. It can't hurt to check." Piper's interest in his theory was waning.

"Do you think their argument is related to the missing package?" He kept pressing her with more questions.

"Listen, Jay. I appreciate you filling me in, but I can't see how Representative Barnes's fight with his wife has any relevance to locating the person behind the strip club's opening. That's our main goal. Remember? What we need to find out pertains to dollars and cents. Not some domestic squabble. Let me hook up with you later. We can dissect any morsels of information you've got when I'm not so rushed. Okay?"

Clearly deflated, Jay shrugged in agreement and sulked away.

Piper hadn't meant to hurt Jay's feelings, but sometimes his so-called theories were a tad bit far-fetched. Damage control would be a necessary by-product of their unfortunate encounter. And to think at one time Piper had been called high maintenance. Nowadays, Jay had her beat hands down.

Piper sensed she was way over her allotted time limit, so she barreled through the door of the locker room hoping to make it quick. Looking for the key to her locker among the numerous others she had on the key ring, she nearly bumped into the wall. "Darn it!" she exclaimed. She was definitely out of sorts. As she approached the back wall, Piper noticed the shower area was lit up. Knowing that the club used energy-saving lights attached to a sensor she shouted, "Hello?" She hadn't thought anyone was in there but evidently she was wrong. "Hello? Anybody in here?" she called out again. Still no reply. An eerie feeling crept down her spine. She remembered having this same sensation not too long ago, and its aftermath had changed her life forever.

Walking towards the far area, she braced herself for the unknown. Like it or not, she had to finish what she had started. On the left stood a row of sinks adorned with mouthwash and small paper cups. To Piper's right was the illuminated shower area. Piper tiptoed closer to take a peek. Thankfully, the first stall was empty. Just some sparkling white tile staring her in the face. Relief swept over her. Piper exhaled and took two more steps. The second was empty as well. Piper started to relax. Her mind was playing tricks on her. *No need to be dramatic,* she thought. On the third and final one, the pink polka dot curtain was drawn. Piper drew in her breath, pushed it aside, and peered in. One look was all she needed. Piper spun right back around and darted towards the door. With full force fueled by fear, she unintentionally wound up catapulting herself out into the hallway landing right smack into the arms of Jay.

"You were right," Jay exclaimed as he untangled himself from her embrace. "His car is still in the parking lot. Representative Barnes is in the building."

"I know," answered Piper, barely able to spit the words out of her mouth. "I just saw him."

"Really? Where?" asked Jay.

"In the shower stall." Piper had a hard time catching her breath.

"Get out!" he exclaimed. "In the women's locker room? What's he doing in there? Did he see you?" Jay's voice cracked.

"Evidently not," she said while glancing up and down the hallway.

"How come?" He tilted his head.

Piper took a moment to catch her breath. "Well for starters, he's dead."

Hole 5

The dynamic duo stood riveted to the spot, each wishing the other would take command of the situation. Having just found a man bludgeoned to death took the wind right out of Piper's sails. She stood there with a dazed look on her face. As luck would have it, Jay just happened to have been assigned manager on duty for that morning so he took it upon himself to lock the locker room door. The angst on his face said it all. With a dead man sprawled out on the shower floor, the likelihood of him finally getting that promotion he thought he so justly deserved went right down the drain.

"Has the cat got your tongue?" chided Beth, the club's favored barmaid, who was passing by. "You both look like you've seen a ghost."

"You're not too far off," replied Jay. Turning towards Piper he continued, "Should we tell her?"

"Tell me what?" replied Beth playing along. The perky blonde could smell gossip permeating the air. She stuck her hands into the pockets of her black and white uniform.

Piper nodded her head in agreement.

"Beth, Representative Barnes is dead. Piper found him in the women's locker room."

We need to call 911." Jay made the announcement with an air of authority.

The barmaid's face turned ashen. "OMG! Yes, sir. I mean…on the double. Right now. I'll go make the call from the bar," stammered Beth while scurrying away.

"While she's doing that, I'll head downstairs to the pro shop and blow the horn. All of the golfers need to vacate the course ASAP. I'm sure the police will want to speak to them as soon as they arrive. Piper, why don't you go to the courts and gather up everyone you can find? Everyone here this morning is a potential suspect, including you and me. So, we'd better get our story straight."

Piper glared at him and said, "Did I miss the television cameras or crew guys? For a moment there, I thought we were taping an episode of C.S.I. Get a grip, Jay."

"What? It's the truth. We'd better be prepared. Remember what happened last time?"

His mentioning of her husband Charles's murder opened the floodgates of unwanted emotion. Finding her husband dead on their bathroom floor was etched in her memory forever. "Why me?" answered Piper. "Why couldn't you have found him instead? Truly, I love being first except when it involves finding dead bodies."

While the club was waiting for the authorities to arrive, Jay took it upon himself to usher the members inside the grand ballroom. His actions reflected his innate desire to gain some respect from those around him. The members guffawed at his suggestion to remain quiet. A dead representative in their midst was a hot topic that needed to be discussed. Despite the fact that each member potentially could have committed the murder, the consensus of the group was that Danielle was the likely suspect.

As for Piper, she did what any sensible, single woman would do. She called upon her boyfriend for back-up. If Rusty was truly serious about starting up this detective agency, it was time to put his skills to the test. Who more qualified than the man sharing her bed to help solve this case?

The roar of the sirens deafened the assembled crowd. From the sound of it, all available units were on their way. News this tantalizing could not be missed. Even the off-duty cops wanted a piece of the action. All eyes were fixated on the entrance of the ballroom. The next few minutes would set the tone for the entire investigation. Who would be in charge of the hottest political murder case bestowed upon the tony suburban town of Woodlawn? All inquiring minds wanted to know.

"Move aside, move aside," bellowed a deep, officious voice. A man dressed in a plaid shirt, jeans, and a New York Yankees ball cap pushed his way inside the door. "Let me in, people," he ordered. "I can't do my job standing outside, people."

"Oh, you've got to be kidding me," whined Piper. "This day has gone from bad to worse."

"You," the man shouted as he approached Piper. "Why am I not surprised to find you here? Where there is murder, there's Piper O'Donnell."

Holding her ground, she grumbled, "Lt. Morgan. Long time, no see. I thought you'd fallen off the face of the earth. No such luck, huh?" Piper smirked.

"It's Captain Morgan now, my dear," he replied as he made his way over to her.

Bursting out with laughter, Piper said, "How apropos! You wouldn't happen to have a shot hidden under that hat of yours, would you? I think I could use one right about now."

"Very funny, little lady," he quipped back at her. "I'd be careful who you mess with. Let me take a wild guess. Once again, you are a prime suspect in a murder case."

"Leave her alone. She has nothing to do with it," shouted a voice from the back of the crowd.

"What did you do? Drug the mob?" asked Captain Morgan.

Shrugging her shoulders, Piper turned to the group. "Who just said that?"

"Me!" Like a windup jack-in-the-box, Rusty popped up.

"You, too?" Captain Morgan couldn't believe his eyes. "Just like old times."

As the police sequestered the suspects, Captain Morgan and Piper traced her steps leading up to the discovery of Representative Barnes. Rusty was perturbed he couldn't be privy to the conversation, but he understood procedures must be followed. There would be plenty of time to get the exact details from Piper later on when they were alone. Rusty heard the members griping about being kept so long, but it couldn't be helped. Testimony needed to be taken now in order to set the investigation in motion.

The detectives sectioned off the area in front of the locker room using the standard yellow police tape. Inside, the police photographers took their time snapping photos for documentation. Following protocol, the crime scene investigators dusted the area for prints and checked for any signs of entry. Evidence samples were collected and tagged for further examination. Once the police felt the area had been fully searched, the coroner came in and proceeded with his analysis of the body.

About an hour or so later, Danielle showed up at the club. Her first order of business was to see her husband. From her demeanor, she appeared to be distraught. Her hair resembled a rat's nest and her face was quite blotchy. *Not a good look for a representative's wife.*

Piper had been down that road before, so she greatly empathized with the woman. Losing a spouse was never easy, especially when said spouse had been brutally murdered.

"Piper! Piper! Where are you?" stammered the grieving widow. Weaving in and out of the groups of people, Danielle was determined to find her new friend.

"Over here," shouted Piper as she waved to the woman. "I'm over here with uhm…Lt. Columbo…I mean Captain Morgan. Whatever his name is."

As soon as Danielle reached Piper, she grabbed hold of her and held her tightly in a bear hug embrace.

"I know, I know," soothed Piper while gently stroking Danielle's hair. "It's going to be okay."

"Yeah, I know," she whispered into Piper's ear. "I never have to see that two-timing bastard again! Oh! Joyful day!"

Hoping no one had heard what Danielle had said, Piper answered, "Have you been drinking?"

"Celebrating is more like it," Danielle hiccupped. "How can I thank you?"

"For what?" Piper asked. *What is she talking about?* she thought.

"For killing my husband. Don't worry, dear. I won't tell anyone. It's our little secret."

Arching her back, Piper struggled to break hold of Danielle's embrace. No luck. The woman had her in a death grip.

"There, there. It's okay, Piper." Danielle inhaled deeply and then continued on, "Calm down, honey and don't say a word." Danielle surveyed the crowd. Realizing all eyes were upon them, she whispered in Piper's ear, "After the police let everyone go, meet me back at my place. We can strategize about your alibi then. In the meantime, I suggest you say as little as possible. I owe you one."

Taking a step back, Danielle announced to the crowd, "Who among you killed my husband? Step forward, you coward." Her level of sobriety needed no questioning. The woman was clearly hammered.

By the time Captain Morgan had questioned all of the suspects, night was drawing near. The only ones left in the building were Jay, Piper, and of course Captain Morgan. As for Representative Barnes, his corpse had been taken away by the coroner's office. All the evidence had been collected to the police department's satisfaction. The hazmat team was on the way to facilitate the clean-up process. There was nothing left to be done.

"Remember the drill?" Captain Morgan said to Piper. "You can't leave town."

Walking towards the main hallway side by side with Jay, Piper responded, "I have no travel plans so you're in luck. May I give you some words of advice?"

Following closely behind, Morgan answered, "Feel free. Although had I said no, you still would have told me anyway. Have at it."

Piper stopped short and looked him squarely in the eyes. "Don't waste your time with me. You have bigger fish to fry. Word around town is that the representative was somehow involved with the opening of Peeps & Petals. I can't think of a single, moral person who wanted that kind of establishment in our quaint town. Mostly all of its clientele comes from the other side of the tracks, give or take some hormonal guys like Jay and his buddies. No offense, dear."

"None taken," Jay quipped back. The two had forged an unspeakable bond brought on by murder. Catty little comments no longer ruffled their feathers.

"You don't think I know that? Really?" said Captain Morgan. "Believe it or not, I have earned the stripes on my uniform. Representative Barnes was not a well-liked man around these parts. Plain and simple. It's my job to find out who killed him. That's why they pay me the so-called big bucks, Piper. I don't need you two nosey bodies messing with my investigation. Hang up your detective hats and let the professionals do their job."

"I couldn't have said it better myself," Piper declared. "First thing in the morning, P.I. Rusty O'Brien will take the case. I have no doubt he'll get to the bottom of this mess. Good night, Captain Morgan. Sweet dreams." Motioning to Jay, she continued, "C'mon Jay. Tomorrow is going to be another long day."

The trio briskly walked towards the front door in silence, each with various sugarplum murder fairies dancing around in their heads. Woodlawn had officially seen its second murder. Two in two years. The stats proved to be disheartening. Without a doubt, the town had lost its innocence. The death of an elected official would bring unwanted scrutiny by outsiders. Within hours, their precious enclave would become the talk of the nation. Pundits from both sides of the aisle would offer up their opinions, each with a purported political agenda. Media crews would swarm the area while unknown entities would surface at the most inopportune time. As expected, the local television crew was already lined up outside under the entrance's awning. Having been down this road before, Piper told the vultures no comment. Jay followed suit as he secured the lock on the door. Captain Morgan stopped briefly and gave them the usual innocuous official statement that further details would follow at an appointed time. The trumpet had sounded. The media hounds were on the scent and there was no turning back now. The hunt had officially begun.

Hole 6

The next day brought an influx of media personalities to Woodlawn. Not surprisingly, news of the state representative's murder spread like wildfire simply due to the stature of the victim. Once unheard of, the tiny town of Woodlawn finally earned its place on the map. Like ants on their way to a picnic, an endless stream of news vans rolled into Woodlawn all looking for the hottest scoop to report to their viewers.

Still reeling from yesterday's events, Piper overslept, missing her morning cup of coffee and daily news show. Much needed sleep took over as her number one priority. Facing yet another murder case as a potential suspect sent Piper high-tailing it under the sheets. With the ornery Captain Morgan on her tail, who knew what the day might bring?

All too soon, her dreamy reverie was cut short by the constant ringing of her doorbell. Once. Twice. Three times. Whoever stood on the other side of the door was awfully persistent. With no choice but to answer it, Piper lazily tumbled out of bed, threw on a pink, fluffy bathrobe, and headed downstairs.

By the time she approached the front hall, her visitor began knocking with vigor and vehemence. Curiosity took hold of Piper as she swung the door open.

"Well, it's about time," said Penelope. Dressed in a floral top with bright yellow pants, Penelope looked as fresh as a spring day. "For a minute there, I was worried." Looking her sister over, she continued, "What's up with the pink bathrobe? It's ten o'clock,

Piper. Don't tell me you're depressed again. I thought we worked through that, sis. You're sleeping the day away." Penelope pushed her way into the house as if she owned the place. "We have lots to discuss starting with the gory details. What happened to Representative Barnes? And more importantly, tell me you weren't involved."

By the time Piper had filled Penelope in, it was nearly noon. Penelope insisted her sister take a quick shower amid the retelling of the gruesome details. While in the shower, Penelope pressed her sister's Lilly pants and polo shirt so that she had something fresh to wear. She even cleaned up the leftover breakfast dishes in the sink and managed to throw a load of clothes in the high efficiency washing machine. Anything to get Piper back on track. Penelope wasn't the least bit surprised that her sister was up to her eyeballs in trouble. With Piper, it was just par for the course. As long as Piper stayed clear of the fray, Penelope would be able to put her mind at ease.

Refreshed and invigorated, the girls decided to head to the diner for a bite to eat. As they made their way to the front door, a loud mumbling of voices outside could be heard.

"Were you expecting anyone?" asked Penelope.

Choosing not to mention her run-in with Danielle, Piper shrugged her shoulders.

"Well, evidently someone is out there. C'mon, let's go see."

The two grabbed for the handle simultaneously yanking the door open wide. Within seconds, they were blinded by the steady stream of flashbulbs going off in their faces.

"Piper! Is it true you found the representative's body? What can you tell us about him?" yelled a scrawny young man with a red baseball cap on his head.

"Piper! This isn't the first time you've found a dead body. Are you somehow connected to him?" The bleached blonde reporter looked as if she'd fallen head first into a vat of make-up.

"Were you two secret lovers? Does his wife have any idea of your scandalous affair?" asked a dark-haired raven in search of her next road kill.

Before they'd had a chance to interrogate Piper any further, Penelope heaved her back inside and slammed the door in the crowd's face. With her back up against the door, Penelope took a few deep breaths.

"Wow! I didn't see that one coming," proclaimed Piper. "How do you think I looked? Is my nose oily? I think I may be using the wrong type of foundation. My other brand has been discontinued. I hate when that happens, but…."

"What the heck was that?" Penelope cut her off mid-sentence looking a tad bit shell-shocked. "Is there something you're not telling me, sis?"

"I did not sleep with Representative Barnes if that's what you're asking." Piper beamed with pride.

Rolling her eyes back into her head, Penelope continued, "Okay, well that's a good start. Just tell me…what did you do?"

The thought of Danielle's unfortunate comment at the murder scene took center stage in Piper's head. "Well, Danielle seems to think I killed her husband as some kind of favor to her. Where she would have gotten that idea is beyond me. Just because my husband was murdered, too, doesn't mean that I'd have experience whacking people off."

If it were physically possible, steam would have escaped from Penelope's head. "Get your mind out of the gutter. We're not talking about your sexual habits here, Piper."

Piper just stared at her sister in complete befuddlement.

"Stick to the program. And what makes her think that you're involved, dare I ask?"

Piper knew her sister well enough to realize the boiling point had been reached. Now might be a good time to call in some help.

Scuttling back towards the kitchen, Piper said, "I think I better get Rusty over here to help. Did I mention the private eye business he's thinking of starting? Good timing, huh?" Her voice quivered. "Let me just give that sexy hunk a holler and see if he is available." She paused. "Then again, I can't think of a time when he wasn't ready and willing."

"So that's what you say about me when I'm not around?" bellowed a voice from the far side of the kitchen.

"Ah!" screamed Piper. Sure enough, Rusty stood leaning on the counter with a Diet Pepsi in his hands. His sexy demeanor made Piper's heart skip a beat. "What are you doing here?"

"Is that anyway to greet your knight in shining armor?" The look in Rusty's eye said it all as he looked her over with a slow, sensual glance.

"Sorry, no time for dress up, babe." She knew exactly what he wanted. "I've spent too much time in fantasy land today as it is. Maybe later?"

Rusty couldn't help but laugh. "I thought you might need some reinforcements, Piper," he chimed in. "I drove by on my way to the club and I saw the frenzy of press outside your door. You know I'm a sucker for a damsel in distress."

Piper tilted her head to the right in a sly, seductive way while saying, "Thanks, babe." Throwing her arms around his neck, she planted a luscious, wet kiss square on his lips.

"Okay, okay!" interjected Penelope. "Enough of this role playing garbage, you two. Too much information, as far as I am concerned."

The couple chuckled then turned to face Penelope.

"Your so-called damsel in distress has gotten in way over her head this time, my friend. Did you happen to notice that the news crews out there are not just local? I could have sworn I spotted Natalie Morales in the crowd."

"I just love her," squeaked Piper. "That woman is so poised and professional. Nothing ever seems to rattle her cage. Sis, you mind peeking out the living room window to see if she is still here? I'm just going to run upstairs and put on something more appropriate for television. I hear black looks best on the little screen."

Before Piper had a chance to sneak away, Rusty piped up, "Not until you take a look at this first." He reluctantly handed her a piece of paper. "I was going to wait until later to show you this, but it looks as though now is as good a time as any. You may want to take a seat and read it aloud."

Carpool Chatter
What's pink and green and guilty
all over? Why it must be the
number one suspect in the murder
of Representative Gus Barnes.
Haven't you heard? Found dead as
doorknob at Woodlawn's exclusive
golf club by one of its own
members! Who knew our tony
little suburb would harbor such a
devilish little maven? From
mistress to murderer, our sexy

seductress shows no mercy.
According to reliable sources, the
victim's family can identify the
killer. Who in their right mind
would set up a clandestine meeting
with the widow in order to strike a
deal? Will justice be served? One
can only hope...

Piper crumbled up the paper and threw it over into the kitchen sink. Feelings of disgust, anger, and fear all welled-up inside of her. Everyone in town read the popular Carpool Chatter blog. It dished up the hottest local scoop on the Internet with a no holds barred approach. The identity of the blogger remained a mystery; however, the person had his or her pulse on the heartbeat of Woodlawn. Piper gathered the pink and green reference would be a dead give-away to her identity. Her fondness for Lilly Pulitzer clothing was a well-known fact. How the blogger obtained news of the supposed clandestine meeting puzzled Piper. *Had someone overheard my conversation with Danielle?* Even Piper had trouble deciphering Danielle's alcohol-induced speech. Once again, Piper was in over her head.

As Piper let out a huge sigh she mumbled, "Well, I guess we need to come up with some sort of plan."

Piper lifted her eyebrows in a questioning glance at Rusty. No luck. His anger was apparent. Throwing her hands up in the air, "I never planned on following through with meeting Danielle. I'm not an idiot, you know. I realize that wasn't a good idea to begin with."

Shaking his head, Rusty asked, "Is there anything else we need to know before we go any further?"

"No!" Piper insisted, "that's about all I can think of right now. If anything else comes to mind, I'll be sure to let you know. Scout's honor." She held up two fingers to reaffirm her point.

Satisfied with her response, Rusty stood up and took a couple steps towards the door. "Okay. We need to get out of here. My truck is parked on the side street behind your house. We can cut through your backyard to get there. Hopefully, no reporters will spot us. Let's all head over to my new office so we can strategize." Rusty grabbed his keys from his front pocket. "Do you both want to ride over with me?"

Penelope rose from the table. "I'd love to come, but I need to get to work. I'm sorry to say but it's about that time. Why don't I be the decoy? I'll head out through the front door with a scarf over my face. Piper, will you hand me the one in the hall closet? The pink one with flowers on it?"

Piper jogged to the front hall, rummaged through the top shelf, and came up with the scarf. Walking back into the kitchen she said, "Here you go, sis."

"Thanks." Penelope grabbed it from her hands. Wrapping it around her head she continued, "With any luck, they'll follow me over to Dr. King's office. I'm sure he'll get a kick out of the news vans. He's such a celebrity newsmonger. It'll probably make his day."

By the time Piper and Rusty traveled across town to the liquor store, she had filled him in on all of the gruesome details of the murder scene. Despite the rather unnerving topic, Piper left no stone unturned, even throwing out names of possible suspects. The list was rather long due to the mass of angry citizens opposed to the opening of the strip club. From soccer moms to church-going blue-haired ladies, Peeps & Petals did not receive many Likes on Facebook from that crowd.

As soon as they pulled into the parking lot, Piper spotted Janie exiting the liquor store. "Look who's shopping for booze. My favorite frenemy. Must have a big night planned. Did I tell you she hired a nanny?" Piper raised her eyebrows.

Shaking his head no, Rusty replied, "Did she get a job or something?" They both exited the vehicle and started walking towards the store hand in hand.

"Or something is more like it. Tanya seems to think I'm way off base, but I think little Miss Perfect is having an affair. Shh! Here she comes. Let's see what we can find out."

With an armful of booze, Janie tried to side-step the couple, but to no avail. Piper had her cornered. "Hi, Janie. Fancy meeting you here."

"Well, hello there. I'm surprised to see you two out and about after such a harrowing day yesterday. Any clues as to who killed Congressman Barnes?" Garbed in a flirty dress with pearls and designer heels, she looked every inch the corporate man's trophy wife.

Piper totally ignored her question and went in for the kill. "How's that nanny working out for you, Janie? I hear you needed an extra set of hands around the house. I didn't realize you'd gone back to work."

"I haven't really." Her hesitation signaled uneasiness. "Just a little side job doing some freelance writing here and there. The extra money comes in handy."

Rusty and Piper exchanged quizzical looks. Neither had anticipated that response.

"Well, I know we all can use the extra money nowadays, but since when have you been a writer? I thought you were a pharmaceutical rep or something salesman-like before you trapped...I mean married Ed." Piper nudged Rusty.

Annoyed by Piper's obvious dig, Janie insisted, "You are confused, Piper. Too much information rolling around in that pretty little head of yours." Janie made circles with her index finger to drive the point home. "Perhaps you need to keep note cards on all of your acquaintances. Carolyn graduated from Vanderbilt with a degree in chemistry. Quite frankly, not sure how she finagled that one, but that's not my story to tell. She worked for a couple of drug companies as a rep until she married Donald. I, on the other hand, graduated from Sewanee. I worked as a local reporter in Tennessee for a few years and then became a morning news anchor."

"Really? What caused you to relinquish your television tiara?" Piper just had to know.

"The long hours kept me away from Ed too long which is never good for a married couple, especially newlyweds. Plus it didn't pay enough to warrant me getting up before his cock crowed. I mean *the* cock crowed. Whatever. I gave it up when we moved back to Woodlawn. Now I just keep myself occupied with some freelance work. Why the sudden interest in my employment history? Has Charles's money run out already? Oh, don't tell me. You're looking for a job?"

"No, it hasn't. Not that it's any of your business anyway. Actually, I, too, am employed, part-time. You're not the only one in town earning a little cash on the side." Piper chimed.

"Since when?" snapped Rusty.

Piper rolled her eyes at him. His master plan involved Piper barefoot and pregnant in the kitchen. Not bringing home the bacon and frying it up in a pan. "I told you all about it the other day. Guess you weren't listening again."

"You did not! I would have remembered that! First, you find a dead body. Now you're telling me you have

a job. Dare I ask...do you have a new boyfriend, too?"
Rusty threw his hands on his hips like a defiant two-
year-old.

*Really? We're going down this road right now in
front of the town crier. Give me a break.* The whole
point of the conversation was to grill Janie. Not her.
Rusty was acting like a spoiled brat. "If you remember
correctly, when you came over to tell me about your
brother I filled you in on my news, too. I've had a lot
of stuff going on lately. You know...dead body.
Hysterical, lunatic wife. You're not the only one with
issues. And, why would you think I had another
boyfriend?" Piper furrowed her brow in disbelief.

"So are you going to tell us or not?" said Janie. She
switched the box to her other hip. "This box is getting
heavy, and I need to get home to relieve the nanny."

Piper felt trapped. Two against one with nowhere to
hide.

"Well, if you must know...Peeps & Petals." There.
She had said it.

Janie spewed a raucous laugh. "Finally, a job
perfectly suited for all of your talents. I wish you the
best of luck." Before Piper had a chance to respond,
Janie hightailed it to her car, click clacking along the
way in her three-inch heels.

"Peeps & Petals? C'mon, babe. Why didn't you tell
me you needed some money? The only person who
should be seeing you naked is me." Rusty reached out
to Piper embracing her in a tender hug.

"Get over yourself!" Piper pushed him away. "I'm
not stripping, you fool. I'm doing some secretarial work
for Chad. He called me on Tuesday night and asked if I
could spare a few hours a day to help him straighten
things out. From what I understand, the books are a
mess. I told him I could start next week. What better

way to find the killer than to be on the inside track. Now that Janie knows, my cover has been blown."

"Not necessarily, babe. If anything, the killer might be breathing a sigh of relief knowing that you're otherwise occupied. But, the thought of you stripping …"

"Stop right there. Let's go in the store and check up on your little brother. I'd be happy to show you my so-called pole moves later in private." His childish rant was all but forgotten. Piper's devilish grin gave him a ray of hope that future sexual favors were a definite possibility.

"Am I glad to see you two," Tom said with a sigh of relief as the couple walked into the store.

"Business that slow?" asked Rusty. He threw his keys and wallet on the counter.

"Yes, I mean no." Tom paced back and forth behind the counter like a rat in a maze.

Piper and Rusty turned toward each other with puzzling looks on their faces.

"Which is it?"

"Well, business has been slow but steady. It's not the customers I am talking about. It's the visitors."

"Spit it out, boy," Piper insisted. She hopped on the barstool behind the counter as he moved out of her way. "Are you looking forward to taking my sister to the Member-Member tomorrow night? She's counting on you to show her a good time." Piper slapped him on the shoulder.

"No, I don't think that's going to be happening," he retorted. "She has much bigger problems on her hands right now than attending the Member-Member party at the club with me."

"What the heck? You said you'd go. I can't believe you're bailing on her at the last minute!" Piper turned around and faced Rusty. "I told you I shouldn't have agreed to this match-making. She claimed to be ready to dip her toes into the dating pool, but I had my doubts. I should have set her up first with someone dependable from the club rather than your wayward brother. Now what's my sister supposed to do for a date tomorrow night? Evidently, your brother is cuckoo for Cocoa Puffs."

Rusty sighed. "Enough. Both of you are driving me crazy. Tom, what are you talking about? What has happened that changed your mind about taking Penelope to the club? Did you two have words?"

"Not directly." Tom haphazardly ran his hands through his blond hair. The man appeared dazed and confused.

"That's great. You decide to ditch her without giving her the courtesy to tell her face-to-face. What did you do? Drive by her house and put a note in her mailbox?" Piper jeered. "Nice brother you have, Rusty."

"I never said I didn't *want* to go with her," insisted Tom.

"Well, then, what gives?" said Rusty.

"You may want these," stammered Tom as he threw Rusty the car keys.

"And leave you here running the store, I don't think so. You're a mess, bro. What's going on?" Rusty's obvious concern for his brother temporarily cooled Piper's jets.

Tom took a moment to gather his thoughts. "About fifteen minutes ago, Dani Barnes stopped by looking for you two. She said something about needing to talk with Piper about an alibi. Not sure what that meant."

"Dani?" She thought it odd he used her nickname.

Rusty glared at Piper. His disappointment in her involvement with that woman was loud and clear. "Go on."

"Well, before I had a chance to answer, her cell phone went off. It was Penelope looking for you guys."

Piper chimed in, "Evidently we're quite popular these days. I didn't realize she and Penelope were friends. I wonder why she just didn't call me on my cell." Making light was her way of try to diffuse the situation.

Rusty just shook his head as if to say enough already.

"She said she called and texted you, but you never answered. And, I don't think they are really friends, Piper, but they may be now. Penelope just needed someone with connections and fast."

"Why?" asked Piper. Looking through her purse she added, "I must have left my phone charging on the counter."

"I hate to be the one to tell you, but Penelope was pulled over for going through a stop sign this afternoon." He looked fidgety.

"So what? My sister rolls through them all the time. Did Captain Morgan give her a ticket? Wait 'til I get my hands on him." Piper was wringing her hands.

"I wouldn't go slinging any mud around right now." Tom's forehead started to sweat. An eerie feeling crept up their spines. Something was not quite right.

"I can't take this anymore, Tom. Just tell us," Rusty demanded. Piper nuzzled up to Rusty rubbing his arm in support.

"Fine, but don't shoot the messenger. When Captain Morgan pulled her over, he decided to do a random search. In the trunk of her car, he found something," he grimaced.

Piper gasped in horror. Rusty appeared mortified. "What? What did he find?" shrieked Piper.

"A bloody golf club." Tom hesitated for a brief moment. The news had to be told. Too bad he was the one who had to deliver it. "He has reason to believe that it may be the murder weapon used to kill Representative Barnes."

Hole 7

By the time Rusty and Piper were able to spring Penelope from the county jail, the sun was just coming up over Woodlawn. Preliminary results from the lab had indicated the blood to be from an animal not a human. Most likely a pig or chicken. Evidently someone wanted to put the fear of God into Penelope and her sister. It had worked. The girls were trembling like frightened church mice in search of a lost nibble of cheese.

Meanwhile, preparations were underway for the evening's big event. Red carpets were laid, tables set, and flowers delivered in order to transform the ballroom into a magical wonderland. The who's who of the club was preoccupied with last minute details. From wardrobe selections to hair extensions and shellac nails, the women of Woodlawn were primping with excitement for what surely would be a memorable night.

Piper insisted Rusty rectify Penelope's date situation with Tom. This he did. The two were back on as previously planned even though Penelope's attendance at the night's event was not yet confirmed. As for Tom, he had no choice in the matter. His presence was mandatory according to Piper. She insisted Penelope's psychological well-being depended on it. It was bad enough her sister had been wrongly accused of murder. To also be dateless in Woodlawn would have been the kiss of death. No pun intended.

The proposed plan had the foursome meeting up around five for some pre-party cocktails at Penelope's which was the former residence of Mrs. Haigley…the woman found guilty of killing Piper's husband. As a sign of atonement, Mrs. Haigley had given Penelope permission to reside there in hopes of earning some points with Piper. Due to prison overcrowding, Mrs. Haigley had the chance of being paroled early for good behavior despite her crime. The wise old woman intended to keep her options open should that day come, hopefully sooner rather than later.

Piper crashed at Penelope's upon their return simply due to convenience sake. Being faced with drama in the wee hours of the morning had wreaked havoc on her face. From puffy eyes to blotchy skin, her complexion looked horrific. Thank goodness she was well versed in make-up application. She would need all the tips and tricks she could muster up in order to make herself presentable by five.

Rusty chose to head home rather than joining Piper in the guest bedroom. With the liquor store and his budding private eye business needing his attention, he couldn't possibly afford to waste any more time. Having Piper lying next to him wouldn't bode well in terms of actually getting some sleep. Thoughts of hot sex surely would have clouded his mind. Plenty of time for that later on tonight. An open bar at the club guaranteed some fooling around for married and single folks alike.

Rusty went to his makeshift office above his mother's garage. Her offer to loan him the two rooms made sense although he was well aware that it came with strings attached. He needed space. She needed a viable excuse for keeping tabs on him. Being paralyzed from a car accident years ago precluded her from using the area. The rest of the house was equipped with handicap accessible equipment. From higher toilet seats to handrails strategically placed on the walls, the ranch style house was a comfortable haven for his mother. All that was missing was the sound of another human's voice. The intercom system she'd installed enabled her to check on Rusty's comings and goings without being overtly obvious. Most times he didn't even realize she was eavesdropping. Of course, when caught she blamed it on faulty wiring. Thank goodness for modern inventions. There was no escape. She had him right where she wanted.

Luckily, she spotted Rusty pulling into the driveway. Having retrieved the morning paper, she was just heading back into the house. As she waited for him to park, she took the newspaper out of its plastic bag. Strewn across the front page was a disturbing headline. "Sister Sacks State Rep." *What is Rusty's girlfriend up to now?* she thought. Helen had her doubts about her son's latest paramour. Sure, Piper had been cleared of her wealthy older husband's murder, but now she was connected to another dead body. *What if my son is her next victim?*

Jumping out of his truck, Rusty smiled as he approached his mom. Admiration is what he felt towards this woman. The cards she'd been dealt did nothing to deter her will as of late. Sure, the early years had been tough for her but now she was like a new woman. Positive and downright pleasant. His mom had really turned herself around for the better. Rusty was just thankful she'd hung in there as long as she had. Not every tragic accident had such a happy ending.

"You're up bright and early today, son," she shouted. The tone of her voice gave away her sheer joy of seeing him.

"More like never went to bed." He leaned down and kissed his mom on her cheek.

"Has that new girlfriend of yours kept you out 'til the wee hours of the morning? I thought you were passed those reckless party days. By the way, you might want to take a look at this morning's headlines. What kind of company are you keeping, dear?" She had a worrisome look in her eyes.

Rusty grabbed hold of the newspaper. No need for him to read it. He could have written the story himself. Piper and her sister were in over their heads as far as he was concerned. Asking them to lie low while the dust settled wasn't even an option. The girls loved the limelight whether it was positive or negative. Like moths to a flame. It was up to Rusty to put the brakes on this murder investigation before the girls wound up spinning out of control.

Typical in their don't ask/don't tell relationship, Rusty ran circles around the truth giving his mom just enough information to keep her satisfied. He knew she meant well; however, he could do with one less female meddling in his affairs. There was too much to accomplish in such a short amount of time. Each hour brought with it another twist in the case. His top priority involved eliminating suspects in order to pinpoint the killer. His most obvious choice was Danielle. From what Piper had shared, Danielle had both motive and opportunity. It was up to Rusty to bring her to justice.

Interrupting his thought process, Helen said, "So how does Piper feel about having Danielle around? Personally, I'd rather not have to compete with yet another woman for a tiny morsel of your attention. It's hard enough as it is."

Rusty snapped to attention. "Don't you think you're being a little melodramatic, mom? I stop by on a regular basis. If you need me, you know where to find me."

With a slight chuckle she added, "You didn't answer my question, son. Are you still harboring feelings for that fiery redhead?"

"Really, mom? You have to go there? Let's just forget you ever brought that up." Rusty shifted from one foot to another. A telltale sign he felt uncomfortable.

"You haven't mentioned the fact that you were once engaged to that woman? Rusty, I thought I'd raised you better than that. If I were Piper, I would be angry beyond belief if I…"

"No need to go there, mom. The relationship was doomed from the start. Dani used me to get to Gus. End of story. My ego took a beating. One which I choose to forget, thank you very much. Dani moved on. So have I."

"It's not as simple as you make it out to be," Helen sighed. "Your ex-fiancé's husband was murdered. Don't you think someone's going to find out that you two were connected? What if Captain Morgan believes you had a hand in this gruesome mess? A scorned lover seeking revenge. Her husband was a state representative for goodness sakes, Rusty. The information is out there just waiting for some nosey reporter to uncover. I think it's best to be forthcoming before it's too late. Or, if you'd rather be behind bars for a murder you didn't commit, then have at it. It's your call, son."

Rusty hated to admit it, but his mom did have a valid point. He and Piper had briefly discussed past love interests. He had conveniently neglected to mention Danielle. Never in a million years did he think their paths would cross. Damn her. Things had just gotten a whole lot more complicated.

Meanwhile, Piper and Penelope were just sipping their first cup of coffee when the doorbell rang. "Expecting company, sis?" asked Piper.

"Actually no, I'm not. Would you mind getting the door? I'm not in the mood for another surprise." Penelope rummaged through the newspaper in search of the entertainment section.

Rising up from her chair, Piper gingerly stepped towards the door. Pushing aside the curtain ever so slightly, she peeked through the window pane. "Not now."

"Who is it?" shouted Penelope from the kitchen.

"My new best friend." Opening the door, Piper said, "What brings you here so bright and early, Danielle?"

"I thought you could use some reinforcements. What'd you think? I'd leave you high and dry? Word on the street is that you and your sister are prime suspects in my husband's murder. Don't worry, honey. I've got connections. We'll figure something out." Danielle breezed right by Piper and bee-lined it for the kitchen. All that could be seen was a flash of bright red hair. "I smell coffee brewing. Gosh, I really could use a cup."

As Danielle veered around the corner, she practically knocked Penelope right off of her feet.

"Whoa! Danielle! What are you doing here?" The sisters exchanged puzzling glances. Danielle looked refreshed and relaxed dressed in black yoga pants with a purple blouson top.

"As I already mentioned to your sister, I'm here to help. Why are you both acting so surprised?" The three of them huddled together by the sink each waiting for the other to speak first. Danielle looked rather put out as if her being there should have been an obvious assumption. Piper and Penelope on the other hand looked dazed and confused.

"Fine," said Danielle. "I'll go first. Girls, I really don't need to know which one of you is responsible for Gus's death. I just want to go on the record as saying thank you. My life will be so much better without that egotistical pig breathing down my back."

"But…" interrupted Piper.

"Let me finish. If I were you, and thank heavens I'm not, I'd take advantage of being at the club tonight and put my feelers out. There has to be someone you can pin this one on. I'll do my best to snoop around and see what I can find out. I'd hate for one of you pretty girls to wind up behind bars. Of course, you've already been there, Penny. And you, Piper. It would be a shame for Rusty to have to lose yet another fiancée. Oh, sorry. I forgot. You all are just dating. Poor guy. He just can't seem to find Ms. Right. Perhaps now he'll finally get his second chance. Okay, enough about me. I need to go. See you tonight." Danielle air kissed both girls and then scooted out the front door.

"Mind explaining to me what the hell just happened there? Is it me or is that woman absolutely insane?" Penelope sat down at the kitchen table. "And why does she think we offed her husband? I wasn't even at the club when it happened."

Piper neglected to respond.

"Maybe we should give Rusty a call and see if he can make any sense out of what Danielle had to say. And did you catch that fiancée comment? What was that all about? I didn't know Rusty had been engaged before. Did you?" Penelope scrunched up her nose in bewilderment.

"Oh, no. He must have forgotten to mention that little fact. Don't you worry, sis. I'll get to the bottom of this. That man has some explaining to do." Piper balled her fist, and off she went.

It took Piper less than fifteen minutes to arrive at Helen's doorstep. Her finesse on the roadway could have easily rivaled that of Danica Patrick. As she swerved out of harm's way and dodged oncoming traffic, Piper meticulously rehearsed her speech in hopes of not sounding too emotional or over the top. Driven by raw emotion, she felt like a scorned lover right out of some steamy romance novel.

Piper had never been to Rusty's mother's house. For one reason, she wanted to keep their relationship at arm's length. Once family became involved, breaking ties was not as easy. Her fear of betrayal prohibited her from simply letting go. Evidently her instincts were right on the mark. Piper kicked herself for not following her gut in the first place. Rusty was just like all those other losers from her past. He could not be trusted.

As soon as she turned the corner, Piper spotted Rusty's dirty pick-up truck. Taking deep breaths, she gathered her thoughts one last time. She wanted to make sure she had her questions down pat in order to beat him at his own game. If there was one thing Piper knew better than anything else, it was how to catch a cheat. If truth be told, Piper was a tad bit nervous about what was about to go down. She feared Helen might jump to her son's defense which would make their confrontation twice as hard. To avoid that, she zipped into the driveway, hopped out of the Mercedes, and dashed up the stairs to the loft apartment in three seconds flat. Not too bad for a twenty-nine-year-old widow. Thank goodness for Denise Austin. Piper was fit as a fiddle, despite the few extra pounds of late.

Taking him by surprise, Piper bolted through the door. "There you are," she shouted.

Rusty flashed his girlfriend the biggest smile and replied, "Well, hello babe. What are you doing here? I thought you were getting ready for tonight. This is a nice surprise."

Piper snarled, "Oh, yes indeed it's a surprise. Nice? I'm not so sure. We need to talk."

Rusty quickly surveyed the situation. Something was going down and from the vibes he was getting from Piper, he sensed it was far from good.

"Did Captain Morgan stop by or something? Is there some news about Gus's murder?" he asked. She haphazardly fiddled with the tassels on her shirt.

"Oh, I had a visitor alright, but it wasn't him. Danielle dropped by. Want to take a guess what she had to say?"

Rusty may not have been the sharpest tack in the box when it came to women, but he was no fool. From Piper's demeanor, he knew hell was about to freeze over. If he didn't play his cards right, he'd wind up with a one-way ticket. "Uh, about Danielle."

"Yes, about Danielle. Remember on Tuesday when I told you that she and Gus were back in town? And, I asked you point blank if you knew her? What did you say?"

"I don't remember," he stammered.

Piper eyed him furiously, "Yeah, well I do. Let me refresh your memory, babe." Her words sounded like nails on a chalkboard tearing right through his heart. "You said something along the lines that you and she never met. You only knew *of* her. Isn't that what you said, babe?" Her fixated gaze made him even more uncomfortable.

"Well...what I meant to say," he scrambled for the right words to redeem himself.

"Don't even go there, Rusty. You're already way in over your head. Let me fill in the blanks for you. You boinked her. You dated her. You even asked her to marry you. And, you couldn't remember all of that?

What are you suffering from amnesia?" Piper stared him down as if daring him to come up with some viable excuse.

"Piper..." Rusty pleaded. He took a step towards her.

"Save it for someone who cares. We are done. Over. Finished. I want nothing more to do with you. I'll pack up your clothes and drop them off at the store within the next few days. Don't bother coming by. You are person non gratuitous." Piper reached for the door.

"What? Do you mean persona non grata?" Rusty asked trying to insert a little humor into the tense situation.

"Whatever!" she pouted.

"So, what about tonight?" He held his arms opened wide.

"Oh, I forgot about that. Please let your brother know Penelope will no longer be in need of a date, but thanks anyway. And as for us, there is no us. Although that shouldn't be a problem for you. Why don't you go ahead and give Dani a call? With Gus dead as a doorknob, I'm sure she'd love to pick up where you two left off. Good-bye, Rusty." And with that, Piper closed the door to what was once a promising future.

Hole 8

Due to the fallout from the morning's events, Rusty was forced to come up with Plan B. After filling Tom in on his precarious situation, Rusty suggested they head back to his brother's apartment to rest up before the party. Rusty didn't want to risk Piper finding him at the store or his office just in case she had more to say. The emotional strain plus the constant stress surrounding Gus's murder had taken its toll on Rusty. As far as not having a date, it didn't faze either one of them. A non-issue was Tom's exact word. He really had no interest in a relationship with Penelope. As he said, there was no upside in getting involved with her. Better to keep things on friendly terms than jeopardize his brother's future with Piper. As for Rusty, he felt sure Piper would forgive him…eventually. A little begging and pleading might be in his imminent future, but in the end it would work out okay. He knew all too well being in a relationship took lots of hard work. With nothing better to do, the guys decided to watch *The Hangover II*. A little raucous humor and a couple of beers would certainly lighten the mood.

Around five o'clock, the guys got dressed and headed out. The infamous pre-parties were starting to swing into high gear. Similar to a food crawl, various club members opened their homes for all to attend. From cocktails to savory appetizers, this portion of the evening sometimes overshadowed the actual big event. In years past, some members had actually skipped the

Member-Member cocktail party entirely in hopes of catching a glimpse of alleged rendezvous' between rumored swingers. Having such scandalous players among their own drew quite the crowds.

Despite all of the nuttiness, the coveted invitation for the night was for the party being held at the home of the illustrious Donald and Carolyn DeWitt. Every year, they threw an extravagant après-soirée party catered by the renowned Chef Henri Samuel. The guest list included the who's who of Woodlawn. This year, Rusty, Piper, Tom, and Penelope made the cut. After everything that had happened that day, it would be quite interesting to see what would transpire.

Rusty and Tom chose to stop by Jim and Laura Wagner's house first before heading over to the club. Since the Wagners were new members, Rusty anticipated a small turn-out. It was a given that Piper and her sister would not be there, so no drama would be involved. The Wagner house was a modest two-story home with black shutters. No grandiose staircase or breathtaking architecture to speak of. Just ordinary, like its owners. Upon arrival, Rusty counted maybe twenty people in attendance. The food was also light...pigs-in-a-blanket, chips, and various homemade dips. Man-food as Rusty liked to call it. Rusty made a point of saying hello to Tanya and her husband Johnny due to their connection with Piper. They were all hyped up about the evening's events which was no surprise. They lived and breathed the club as it served as the center of their social universe. The brothers stayed just long enough to not appear rude. Rusty had plans to do some investigating into the murder before the party swung into high gear. Unable to access the women's locker room prior to this evening, he felt the need to do some snooping tonight. If all went according to plan, he would be in and out before anyone even noticed.

As for the sisters, they were on a mission of their own sort. Piper was still seething from the news of Danielle's supposed "history" with Rusty. Indeed, she was overreacting, but what else was new? In Piper's eyes, any relationship at all was unacceptable even if it took place prior to Piper knowing him. In order to get to the bottom of this mess, the girls intended on catching Danielle off-guard. Danielle had lots of explaining to do. Simply neglecting to divulge her past was unacceptable even if she was newly widowed. Plain and simple...Piper was out for blood. Whether tiger or pussy cat was yet to be determined.

First on the agenda involved a stop at Janie's house. The golfing ladies were notorious for the pre-party bash hosted by the Vanhorsts. From tequila shots to various shooters, these supposedly dainty women let their hair down when not in front of the upper echelon, i.e. the crotchety, old ladies of the club. There would be plenty of time to impress the Joneses, so to speak, at the event. No better time than the present to get all liquored up. Not to mention, Piper was dying to get inside Janie's house. With all of the rumors circulating around about Janie's hot nanny, she wanted to see for herself how Ed interacted with his hired nymph. Carolyn would not likely be in attendance, though Danielle was rumored to be going.

As the girls turned onto Janie's street, they were surprised to see their hostess huddled by the curb. From a distance, it appeared as if she were talking on her cell phone. And, if her hand gestures were any indication, she looked irate. The alarms went off loud and clear. Something was up! Within seconds, Piper jerked the car towards the curb, threw it in park, and hopped out. As she hustled towards Janie, Piper couldn't help but notice her poor sister behind her sucking wind just trying to keep up.

Right as they reached Janie, they overheard her saying, "Of course, I realize what I'm saying. If you're not going to do anything about it, then I'll have to take matters into my own hands. She's your daughter, not mine. Fix it now." Janie snapped her phone shut. Startled by the sisters' sudden appearance, Janie stammered, "Well, hello, ladies. Do come in. The party is just starting. You're right on time."

Piper could see panic in Janie's eyes while Penelope surmised by the mere sight of her body language that all was not well. "Hi, Janie," said Penelope. "Is everything okay? You don't look so good."

"I look about as well as a person in my situation can be. It's been a long afternoon. Please. C'mon in the house. Danielle is here and she's already pretty looped. She's not taking the loss of her husband very well. The woman needs a shoulder to cry on, not a bottle of booze."

"I know just the person for the job," mumbled Piper under her breath.

"Did you say something, dear?" Janie held the door open for them.

"Oh, nothing." Changing the subject she continued, "Wow! Look what you've done with the house. You are such the decorator, Janie."

Taking the bait, Janie offered them a grand tour. As they meandered from room to room, Janie gave them a play-by-play account of where she had bought every single knick-knack as well as swatch of fabric known to man. The girls placated her with just the right number of *ooh's* and *aah's* when all they really wanted to know was whose daughter Janie was referring to and where the heck was Danielle. By the time they'd finally made it to the screened-in porch, Piper's face felt as if she'd been overloaded with Botox. Her mouth was frozen into a permanent smile. Upon entering, Janie noticed a few new guests, so she politely excused herself which suited the two sisters just fine.

"What do you think is going on with her?" asked Penelope. "I didn't realize she had a step-daughter."

"Neither did I," replied Piper. "Janie has three precious girls. I'm not sure of their exact ages, but if I had to guess they're about ten, eight, and six. Something like that. Of course, I wasn't around when she was pregnant so for all I know, they could be Ed's from a previous marriage. Although, those girls are the spitting image of Janie."

"Oh, look-out!" warned Penelope. "Danielle is stumbling towards us. Janie's going to be livid when she realizes the mess Danielle has made. She's sloshing her drink all over the floor."

On cue, Danielle sloppily approached them. "Yoo! Hoo! Piper! Penelope! Darlings, what a nice surprise! I had no idea you'd be coming." Her bold, geometric dress looked as if it had a life of its own as it swayed back and forth.

The girls stood watching her approach, one splash at a time.

"We must find a quiet corner so that we may have a chat, I mean strategize. Poor Piper being accused of yet another murder. How frightening! Penelope, you must keep a better eye on your sister. It seems trouble hovers over her like a sinister black cloud."

Before Piper could respond, Penelope jumped right in. "Danielle, let's all head outside. It looks like you could use some fresh air." She gently placed her hand on Danielle's shoulder.

"Splendid idea! Let me just freshen up my drink and I'll meet you by the pool." Not waiting for a response, Danielle proceeded to make her way to the bar in order to keep her pleasing buzz afloat.

Penelope had noticed the devious look in her sister's eye, sensing that she was up to no good. Time for an intervention of a sisterly kind. No one had a better handle on Piper's emotional gauge than her. "Let me take care of this, sis. She doesn't have an axe to grind with me. If you confront her about Rusty, things will turn ugly real fast. I think I know a way to get her to talk without making her feel as if she is on the hot seat. Trust me," she nodded.

"Okay fine, if you insist, but I need to know exactly what went wrong with their relationship, and why she didn't bother to mention it to me when she had the chance. We played golf together for over two hours for goodness sakes. We talked about everything under the sun including Gus's nail fungus problem. I think her having a previous relationship with my current boyfriend is of a little more importance. She knows what a small town Woodlawn is. Like I wouldn't find out? Really?" Piper accentuated her point with her hands.

"Calm down. I'm not the least surprised she kept her trap shut. C'mon, sis. You're not the most rational person when it comes to emotional issues. Why don't you go find Janie and see what's up with her daughter? That's more your speed." Glancing at her watch she continued, "Yikes! It's getting kind of late and I do want to head over to the club at some point to hear the latest gossip rocking Woodlawn. You've got twenty minutes. Meet me by the hedge in the backyard when you're done and we'll slip out like two thieves in the night."

"Or like a fledgling starlet with a brand new diamond ring. Thanks, sis. I do appreciate you helping me out." Piper gave her sister a quick peck on the cheek.

"Don't mention it." Penelope smiled.

As Piper made her way to the kitchen, she bumped into Liz Monroe, owner of The Cardinal Shoppe. The sisters spent beaucoup bucks in her store buying the latest Lilly fashions as well as an occasional Vineyard Vines skort or cutesy top. When Piper first moved to town, no one had even heard of the preppy label, but that didn't last too long. Known for her keen business sense, Liz invested in some signature pieces and the rest was history. Her small boutique stuck in the middle of the cornfields in Ohio was now the hottest shop in town. Who knew Piper O'Donnell's fashion sense and style would influence Woodlawn's most beloved establishment?

"Oh... hi, Liz! How are you?" Piper gave her friend a gentle hug. Dressed in a signature pink patterned Lilly dress, her svelte figure was the envy of many women in town.

"Piper! So good to see you, as always." Liz returned the embrace. "Love your outfit."

Piper smiled. It was no secret where she bought it.

"I don't need to take out any ads for my store. You're my walking billboard, darling," Liz proclaimed.

"Glad to be of service. You always make me look so chic. You wouldn't have happened to see Janie, have you? I can't seem to find her." Piper was always happy to chitchat with Liz, but not at that moment. She was on a mission within a limited timeframe. Every second counted.

"No, I can't say that I have. Do you have a couple a minutes to spare? I have something I want to talk with you about." Liz stepped closer to her.

Piper sighed. There was no escape. Liz always had a secret agenda up her sleeve. If it wasn't some charity event in need of sponsors, it was something else. Piper wasn't really in the mood, but she figured it was better to get it over with now rather than later. Liz had a way of hunting you down at the least opportune times resulting in a wad of unwanted raffle tickets or superfluous cookware. "Of course, Liz. I always have time for you. What's up?"

Peering over her shoulder in search of inquiring minds, she whispered, "I'm not one to gossip..."

That's a gross exaggeration, thought Piper.

"but...word on the street is that Janie may be leaving Ed for another man," she said in a low voice so not to be overheard.

Now this is something worth sticking around for, thought Piper. *I knew it.*

"What makes you say that, Liz? Has she mentioned something to you in confidence, or is this just based on conjecture? There's a big difference in my book." Piper glanced over her shoulder to make sure they were not in earshot of gossiping hens.

Liz's Cheshire smile said it all. "Ed and my hubby Rob played a round of golf last week with Gus and our unscrupulous County Executive Jack Conway."

"Oh, how is his ex–wife Kat doing these days?" inquired Piper. "Last I heard she bought a summer bungalow in Duck, North Carolina. Must be nice being her." The word *bungalow* Piper emphasized with finger quotes. Kat's divorce settlement from the philandering politician had made her quite the wealthy divorcée. "I can only imagine how many thousands of square feet it must be."

"I'll let you know," said Liz. "She has graciously invited everyone in our book club for a long weekend in July. Feel free to stop by the store when I return and I'll gladly fill you in room by room. Anyway, back to Janie. According to Ed, he thinks she may be seeing someone else. He asked Rob if he'd heard anything."

"Really? How did Rob feel about that?" Cheating spouses were Piper's specialty. In her experience, there were no happy endings, well, then again…that's not what he said.

Despite being engrossed in the conversation, Piper's eyes drifted to the mantle clock in search of the time. Fifteen minutes had flittered by and she was no closer to finding out any scoop. Then out of the blue it hit her. Liz! Who better than the town gossip to know the skivvy on Janie's personal life?

"Well, Rob said…"

The deafening sound of the clock ticking sent Piper into overdrive. No time for manners. Like it or not, Piper was going for it. "On our way into the house, Penelope and I overheard Janie in a heated conversation on her cell phone. She was saying something like she's your daughter, not mine. Fix it. Any idea to whom she was referring? I didn't realize Janie had a step-daughter. Am I missing something?"

Liz paused as if contemplating how much she should say. "Um…I thought you two were close friends. It's really not my place to…"

Now is not the time for being coy, Piper thought. "Is Janie in some kind of trouble? Liz, you have to tell me. Maybe I can help."

"Well, if you insist. Please don't tell anyone you heard this from me," Liz insisted.

"Of course. I'd never throw you under the bus," Piper assured her.

"The nanny helping Janie out is not just some hired help. She's Gus's daughter."

"Daughter!" exclaimed Piper.

"Shh!" replied Liz with her finger held to her lips. "No need to draw attention to us." A group of ladies looked up from their conversation. Liz gave them a little wave and then continued on.

"That's why Danielle and Gus moved back here in the first place. The girl's mother had a change of heart and wanted the young woman back in her life. For years, she'd been in a boarding school on the East Coast somewhere, but she graduated last spring. That's when everything started to fall apart for Gus. Of course, the woman held all of the cards so it had to be on her terms. The thought of another scandal in Gus's political career was her ace in the hole. She wanted the girl close. Janie volunteered to hire her as a nanny in order to help the woman out. Evidently, this girl has quite the body. She has started hanging out with the wrong crowd. I don't know if this is true, but supposedly she was dancing at Peeps & Petals."

Piper was flabbergasted. How did she not know this? She was going to be working at the joint for goodness sakes. "Seriously? You've got to be kidding. I had no idea Gus had a daughter from a previous marriage."

"Well, darling, until recently, no one else knew either. With Twitter and Facebook, everything comes out sooner or later." Liz stated the obvious.

"I thought Gus never had any children. Didn't one of his wives die from cancer or something like that? I never heard about a daughter." Piper shook her head in astonishment.

"Yes, wife number two died. Very tragic story. No, this child is not from a previous marriage."

Piper looked very confused. "What do you mean?"

"This girl is Gus's love child. He impregnated his second wife's personal assistant. Imagine that! He just couldn't control his urges. Typical politician. I guess I shouldn't be talking ill of the deceased. It's probably bad karma or something." Liz cringed.

Piper was having trouble taking in all of the news. *Love child! How could this be?* she thought.

"Hard to believe, huh? Makes Gus's death that much more complicated," said Liz.

"You don't say! But, Liz. Who is the girl's mother?" Piper couldn't help but ask.

"Carolyn's little sister."

Piper shrieked, "Holy shit! I'm sorry. Please excuse my potty mouth."

"No offense taken. You should have heard what I said. If you don't mind, please keep my name out of this. I would hate for it to get out that I'd had a hand in this news. I need all the business that I can get right now. As you know, the economy stinks."

With a head full of scandalous news, Piper hurriedly thanked Liz while promising to keep her source confidential. Piper could only imagine what her sister would have to say, although that would have to wait for now. At the moment, there was only one person in Woodlawn whom she wanted to tell, and she knew exactly where to find him.

Hole 9

As Piper waited to turn onto the familiar tree-lined driveway of the club, she was sidetracked by a peculiar looking tombstone planted firmly at the entrance. Granted, it was dusk, so her vision was somewhat impaired. Upon further inspection, she recognized the crest and WCC initials engraved right smack in the middle. Then it dawned on her. In order to drum up some much needed funds, the latest board of directors ran a campaign to purchase markers for each hole as well as a new sign for the entrance. Perhaps their time would have been better spent screening new members rather than purchasing castoffs from the local monument works.

The parking lot was already jammed pack with cars and it wasn't quite seven o'clock. Piper figured she'd better text Penelope to give her a heads-up. Penelope preferred to park as close to the building as possible. Despite living out in the cornfields for over a year now, she couldn't shake her fear of lurking predators. Normally, Piper would rib her sister over her silly paranoia; however, just two weeks ago, five cars had been broken into down by the driving range. Now of course, with Representative Gus Barnes's murder still planted firmly in everyone's mind, it was best to be safe rather than sorry.

After squeezing her Mercedes into a tight spot next to a rather luxurious Lamborghini, Piper sent Penelope a brief text letting her know that she was at the club. Figuring she better 'fess up, she also included a tidbit of news from what she'd heard from Liz. Of course, she promised more details to follow. It would have to suffice for now.

In order to dodge the crowd, Piper entered the building through the staff's entrance. The workers all seemed to think she had a loose screw anyway, so she figured no one would dare to question her presence. On cue, she passed three members of the wait staff. They threw her a puzzled stare and went along their way just as she had anticipated. Piper threw them a phony smile and then darted into the women's locker room in search of Rusty. She had no doubt he'd be there snooping around for clues. Granted, she'd only told him off just that morning; however, she already missed him. Call her crazy, but Piper was lusting after her naughty ex-boyfriend.

As luck would have it, the coast was clear. Piper managed to slip into the locker room without being detected. In spite of her best intentions, her cover was immediately compromised due to the eco-friendly lights. Like the Fourth of July, she was instantly lit up for all to see; however, luck was clearly on her side that evening. Although Rusty was nowhere in sight, she felt he was close by. To be safe, she dodged behind a row of lockers which provided the ideal look-out spot. Just then, her cell phone went off. Piper silenced it but to no avail. Rusty had apparently heard it. He came barreling out from behind the shower stalls with his faced locked in a grimace. He seemed very perturbed to have been disturbed. Piper, on the other hand, loved every minute of it. It wasn't her style to play such head games, but her wounded heart was clearly in the driver's seat. She slowly peered around the corner and watched him walk back. Quiet as a church mouse, she followed behind.

Sensing something amiss, Rusty stopped dead in his tracks giving Piper just enough time to duck down behind the dirty towel bin. Holding her breath, she listened for the sound of his footsteps, but all she heard was dead silence. *Does he know I am here?* she thought. Just as she was peeking around the corner, a strong hand grabbed the collar of her shirt jerking her to an upright position.

"Piper! What the heck are you doing?"

Piper stood face-to-face with her ex-boyfriend fully expecting to plead her case, but his dark blue suit transformed him into Woodlawn's version of a debonair James Bond. Not able to control herself, she gave in to her desires, grabbed him by the shoulders, and drew him in for a long kiss.

"But, I thought...," he tried to resist, most likely due to pride, but Piper proved to be quite persuasive. Within seconds, the two found themselves jammed up against the lockers. Rusty's pent-up frustration was exactly what Piper was looking for. Nothing like some hot and heavy make-up sex to soothe things over. Their usual sensual love-making turned into a college student's drunken lovefest. Piper's new yoga moves came in handy as Rusty devoured every inch of her body. The two couldn't help themselves as each piece of clothing was quickly peeled away. To spice things up, Piper guided him to the cold tile floor and made him lie flat on his back. Starting at his navel, she teased him with her tongue moving slowly towards his...

"Oh! My! God! Have you two no shame?" shrieked a female voice.

The startled couple looked up and saw Penelope standing less than three feet away. Their facial expressions mimicked those of deer staring straight into headlights. They remained motionless in hopes their predator would quickly disappear.

"Is this how you two think you're going to find Gus's killer? By screwing each other's brains out?" Penelope reprimanded them.

The two scrambled to their feet in search of their respective clothing while avoiding eye contact with Penelope.

With her cell phone in hand, Penelope scrolled through her messages. "Let me see. If I remember correctly, your text message said something like 'I'm done with that lying son-of-a-bitch. I'd hate to see what you'd do if you actually liked the guy."

"Okay, okay," answered Piper in the midst of fastening her bra with her silk dress in hand. "You caught me at a weak moment."

"A weak moment?" bellowed Rusty as he yanked on his trousers. "Is that what you call it?"

"Cool your jets, big man. You're lucky I'm even talking to you." She managed to zip up her dress without any help.

Rusty smirked. "Well, if I had a choice in the matter, I'd take the non-talking Piper any day. It was just getting good when..."

"No need to go on any further," insisted Penelope. "I know exactly what was going to happen next. Thank God I arrived when I did. It's going to be hard enough...no pun intended, to erase the image of you lying..."

Blushing, Rusty chose to keep quiet rather than come up with some witty rebuttal. He buttoned his shirt and then threw on his jacket.

"Enough already. Let's move on," interrupted Piper. "I have some big scoop I need to fill both of you in on that might help lead us to Gus's killer. That nanny Janie hired is not just some girl."

"What do you mean?" asked Rusty. "Is she some runaway or something?"

"No! I've got it!" interjected Penelope. "Janie's involved in a human trafficking ring. I saw a story about that on some news show the other night. What did I tell you, sis? You never know what your neighbors are up to especially in the suburbs...or cornfields."

The noise from the band was making their conversation nearly inaudible. The group needed to head into the ballroom soon before someone discovered them tampering with the crime scene.

"Hush! Listen to me! Janie's nanny is Candace Bailey's daughter," shouted Piper.

"So?" said Rusty. "Why is that such big news? What does that have to do with Gus's murder?" He straightened his tie.

"Aren't you going to ask me who her father is?" replied Piper in a loud and firm voice.

"Okay. I'll bite," answered Penelope. "Who is the girl's father? And by the way, what is the girl's name?"

"I am glad you asked. Her name is Willow Barnes."

"Gus!" shouted Penelope and Rusty in unison. The plot had just thickened.

With no time to spare, the trio discreetly exited the locker room one at a time. There was no need to cause suspicion among the crowd. The party was already in high gear. With budget cutbacks, the appetizers were few and far between. As soon as the wait staff exited the kitchen, the vultures were already on them swooping in for any morsel they could find. It came as no surprise that the bubbly twins were strategically placed front and center. These two twenty-something sisters were permanent fixtures at the club. Always looking for the next best thing, they threw an elbow or two at some feeble, old ladies while trying to snag some hors d'oeuvres.

As soon as they entered the ballroom, they couldn't help but notice Danielle. Playing the widow card, she had a group of about six men at her beck and call trying to gain favor with the wealthy widow. With a half-empty drink in hand, there was no doubt it was one of many for her. The volume in which she spoke echoed within the room. From fake tears to vivacious laughter, the woman spared no expense in entertaining her devoted crowd. As if she needed an excuse to be the center of attention, Danielle orchestrated a cacophony of chaos in order to monopolize her fans.

Directly opposite the group was County Executive Jack Conway. Over the shrill of Danielle's voice could be heard his nearly one hundredth rendition on how he managed to finish eight under par at last year's Glow Ball Tournament. Despite the chilly October night, Jack weathered the elements by staying warm with the help of his blackberry schnapps. His foursome's victory earned them a place on the coveted club trophy. What he conveniently forgot to mention was how Jay had to search the course near midnight for Jack's lost car keys due to his date throwing them into the woods. It's never smart to fool around with your lover's sister and casually mention it with everyone present. You'd think he would have learned his lesson from his notorious indiscretion with his secretary that caused his divorce from Kat. Perhaps he'd have been better off sticking with club soda. Details, details.

As the three made their way into the crowd, Piper couldn't help but feel that someone was watching her. With the killer still on the loose, it made sense to figure that he or she would be among them. Members nonchalantly trickled in and out of conversations depending on the importance of the person holding court. Penelope meandered over to a bunch of co-workers who were gathered around Dr. King, hanging on his every word. Piper gave her the nod as if to say go ahead. She knew her sister well enough to know her priorities were in line. Socialization and investigation went hand in hand. Grabbing Rusty's hand, she sensed it was time to head towards the bar in search of some alcohol to calm her nerves.

Evidently, Danielle needed a refill because she was heading in the same direction. Piper nudged Rusty, and the two darted towards a few empty seats at the end of the bar. When Danielle spotted them, Piper eagerly waved her over. As soon as they were situated, Rusty signaled Beth for service.

"What can I get you, folks?" Beth asked as she wiped the bar clean.

"I'll have whatever they're having," slurred Danielle. It was a wonder she could even sit up straight in her condition.

"Make that one gin and tonic and two cranberry cosmos, Beth," said Rusty.

"You got it!" Beth flashed him a toothy smile which was duly noted by Piper.

"Danielle, have you given any more thought as to cancelling book club on Saturday? Maybe it would be best if you rescheduled it." Piper was trying to be a supportive friend despite her dislike for the present company.

Beth was back in a flash. She gently placed their drinks on the bar, and then pretended to be cleaning some glasses as she listened in on their conversation.

"Why the hell would I do that? It's not like I have any place to go. My husband's been murdered. The police can't find his killer..." Danielle paused for a moment and winked at Piper conspiratorially. "I can't think of a better thing to do. Hey, Beth! Got any plans for Saturday night?"

Beth looked up and replied, "No, I don't."

"Well, now you do. Piper, fill her in on the details. I need to go find Captain Morgan." They all watched as Danielle hastily slipped off of her barstool and stumbled away with her drink in hand.

Rusty just looked at Piper and shook his head.

Beth didn't have time to schmooze as members were now swarming the bar area for drinks, so Piper gave her the pertinent information and then she and Rusty excused themselves. Piper suggested they go find Penelope, so they turned around in the opposite direction and literally bumped right into Candace.

"Oh! No! Candy, we're so sorry!" Candy's drink splashed all over the floor. *Better than on her dress*, thought Piper. For as long as she'd been living in Woodlawn, Piper never had said more than two words to this woman. Their social circles had never crossed. Before tonight, Piper had never questioned it. Come to think of it, Carolyn kept her sister as far away from the club as possible. Strange that she would show up here tonight, especially on the heels of Gus's death. Perhaps this was their much anticipated break. Piper could see the twinkle in Rusty's eye. He seemed to agree.

"Well, who the hell are you?" Her slurred words splattered all over Piper's face. *Truth serum,* thought Piper. There was no doubt in her mind. Candy was totally liquored up. Time to put the squeeze on and get some information. "Baby, get me another drink." Her so-called baby was a man Piper vaguely recognized. Racking her brain for clues, she was certain he was somebody important...but who could he be?

"I do apologize, Candy. I'm usually not this clumsy. Let me introduce myself. I'm Piper O'Donnell and this is..."

"One hot ass dude." Candy certainly had a way with words.

"I prefer to call him my boyfriend Rusty, but your name works just as well." Rusty extended his hand which was pushed aside for a sloppy kiss on the cheek.

"Friendly, aren't we?" Piper's annoyance by Candy's forwardness made Rusty crack a smile.

Candy totally ignored Piper's comment most likely due to her inebriated state...or perhaps simply rudeness. "Well, are you gonna get me something to drink, honey, or do I have to get it myself? It's an open bar tonight. We can't let the booze go to waste."

"Of course," the mysterious gentleman answered. The two didn't look as if they belonged together. Her date appeared to be in his early fifties and very well-kept.

"I'm sorry...your name is," asked Rusty extending his hand.

"Councilman Marc Bennett." He shook it in return.

Piper and Rusty exchange furtive glances.

As the recently elected county council president, Marc Bennett traveled in the finer social circles. As an avowed bachelor, he made sure to be seen with the most attractive woman affixed to his arm, though it was also rumored he might be gay. How he wound up with Candy was puzzling. Unless...the two were somehow involved with Gus's murder. When Gus was up for reelection early in his career, Marc Bennett had decided to challenge his seat and ran against him in the primary. According to what Piper had heard around town, the election was one of the ugliest in Ohio state history. Back-stabbing accusations hurled from each candidate made even the staunchest of voters hesitant to cast a vote for either side. In the end, it came down to Danielle's connections. Through networking among the women, she was able to garner enough votes to send Gus onto victory lane. Since then, Marc Bennett had stayed active on the local level with some minor appointed positions. His latest coup was certainly his most impressive. Why he would want to tarnish his reputation by being seen with the likes of Candy remained to be seen. Perhaps the bad blood from years past remained an issue.

"How do you two know each other?" Piper figured it was best not to mince words. The facts were the facts. And, knowing them was of the utmost of importance.

"We go back a long way," offered Marc. He seemed a bit uncomfortable. "Please excuse me. Candace, I'll be right back."

As her date made his way over to the bar, Candy locked arms with Rusty. She needed someone to hold her upright...might as well be him.

"Candy, are you two dating?" Piper was relentless.

"You could call it that. My buddy Marc needed a date for tonight and seeing as how I owe him, I decided to honor him with my presence. Have you slept with him, too?"

"No, I'm afraid I can't say I have."

Rusty glared at Piper. That was not exactly what he wanted to hear.

"Well, I'm sure if you want to it might eventually happen. Although Rusty here might have a better shot at it than you. Just saying..." She gave Rusty a little nudge to drive home her point.

"A shame about Representative Barnes being murdered," Piper said. "Did you happen to know him?"

"That son-of- a ...."

"Here's your drink, Candace," interrupted Marc. "One skinny margarita on the rocks with just a hint of salt. Just the way you like it." He returned just seconds too early.

"We were just talking about the tragic death of Representative Barnes. Candy here was telling us how they knew each other. Right, Candy?" Rusty and Piper sized up Marc looking for the slightest hint of guilt.

"That's my job, thank you very much." An authoritative voice insisted on putting a damper on their interrogation. "Why am I not surprised that you two are sticking your noses where they don't belong?"

"Who asked you?" No need for Piper to turn around. She knew exactly who was putting the kibosh on things.

"Well…seeing as I'm the one in charge of this investigation, I believe I do have the right to question folks when they meddle in my business." Captain Morgan tapped Piper on the shoulder. She turned around and was handed a fresh drink. "Why don't you spend more time socializing with your frou-frou friends? You better enjoy the party while you can. You're in for a very long night. See you later. "

Piper took a dainty sip of the drink, smiled, and then proceeded to walk away. She knew when she was beat. Captain Morgan raised his eyebrows at Rusty. Not one to challenge authority, he took the hint and followed right along.

As soon as they were out of earshot, Rusty took hold of Piper and said, "That was a bit odd. I wonder what he meant about us being in for long night. He must think we're a bunch of lushes."

"Speak for yourself. But listen…are you thinking what I am thinking? We just found ourselves two prime suspects. Why else would Morgan shoo us away like that? He's not as dumb as he looks. Candy and Marc both had an axe to grind with the representative. Probably one night over a bottle…"

"or two…"

"or three of wine," Piper continued, "the twosome figured out they both could greatly benefit from the representative's unfortunate demise. Wanna bet Marc submits his application to fill Gus's seat?"

"I wouldn't be surprised," he concurred.

"But why would Marc risk actually being seen with her? Wouldn't he have been better off just using her for info and then moving on?"

"Not if the sex was worth it," he stated matter-of-factly.

"Rusty!" Piper shook her head in disgust.

"I'm just saying…"

"What are you lovebirds talking about? Last time I saw you two like that you were discussing a dead body. I'm afraid to ask. What's up?"

Rusty shook his friend Jim Wagner's hand and then grabbed him in a half bear hug. Piper leaned over and gave him a peck hello on the cheek. Standing behind him was his wife Laura, a little hesitant as to how to greet them. Sensing her uncertainty, Rusty made it easy for her. He reached out and embraced her saying a quick hello. Piper just nodded to acknowledge her presence and left it at that.

"We think we may have some suspects in Gus's murder." Rusty wanted to make things right with Jim. By letting him in on their investigation, it would prove he trusted his friend.

"Unfortunately, so do we," answered Jim.

Rusty and Piper looked stunned. That was not what they'd expected to hear. "Really?" they exclaimed in unison.

"Well, yes, but you're not going like what we have to say." Jim looked over at Laura looking as if to say…should I?

"What do you mean?" Rusty did not like the look on their faces.

"It's probably better if you hear it from us first. Have you seen your brother?" Jim inquired.

Rusty shook his head in bewilderment. "Not in the last five minutes, but I know he's here. What's going on?"

Piper put her arm through Rusty's as she pulled him closer.

"Captain Morgan is not here solely for the festivities. He's about to arrest your brother for the murder of Gus Barnes."

"Tom?" shouted the pair in unison.

Leave it to Captain Morgan to come in and spoil all the fun.

Hole 10

The words *brother*, *murder*, and *arrest* were vibrating in Rusty's ears, so much that he couldn't concentrate on what Piper was trying to say. Beads of perspiration were dripping down his face. He'd sensed something was amiss with Tom, but he hadn't been able to put a finger on it. The likelihood he had committed the murder was slim to none. Being caught up in the aftermath was a whole different story. Rusty knew his brother all too well. If someone needed help, Tom just couldn't say no. But, Dani? How he managed to get himself entangled in this mess was anyone's guess. Rusty wouldn't be surprised if Tom even planned on his brother's wherewithal to help him get out of it. Tom's supposed involvement with Danielle had the potential of unleashing some harmful secrets which Rusty preferred to leave alone. Two murders in two years were a bit much. Rusty wondered how his life had come to this.

In the meantime, Captain Morgan was quick to act. Tom was nowhere to be found, which could mean only one thing...guilty as charged. *Fraternizing with a widow was his first mistake*, thought Captain Morgan. His mission was to find the suspect and drag him back to the station for questioning. With all the media attention, this high-profile case could be just the ticket to advance his career. *Major Morgan sounded much better anyway.* He was sick of the Captain Morgan jokes. There was no doubt in Morgan's mind. A big promotion would be in his immediate future if he could quickly apprehend the representative's murderer. The last thing he needed was Piper and Rusty mucking up his case.

With the large size of the crowd, it wasn't difficult for Rusty, Piper, Jim, and Laura to blend in. It looked as though the group were chatting among themselves rather than devising a plan to track down Tom. Of course, Piper purposely kept her distance from Laura positioning herself off to the right from Rusty. No need to risk being seen associating with her unless it was not totally necessary. Sadly, Piper's pride stood in the way of moving forward in their friendship.

Not surprisingly, Piper texted Penelope keeping her abreast of the latest developments. For some reason, her sister was not responding, which really irked Piper. *Of all times to not be checking your phone!* Piper's temper flared. Surveying the room for signs of her sister's blonde locks proved futile. The only person she spotted was Captain Morgan perched on the stage zeroing in on the crowd. He kinda resembled a bird in search of its prey. *Crazy loon!* Just then, her phone rang. Thinking it was her sister she said, "Where are you? I've been looking all over the place."

"Sorry," explained a familiar voice. "I'm in the pro shop. I didn't realize you knew I was here. I had the night off, but decided to come in and do a little spying for you. No need to thank me. Then again, feel free to fill out a comment card and drop it in the suggestion box on your way out tonight. I'm this close to earning a day off for superior service to members."

"Jay?" asked Piper.

"Yeah, it's me. Who did you think it was? Never mind. Listen. I thought you'd want to know that I just saw Danielle and Tom leave the party together."

"Get out! Really?" Leave it to Jay to find Tom.

"Yeah! Danielle was blabbering about something. I heard her saying she was sorry, sorry, sorry. I didn't know Tom was shacking up with the representative's widow."

"Me either. Evidently there's a lot we don't know about Rusty's younger brother. Do you know where they were headed?" she whispered into the phone.

"If I had to guess, I'd say Hole 5. Maybe they were hoping for a quickie in the restroom. Those outside bathrooms can be a little nasty at nighttime with all of the bugs and rodents, dontcha think? Not sure it's the best choice for that kind of activity. Do you want me to go follow them? I mean, I guess I could. Depends on how involved you need me to be. I don't want to be a Peeping Tom, though. Ha! That's funny," he chuckled.

"No!" shouted Piper. "Wait right there. I'm on my way. I'll go with you."

"Fine, but hurry up. My show comes on in five minutes and I don't want to miss the beginning. It's the auditioning part when the judges have their backs to the stage. I think Blake…"

"Alright already. I'll be there in about two minutes. Don't you think finding Rusty's brother is a little more important? And why didn't you just DVR it?" Piper didn't have time for an answer. Instead, she hung up and kept moving.

As she darted through the crowds trying to make her escape, who did she spot on her way down the spiral staircase to the pro shop but Penelope sucking face with Dr. King! *Guess her part-time job just turned into a full-time proposition,* she thought. So much for her claim that their relationship was clearly platonic. Not! His tongue down her sister's throat pretty much sealed the deal on that one. With no time to spare, she chose to let them be. She'd deal with her sister later.

Seconds later, she'd arrived at the pro shop. Throwing the glass door open with all of her might, she landed right smack into Jay.

"That's one way to make an entrance, Pippa." He gave her the once over admiring her svelte figure in the hot pink dress. "Love your necklace. Bold and chunky. Very in style."

"I'm royalty now? What's with the Pippa? And, thank you." Piper caressed her necklace. Jay had a keen eye for fashion. Having three sisters made him an expert on many things most men could care less about. One day, Jay would make some lady thank her lucky stars to call him her husband.

"I think the nickname suits you. Time to break out of your shell. Try something new. With everything that's being going on, you and Penny are kinda like royalty around here."

"I didn't realize I was the shy type. And by the way, nix the Penny. She doesn't like being referred to as a piece of chump change," Piper insisted as they made their way towards the counter.

"Have you seen the latest installment of Carpool Chatter? Whoever is writing it must be a member of the club. He or she knows all too much insider information." He went to grab his laptop.

Piper tugged on his sleeve. "Let's see if we can find Danielle and Tom First. Then you can show me the posting."

Piper had her suspicions as to the identity of the blogger, but she wasn't quite ready to share it with Jay. Finding Tom and Danielle was more important. Something just didn't feel right about Tom's association with Gus's widow. *Had he dated her, too?* she wondered. And, why had Rusty freaked out at the mention of them being together? Did he still harbor feelings for his ex?

"The band is so loud, and so bad. Who hired them? Do you know?" asked Piper.

"Not me. That's for sure. We would have been better off paying an eighth grade garage band instead of spending thousands on this gig. No one would have noticed anyway. With an open bar, it's all about the liquor anyway," said Jay.

"Speaking of booze, I start my new job tomorrow at Peeps & Petals." Piper grinned.

"Wow! You're stripping? What time is your shift?" Jay was obviously impressed.

Piper rolled her eyes. "Is it that hard to imagine that perhaps I'm capable of having a real…"

"I never thought they were fake," interrupted Jay. "I think you're perfect for the job."

Looking down at her chest she said, "not my boobs, you idiot. I have a real job. I'm helping out in the back office with the books. Chad needed an extra set of hands. What better way to find out what's really going down there than to work on the premises."

"I have a pretty good idea what's going on down there, Piper," Jay winked.

"Oh! My! God! Look, Jay!" Piper exclaimed.

Before Jay could continue down his dirty path of naught, Piper pointed out Danielle and Tom intertwined in a compromising position.

"Well, look what we found!" yelped Jay. He could barely keep his enthusiasm at bay.

"This definitely explains a lot. No wonder Rusty has been acting so peculiar lately. His brother is involved with his ex-fiancée." Piper just shook her head with disbelief.

"What did you say? Ex-fiancée? Whose ex-fiancée?" Jay babbled.

"Oh, yeah. I forgot to tell you. Evidently, Rusty and Danielle have a past. A past that he conveniently forgot to mention to me while we were dating."

"Were dating?" Jay was confused.

"Well, that's a long story. We broke up temporarily. He couldn't live without me, so we're back together," Piper clarified.

"Oh." Jay accepted her skewed version of the story.

"So, what should we do? Looks like they'll be naked-wasted in a matter of minutes. Let 'em have at it or stop the action before it gets to the point of no return?"

As much as Piper would have liked to have seen the expression on Danielle's face if they had interrupted them, Piper took the high road and decided it was best for all involved to walk away. Being high on Captain Morgan's suspect list was not a good thing. No need to add fuel to the fire by being caught cavorting with them. For all she knew, Captain Morgan would come up with some crazy story of her being involved in this tryst. Piper wasn't going to be the one to turn Tom in. Instead, Piper opted for scoring some points with Rusty.

"Let's leave them be, Jay. Now that we have found them, we can go tell Rusty. Let him be the one to come talk with them. It's not like they will be leaving anytime soon. I think it's safe to assume they'll be there for a little while longer. Don't you agree?"

"All depends on what Tom has in mind. How long does it take Rusty…"

Piper thought for a minute. "We're good. We have plenty of time. Let's go!" Piper took one more glance at the couple, shook her head in dismay, and then turned to walk away.

Meanwhile, Candy was busy stirring the pot in the main ballroom. Her consumption of alcohol clearly surpassed the legal limit. With no one in sight responsible for reeling her in, she was a fireball of destruction just waiting to explode. Flitting from group to group, she became the center of attention garnering compliments from the single men and married alike. Her supposed escort for the night was in the far corner of the room in a heated debate with County Executive Jack Conway. His absence didn't seem to bother her. Then again, she probably hadn't noticed.

Making her entrance into the ballroom was Penelope, fresh off from her rendezvous in the stairwell. Hooking up with her boss was not on the agenda for the evening, but it sure made for an interesting night. From all the text messages on her phone, Penelope gathered Piper was not going to be too happy when she eventually found her. Thank goodness Piper had no clue about Dr. King, or so Penelope thought. Having to deal with her angry sister on the verge of her boyfriend's brother being arrested was enough drama for one night. Having to explain why she was hooking up with her boss at the club could wait for another time.

"Are you done sucking face?"

Penelope whipped around and stared into the eyes of one seriously drunk woman. "Candy! You scared the living daylights out of me."

"Hmm. That's exactly what Gus said. Famous last words," she hiccupped.

Penelope took a moment to gather her thoughts. *That's what Gus said*, she thought. *Famous last words? Is this woman saying what I think she is saying?*

"I didn't know you had a thing for the doctor. Should have told me before you allowed him to stick his tongue down your throat. He and Marc have a thing going."

"What kind of *thing* are you talking about?" *Sure, leave it to me to hook up with a gay guy.*

Candy snickered. "It's not what you're thinking. Gotcha worried there, didn't I?"

Penelope feigned a jovial chuckle to hide her sigh of relief.

"Would you mind getting me a drink?" asked Candy waving her empty martini glass back and forth in front of Penelope's face. "Looks like I'm empty."

Taking the glass from her hand, "Oh, I think you've had enough, my friend. Why don't we sit down on the couches over there and have a little chat."

Candy was too far gone to disagree. She allowed Penelope to steer her towards the green striped couches in the corner saying hello to a few people along the way.

As the two sat down, Penelope took a quick peek around the room. There was no sign of Piper anywhere. *Darn it!* she thought. She was on her own. Penelope would need to choose her words wisely in order to get the much needed information out of Candy. Time was of the essence. It wouldn't be long before Candy passed out.

"So, you and Gus were close, huh?" Penelope tried the girlfriend to girlfriend approach.

Candy's face turned from happy-go-lucky drunk to cold stone sober. "Why do you ask?"

Yikes, thought Penelope. This was not the answer she'd expected. "Um, just wondering?"

"When it comes to Gus, no one ever just wonders. There's always a motive behind the inquiry," said Candy.

She's a lot smarter than she looks. Or maybe she's not as drunk as she appears. Hmm...

"What is Marc doing over there with Jack?" Candy became angrier. "I told him to stay away from that son-of-a..."

"What are you doing here?" a voice asked from behind the couch. Both ladies turned around. Draped in an expensive gown was Janie looking fit to be tied. "I thought you planned on skipping the party this year. Evidently, you changed your mind."

Indeed, the fireworks were about to go off and still no Piper in sight. "Well, hello Janie. Don't you look lovely this evening?"

"Cut the crap, Penelope. Where's your sister? Looking for her next sugar daddy, I suppose," she sneered.

Her cutting words did little to deter Penelope. The icy daggers in her eyes caused Janie to retreat.

"Let's go!" She grabbed Candy by the arm. "You've had enough partying for one night."

"Who are you to tell me what I can or cannot do?" Candy wiggled loose from her grasp and plopped back down into the chair. "Penelope and I are not through with our conversation."

"Oh, you're through alright." Janie gritted her teeth.

"Penelope! There you are! I've been looking all over for you." Piper flagged her down.

Of course, all three women realized Piper's and Jay's arrival had interrupted what could have been the turning point in Gus's murder case. It only took a matter of seconds before Janie excused herself. Not surprisingly, Candy immediately followed suit. She was no fool. The reality of the situation caused her to sober up rather quickly. Two against one was too risky of odds for a person hiding a dangerous secret. The night had proven to be interesting enough. No need to end on a bad note.

After Piper and Jay filled Penelope in on the recent developments, Penelope in turn did her fair share of divulging information. While they were talking, Laura stopped by to let them know that she and Jim were leaving. They were hoping that Tom would come to his senses and maybe check in with Rusty later on. Needless to say, Piper never bothered to share the news of Tom's little rendezvous with Danielle. She didn't want to risk Laura getting the credit for something she had discovered. For once, Jay kept quiet, allowing Piper to dictate how they were to proceed.

As Piper, Penelope, and Jay made their way to the exit, the sound of loud voices sidetracked the group to the bar. Indeed, Jack and Marc were in the throes of an intense argument. The trio grabbed a vacant table in the corner trying to be nonchalant as if they had intended on ordering a nightcap.

"Can you hear anything?" asked Piper. They were directly behind Jack and Marc.

"I'm trying to read Marc's lips," said Penelope.

All of a sudden, Jack stood up and yelled, "You greedy bastard. If it weren't for me, your political career would be over. I'm running for Gus's seat. Not you!"

Jay's eyes were as big as silver dollars. "Did you hear that?"

The girls shushed him.

"Oh, yeah?" said Marc. "Try to stop me."

Marc stood up and looked Jack directly in the eyes.

"I'd be careful who you mess with, my friend," sneered Jack. "Lest you forget…it doesn't end too well for those who dare to cross me."

That was all Piper needed to hear. She jolted up from the table and summoned Penelope and Jay to follow. As soon as they were in the hallway, Piper squealed, "I knew Jack was crooked all along. I think that's proof enough that he killed Gus. We need to find Captain Morgan and tell him."

"Hold on, sister. You don't know for a fact if he was referring to Gus. You can't go slinging accusations around without solid evidence. If nothing else, it's a solid lead. Although, I think Candy has more of a motive than Jack. Jack just wants his seat. Candy was screwed over by that jerk. There's nothing worse than the fury of a scorned woman."

"Don't I know it," mumbled Piper. Her sister had a point.

After a few more minutes of discussion, they decided it was time to call it a night. The crowd was dwindling plus they'd discovered enough clues for now. As for Danielle and Tom, Piper was too tired to follow up on that lead. Better to let the couple finish what they'd started. Their clandestine rendezvous would most likely be their last, if Captain Morgan had his way. If tonight was any indication of what was to come, tomorrow would be one heck of a day.

Hole 11

By the time Piper finally made it home, she was too keyed up to actually go to sleep. The incessant noise from her mysterious neighbor's lawnmower didn't help much either. Despite the blanket of darkness, he was partaking in his bi-weekly ritual of mowing his lawn. The headlights from his pick-up truck illuminated his property in order to get the task done. Unfortunately, the light shone directly into Piper's bedroom window lighting her room up like the Fourth of July. The neighbor's dogs on her other side added to the dissonance with their frenzied barking. Like usual, she chose to endure the inconvenience rather than to ask him to stop. He was known for quite peculiar behavior such as digging ditches in his backyard late at night. Piper didn't want to take the chance of winding up in the bottom of one. Thank goodness the man was not married. Then again, anything was possible.

After some much needed sexy time with her e-reader and the luscious Mr. So & So, she turned on her iPad to read the latest dribble by the infamous Carpool Chatter informant. Piper had no doubt in her mind Janie was behind it all. Whether she acted alone or had some co-conspirators in compiling the information wasn't clear. Piper wouldn't be the least surprised if she'd even formed her own secret Carpool Chatter club. Knowing Janie came from a news background made it even more likely that she had the wherewithal to make it happen. With all the information floating around on the Internet these days, finding scoop on just about anyone or anything was only a click away.

Carpool Chatter
Who knew two brothers
could share so nicely? Guess if
it involves a representative's
widow, anything is possible.
Now if only we could figure out
why Miss Pretty in Pink is
allowing her man to get mixed
up in the murderous mayhem?
Perhaps their relationship is
yesterday's news. Or better yet,
she is no longer the cat's meow.
With the representative's seat up
for grabs, there's no telling what
past transgressions might
mysteriously come to light.
Then again, if the truth is what
we seek, perhaps it might be
best if we just asked the hired
help.

Unbelievable, thought Piper. The Carpool Chatter informant was dead-on. Yet, Piper was perplexed. If Janie were the source, why would she blatantly mention Willow? Janie and Carolyn were chums. Janie had even hired Carolyn's niece as a favor. Why would she purposely throw her under the bus making her fodder for the general public? Unless Janie had nothing to do with it at all and someone else was responsible for the blog post. But who would be privy to that information was the question. Time to bring in reinforcements! From the police station to the newspaper, Becky Newberry had moles everywhere. It came with the territory. Being a hairdresser in a small town most certainly had its privileges.

Before Piper could continue on her quest to unmask the blogger, she had to first figure out what had happened with Rusty. There were no messages on her phone. *How bizarre*, she thought. Piper also wanted to share her news about the altercation between Jack and Marc. Those two were up to no good. Perhaps having Rusty stop by Jack's office on Monday would be a good idea. Jack's favorite subject was himself, so it wouldn't be too hard to get him talking.

As for Penelope, Piper planned on teasing her sister about the hot and heavy encounter with Dr. King, but that too would need to wait until morning. It was nearly midnight. She was not going to let her sister get off so easily. Combining work with pleasure could lead to a messy affair. Evidently, a little sisterly guidance was in order.

Saturday morning arrived quickly. As the birds began their morning reverie, Piper was awoken by the incessant ringing of her alarm. Grabbing her phone from the bedside table, she checked for a text from Rusty but came up empty-handed. Now she was worried. It wasn't like him to be so out of touch. So, Piper texted him…where r u?

Despite being sleep deprived, Piper was looking forward to her newfound employment for a couple of reasons. First, the bills were starting to pile up. Charles had left her a hefty sum, but Piper knew it would eventually dry up. Better to avoid dipping into savings if not totally necessary. Her hourly wage would not rock her bank account; however, it would finance some much needed wardrobe updates. Secondly, she was hoping to find out some inside scoop as to who was behind the establishment of the club. Piper felt certain

Gus's death had something to do with that. Piper knew she'd landed this position due to Chad's respect for her deceased husband. They'd financed some business deals together in the past, and he'd told her he felt comfortable trusting her with his business. Piper felt a tad bit guilty about her true intentions, but it didn't stop her from taking the job. She needed to find out the truth about the strip club.

After feeding her kitty Ralphie a quick breakfast, she gulped down a cup of green tea and ate a skinny protein bar. Piper had chosen a simple outfit for her first day, slacks and a cotton blouse. Her Lilly scarf and designer wedge heels dressed it up just enough. With a little make-up and a brush of her hair, Piper was all set. Taking one last peak in the mirror, she headed out the door ready to tackle the day.

Across town, Rusty's mother Helen turned over in bed trying to avoid the blinding ray of sunshine.

"Morning came early, huh?" asked a groggy male voice. "Looks like it's going to be a pretty day."

Helen smiled. It had been a long time since she'd shared her bed with a man, especially one with whom she was not married. "Yes, it sure did. Would you like for me to make you some breakfast before you head out to work?"

The man leaned over and tenderly kissed her cheek. "Why don't you sleep a little longer? I'll put your wheelchair right next to the bed and throw the coffee pot on as I head out the door. I think it's best I leave before your son comes around. Not sure he'd particularly like what he might find."

"Aye, aye, captain," she replied. And with that, the man left.

Max eyed Rusty with dismay. The stray dog's persistent whimpering fell on deaf ears. The sun was up, the birds were chirping, and it was way past his time for a walk. Being patient was not this dog's strong suit which was evident by the stains on the throw rug. Luckily for both of them, Rusty's cell phone rang causing him to awake from his deep slumber.

"Hello," he answered. Rusty squinted at the alarm clock. *Eight o'clock sure came fast*, he thought.

"Time to walk the dog," instructed Helen. "Poor Max is probably crossing his legs."

Rising up on his elbow, Rusty glanced over the edge of the bed only to be met by an angry stare.

"Mom, I still can't believe you suckered me into fostering this mutt."

"Sh!" she reprimanded. "Max has feelings. Having a foster dog will teach you some responsibility. It's kinda like having a child. It takes a lot of work. Remember that next time you hook up with that girlfriend of yours."

"How did you know I was still in bed?" He stretched his right arm up over his head.

Fumbling for words, she stammered, "I just figured you'd be with the Member-Member party and everything."

"Your voice sounds different. What's the matter?" Rusty was not up for a heart to heart this early in the day.

"Did you find Danielle and Tom?" she dared to ask.

"No, I didn't. How did you know they were missing? Did Piper call you?" he questioned her.

Helen wanted information so badly that she completely messed up. Best thing for her to do was rebound as quickly as possible. "You know how news travels fast around Woodlawn. Don't skirt the subject. What have you found out?"

"Nothing and he won't answer his cell phone. I stopped by his place, but he didn't come home last night. Most likely he's hiding out somewhere with Danielle. Why he got tied up with her again is beyond me. Sloppy seconds didn't work out the first time. Nothing good ever comes from hanging around that woman."

"You would know," Helen retorted. Changing the subject, she continued, "Will you be picking me up later for mass? I'd like to make it to the 5:30 p.m. Father John is presiding. He's short and sweet. We'll be out of there by 6:15 p.m. the latest. Promise!"

Rusty hesitated for a brief moment. "Sure. I'll pick you up around 5:00 p.m. See you later. Love you, mom."

"I love you, too," she echoed.

Rusty just shook his head. It cracked him up how his mother's choice of mass relied solely upon how long it took for the priest to finish. The quicker, the better. Rusty already had a full day scheduled, but he just couldn't say no. Good thing he wasn't due to tee-off until 9:30 a.m. If he hurried, he'd have just enough time to swing by Peeps & Petals in order to wish Piper good luck. He wanted to be supportive of her new job.

"Get your leash, Max. It's time we boys go for a little stroll." He rolled out of bed.

The happy dog barked in agreement.

As Piper pulled up to Peeps & Petals, she was surprised to see the parking lot was empty. Chad had texted her saying he'd be there no later than 8:00 a.m. Piper checked her watch. It was 8:12 a.m. The storm clouds above coaxed her into retrieving the spare key from under the flower pot. Luckily, Chad had shared its location. Her decision to go in was driven solely by her failure to use anti-frizz serum that morning. The humidity made it difficult to breathe. She could only imagine what it was doing to her hair. As she struggled with the lock, a light sprinkle of rain began to fall. Within seconds, she was safely inside. First problem solved. Her hair was saved. Now it was time to start doing what she did best...snoop.

By the time Rusty made it to the block where the strip club was located, he was out of breath. Max preferred to meander while sniffing and smelling everything in his path. Evidently, he didn't get the memo about the time crunch this morning. Frustrated with the little dog's pokey nature, Rusty swiftly scooped him up and proceeded to carry him the rest of the way. The unexpected raindrops put a damper on his morning due to the upcoming golf game. Trying to get the ball in the hole was hard enough. Unfavorable playing conditions guaranteed a high score from him. Hopefully, luck would be on his side and grant him a hole-in-one.

As soon as the building came in sight, Rusty was able to spot Piper's black Mercedes. Parked right outside the front door, her vehicle was the lone beacon in the parking lot. Rusty was thrilled to see Chad had not arrived yet. Having a few minutes alone with her would be worth the walk over. He needed to compare notes with her about what went on last night. He still had no clue where Tom was which irked him to no end. Common courtesy wasn't much to ask. Rusty had called him numerous times and left a least a dozen messages. Either Tom was fuming about something, or he was in trouble. Rusty was afraid the latter was more the correct guess.

When he reached the door, he went inside and shouted hello. The lights had been turned on in the main bar area, but the rest of the place was pitch black. He guessed the lack of windows was to prevent others from peeking inside. The reflection in the mirrors from behind the bar illuminated the stripper poles. He didn't realize they were directly behind him when he first walked in. Despite being the only person there, Rusty sensed a weird vibe coming from the room. Something was not right. He needed to find Piper and fast.

"Piper!" he shouted in no particular direction. "Where are you?"

No response.

"Piper?" he questioned. "Are you here, babe?"

Taking the silence as a no, he walked towards the wall in search of some light switches.

Where the hell is she? he thought. *She has to be here.*

Rusty went through the building, flipping on any light switch he could find. From the sound of Max's pathetic yowls combined with his incessant squirming, Rusty gathered the dog no longer wanted to be held. Giving in to his request, Rusty loosened his grip. Within seconds, Max torpedoed out of his arms and darted down the dark hallway. Rusty did his best not to trip over the random boxes strewn about the corridor as he followed in hot pursuit of the little dog. Sure enough, Max was on a mission. There was nothing he loved better than Piper in the flesh. Rusty was certain the dog must have smelled her scent. Up ahead, Rusty could see a light shining from under a closed door. *Bingo!* he thought. *He found her.* Max voraciously barked as he waited for Rusty to catch up.

"I'm coming! I'm coming!" he assured the canine.

As soon as Rusty reached the end of the hallway, he pushed the dog aside with his foot.

"Move over, Max. I can't open the door with you standing in my way."

The dog wouldn't listen. He ramped up his barking and even snarled a bit.

"What's your problem, boy?" Rusty had never seen him this agitated. It was then that Rusty caught a whiff of something burning. Looking down, he could see billows of smoke starting to seep from under the doorway. Taking nothing for chance, he immediately dialed 911 and reported a fire while he tested the doorknob for warmth. Sure enough, it was blazing hot. Thinking Piper might be trapped inside, he began kicking at the door. Max sensed danger and obediently moved aside. His barking was muted by the sound of Rusty pummeling down the door.

The sirens from outside gave Rusty a sense of relief; however, the door wouldn't budge. He had to get inside and rescue Piper. He was certain she was in trouble. Rusty headed back to the main area and picked up a metal chair. As he sprinted down the corridor, he prayed Piper would be found safe and unharmed. With one fell swoop, he rammed the chair into the wooden door forcing it to swing open. Not surprisingly, he was met with a gust of smoke which seeped into his lungs. Poor Max was frightened and fled in the opposite direction for safety. While gasping for breath, Rusty stumbled into the room engulfed with flames. It was hard to see more than three feet ahead of him, but Rusty forged on desperate to find Piper. The eerie sound of timber crackling echoed in Rusty's brain, making it difficult for him to concentrate on the task at hand. Piper was nowhere in sight. The thought of losing her made him panic causing him to trip over some seared debris.

His heroic mission was abruptly cut short when two burly firemen picked him up and turned him towards the front entrance. Fire Chief Grant Derbyshire demanded his two young lieutenants move Rusty out of harm's way.

"I can't leave. Piper's in there. She's probably lying on the floor unconscious. I have to save her," he pleaded while struggling to break free from their grasp.

"That's what we're paid to do," the older man replied. Chief Derbyshire was running the show now. He took orders from no one. His reputation for being a fierce yet demanding boss had earned him the top job years ago. The shades of gray around his temples were badges of honor from the twenty plus years of serving on the force. "You need to exit the building now and let us do our job, son. How many people are inside?" He needed the facts in order to safely secure the structure.

"I don't know," insisted Rusty. "I think my girlfriend is in here alone. Today was her first day of work. She came early to open up the place." Rusty just shook his head. "Damn you, Chad Freedom. Why did you have to give her a job anyway?" he spluttered aloud.

"But, you don't know. Is that correct?" the chief verified.

"Yes," he capitulated. The look of fear in his eyes said it all. Rusty was scared to death. He had no choice but to listen to the chief as they escorted him over to the ambulance to get checked out.

Meanwhile, a slew of determined firemen brushed by, armored with rescue equipment and hoses ready to do their job. They certainly didn't need Rusty mucking up their system. The sudden gust of wind brought about by the rain did little to make their job easier. In a matter of minutes, the place was engulfed in flames. What started out as a mere fire turned into a burning inferno of destruction.

As Rusty looked on from the rear of the ambulance, his heart felt as if it would burst out of his chest. The ferocity of the flames could only mean one thing. Piper was not walking out of there alive. Tears welled up in his eyes as his breathing became labored. Sweat trickled down the sides of his face as he struggled to catch a gasp of air.

"Oh my goodness!" shouted a familiar voice. "What the heck happened here? I was only gone for twenty minutes."

Could it be? he thought. *Am I hallucinating?*

Rusty catapulted from the ambulance in search of the voice he thought he heard. As soon as he made it to the front of the vehicle, he came to a complete stop. Standing less than twenty feet away was Piper haranguing Chief Derbyshire about how to do his job. Overcome with emotion, he collapsed on the ground in a heap of pure joy.

Hole 12

Stopping mid-sentence, Piper rushed over to help Rusty. She'd had no idea he was even there. His ashen complexion and smoky clothes alarmed her. Immediately she thought the worse. He must have assumed she was trapped inside with the fire blazing. Her knight in shining armor had come to her aid. How she was going to explain her absence from the building without looking like the fool was yet to be seen. To make matters worse, Rusty smacked his head on an errant piece of rescue equipment tossed aside by a fireman. He was out cold.

Chief Derbyshire looked on with dismay. His friend Captain. Morgan had shared many horrid stories about this notorious power couple during Friday night poker games. Morgan's angst and disgust for their meddling ways was the fodder for playful ribbing by his peers. Now it was his turn. Retirement was just around the corner. Perhaps this was the spark that would ignite his desire to finally extinguish his career, no pun intended. His wife Anna had visions of spending their golden years on a boat somewhere in the Caribbean. Nothing ever turned out to be easy. Chief expected Captain Morgan to arrive any minute. This was going to be a very long day for both of them.

"As I was saying…," Piper interrupted his thoughts.

"Yes, Piper. I heard you. You left the building with your sister Penelope in search of a flat iron." He knew this wasn't going to be easy, yet his patience was already wearing thin.

"Well, yes. That's right. I forgot to use some anti-frizz serum this morning. So when my sister stopped by to say hello, I told her what happened and she suggested we go back to her house. It was only 8:20 a.m. Plenty of time for a quick fix. I planned on returning well before my boss Chad had arrived. My hair would be perfect, and I wouldn't have to spend the rest of the day worrying about how I looked. Bonus for both of us, as I saw it. I wasn't expecting to find all of this. Any idea how this mess started? Quite the fire, huh Chief?"

Chief Derbyshire just stared at her. *Truly this is not happening to me. This has to be some kind of joke,* he thought. Before he had a chance to respond to her gibberish, Piper had walked away. A caravan of television news vans had just pulled up. Evidently, she was going to greet them. Usually, he detested working with the media. This morning, it was a welcomed reprieve.

The commotion from the influx of cars and vans combined with the cacophony among the firemen, woke Rusty up from his accident-induced slumber. Sure enough, Piper was gone. For the moment, Rusty was not concerned. His pounding headache needed his utmost attention. Rubbing his forehead, he proceeded to stand up only to be assisted by a dainty set of hands.

"Looks like you could use some help." The petite blonde coyly volunteered.

"Candy! What are you doing here?" Rusty couldn't help but notice how hot she looked. Dressed in tight yoga pants and some sort of bodice ripper top, Carolyn's little sister looked too good for just a casual morning stroll.

Acknowledging his wandering eyes, she giggled politely and responded in a low, soothing voice, "I was taking my daily walk. The noxious smell of smoke led me here. Any idea how this all started? Looks like Peeps & Petals won't be open for business for quite a while."

On cue, Chad Freedom pulled up. Both watched closely as the owner bolted out of his car and surveyed the damage. His grim expression matched the exterior of the building. Immediately he pulled out his cell phone and began taking photos of the damage. He anxiously patrolled the area as the firemen did their best to put out the flames.

While their innocent tête-à-tête continued, Rusty kept a look-out for Piper. Candy couldn't resist Max's canine charm nestling him in her generous bosom. At least then Rusty had a plausible excuse for his wandering eyes. Rusty thought it was rather odd that Candy happened to be in the area. Sure, she didn't live too far away, but with her past history with Gus and his connection to this place, Rusty had his doubts that her sudden arrival was purely coincidental.

Meanwhile, Piper was doing her best to clear her name. Like a caged animal, she paced back and forth waiting to hear any snippet of information that would exonerate her from starting the fire. The fire chief was busy talking with the news teams assuring each and every member that he'd fill them in as soon as he had some details. For the moment, the fire was still under investigation. It would be a few more hours until the site would be declared safe. Of course, as protocol would dictate, a truck manned with a few firemen would be left overnight to keep watch just in case the fire rekindled.

Piper was satisfied with what she heard. There was nothing more she could do, so she decided to go find Rusty and then head back home.

"Well, you've gone above and beyond even my wildest expectations, Piper." Her discreet exit was now ruined.

Sighing, Piper slowly turned around to face her greatest adversary, Capt. Morgan.

"We meet again. You can't get enough of me, can you?" Piper planted her hands on her hips.

Laughing, he replied, "I was going to say the same thing to you. Playing with matches, I see."

"Really? What makes you think I had anything to do with this?" she challenged him.

"Okay," he retorted. "I'll bite. Where were you when the fire started, Piper?"

Pleased with herself, she stated, "Not here. That's for sure."

Doubting her story he continued, "Alright. Let me rephrase that question. Were you in Peeps & Petals prior to the fire igniting?"

Piper hesitated a moment and then carefully selected her words. "Today was my first day of work. I opened up shortly after 8 a.m., but then left around 8:20 a.m. All was well when I came and went. I can assure you of that."

Captain Morgan was enjoying this way too much. Due to her previous track record, he knew Piper was far from innocent and watching her squirm gave him much satisfaction. Sadly for him, his guilty pleasure was cut short when Chief Derbyshire beckoned him over. "I have to go. Good luck, Piper. I'm sure we'll be in touch."

"Not likely," she argued.

While she watched him join his co-worker, Rusty managed to sneak up behind her. Wrapping his arms around the woman he loved, he said, "I thought you died in that fire. I thought I'd lost you forever."

"Is that why you were cozying up with Candy a few minutes ago? Don't think I didn't see you looking her up and down. Those curves were hard to ignore, even for a man so in love."

Amid playful jabs and stolen kisses, the pair celebrated their reunion in their own special way despite being in the center of the action. The destruction of the town's epicenter of lewdness would set the gossip wheels turning, which might help alleviate the need to discuss Tom's and Danielle's disappearance. Both Piper and Rusty had much to go over, especially Candy's potential involvement in Gus's murder. Rusty was going to have to miss his tee-time. He told Piper he hated to disappoint Johnny Vance, but hopefully Piper could help soothe things over for him with Tanya. Taking advantage of the chaos, they ambled over to Piper's car with Max in tow and discreetly slipped away.

Tom had had enough of Danielle's drama. Spending the night at her place was probably not his best decision. What she revealed to him between the sheets made him question his usual stellar judgment. Okay, maybe stellar was too strong of a word. Level-headed or even sensible would probably be more accurate. Right then it didn't matter which word he chose to describe his own behavior. He'd definitely screwed up big time. His fear of being alone with a possible killer made him jittery, antsy, and a bit insane. He wouldn't let her near the kitchen. Better to leave the knives in the chopping block where they belong, he reasoned. Good thing she didn't have a big appetite. When it was time for breakfast he managed to find some gnarly protein bars in her cupboard which they ate without complaint. Now he just needed a good enough excuse for getting himself out the door. At that moment anything was worth trying.

"Gotta go," he blurted out. Probably not the most creative choice but direct.

"Why?" Danielle must have received the memo.

"I think you know why. Being here with you makes me look guilty for a crime I didn't commit. Captain Morgan has probably figured out we used to be together. My arrival in town around the same time you appeared looks even worse. Heck, he probably ran a credit check on me as well. My mother would cringe if she read that. All roads lead to me, so I need to find another route. You know I care about you, Dani, but I'm not willing to take the fall for Gus's murder. I'm an innocent man, and I plan on retaining my freedom."

Danielle didn't reply. Rather, she seemed to be weighing her options. If seducing Tom would have made a difference, she would have done it. But she could tell from his body language, he was through with her. Danielle hadn't made it to where she was today by allowing a man—any man for that matter—to push her around. She called the shots. Always had and always would. Tom may have thought he had the upper hand in this situation, but little did he know she had yet to play all her cards.

"You need me as much as I need you." She eyed him cautiously.

Tom moved towards the back door. Tiny beads of perspiration started to gather on his brow. Her proximity made him nervous.

"How do you figure?" Tom replied. He collected his wallet and keys from the countertop. He had every intention of bolting as soon as he could.

"Imagine the embarrassment for your family having a murderer...." She dangled a veiled threat.

"You wouldn't!" Tom realized her true intent. Danielle planned on framing him for Gus's murder. The bile swelled up in his throat making him choke on his feelings of pure hatred for the woman standing before him. Hearing her utter those words gave him the strength to finally stand up for himself. "Don't waste your breath, Danielle. I may not be perfect, but you are the devil incarnate. I can't believe I let you suck me back in. You're on your own...you and your conscience. I'm outta here."

Tom didn't wait to hear her response. He left through the screen door and never looked back. Now that he had come to his senses, his next move involved damage control. Big time. If anyone could help him out of this mess, it would be his brother.

On the car ride back to Piper's, all Rusty could think about was sex, or the lack thereof. After his near-death scare, okay, perhaps he was being a bit overly melodramatic, but he thought he'd lost her forever. He was emotionally spent. Nothing would make him feel better than some hot, thank-heavens-I-didn't-lose-you, sex. With some playful chiding, he hoped Piper would agree. With Max in tow, the couple rode along laughing about the absurdity of Captain Morgan thinking Piper had caused the fire. Rusty kept his suspicions to himself solely for one purpose and one purpose alone. The man was in search of a happy ending, and he'd do or say anything to eventually get it.

Since Rusty had bailed on Johnny, he now had his entire day free and clear. He planned on making good his promise to take his mother to church. Perhaps he could persuade Piper to check in with Jesus as well. If nothing else, her presence might score some points with his mother. She made no bones about the fact she wasn't Piper's biggest fan. In the past, Piper had been more of an E & C kind of Catholic, only making appearances at the high holidays of Easter and Christmas. Lots had changed in the past year. Rusty prayed Piper might see the light. It never hurt to have the Lord on your side.

"Any plans for tonight?" Better now than never. It might take a little urging to get Piper to come along.

"Actually, yes. Danielle is hosting book club." Piper rummaged through her purse.

Rusty just shook his head. "I may not be an expert on today's etiquette, but something tells me hosting a book club party while in mourning may be a bit tacky especially for a representative's wife. You agree?"

"Totally, but who am I to judge? I had a BBQ picnic for my husband's memorial service." She found a pack of gum.

"Good point," Rusty conceded. He held his hand out for a piece. "So, what book did you read? I haven't seen anything lying around the house lately."

Piper snickered. "I have an electronic reader these days. I'm super high tech." She handed him one and then unwrapped one for herself.

"You avoided my question. Did you read the book?" he said.

"Yes, I certainly did. It's called *Fifty Shades of Beige*. Quite the titillating read, if I do say so myself." She tossed the gum back in her purse.

Rusty couldn't be more pleased with her response. "Well, by all means, go right ahead. I wouldn't want to stand between you and your literary circle." He raised his eyebrows in a rascally kind of way.

Piper pulled into her driveway and clicked the garage door opener. Max started jumping up and down in the backseat in anticipation of entering the house. The dog shared his owner's excitement. Being with Piper was their common objective. Max relished the fact that she spoiled him with doggie treats and playful jogs in the backyard. Rusty, on the other hand, savored her naughty sexual favors and lively romps in the bedroom in the buff. Each had their own dreams and desires. The question remained…whose wishes would come true?

As soon as they entered the house, Rusty had a sixth-sense that something was off-kilter. The alarm was not set. Ever since Charles' had passed away, Piper was meticulous about activating the security system whenever she left the premises. Catching her by surprise, he forced himself upon her while backing her into the laundry room.

"Can't you wait until I put my purse down?" she complained.

Rusty covered her mouth with his hand and whispered, "Shh! Someone's in the house."

Piper gasped and then squeezed his shoulders tightly. Good thing he'd thought ahead to cover her mouth. He gingerly removed his hand and planted a hurried kiss on her plump, pink lips.

"You stay here. Take out your phone and get ready to dial 911. If I'm not back in five minutes, leave the house and call the cops." He brushed the hair out of her eyes.

Piper whispered okay and then removed her cell phone from the side compartment of her purse.

"Don't do anything silly," he warned. "I don't want you getting hurt. We've had enough drama for one day."

Piper didn't argue.

First thing he did was check the kitchen. On the counter top, he noticed some crumbs. Unless the mice had been busy, someone had prepared a little snack. Moving towards the den, he peered around the corner to find an empty room. Rusty tiptoed over to the couch.

The cushion was warm. Evidently, the intruder had been there, too. The back staircase beckoned him over. As gingerly as his big, heavy feet would permit, he crept up the stairs one step at a time. Rusty couldn't help but think someone was playing a trick on them. Realizing the person was probably hiding in one of the bedrooms, he sneaked into the guest bedroom to grab the baseball bat Piper kept buried in the closet. Signed by some favorite major league player of Piper's ex-husband, she'd saved it just in case it was worth money one day. Rusty put his hand on doorknob and started to ease it open when pop! The closet door smacked him right in the face sending him crashing onto the guest bed.

"Took you long enough!" shouted a cocky voice. "I knew you'd come looking for this fancy bat."

"Damn you, Tom. What the hell are you doing here?" Rusty demanded as he rolled off the bed. In one fell swoop, he pushed Tom back into the closet knocking him on his ass. Then Rusty walked back into the hallway and shouted over the bannister, "Piper! It's okay. My idiot brother is here. Come up here, please."

"I'm right here," she answered from the master bedroom.

Turning in the opposite direction he said, "Does anybody listen to me anymore? I asked you to wait downstairs." Rusty shook his head in disgust.

Piper smiled. "Someone had to watch your back." She sauntered towards him. "No worries. You can punish me later. I'm your prisoner." She clasped her hands in pretend handcuffs.

"Is that my cue to leave?" interjected Tom.

"How did you get in here in the first place?" asked Rusty as the trio made their way back to the kitchen.

"Shouldn't leave a spare key under the front mat. You never know who might use it," Tom warned.

"Ain't that the truth!" tittered Rusty.

"And, you might want to change the alarm code. 90210? Really?" Tom rolled his eyes.

Over the next couple of hours, they compared notes amid generating various strategies to deal with Captain Morgan and the press. The white elephant in the room was Tom's inexplicable sexual involvement with Danielle. Both brothers chose to ignore the issue and focused solely on the insidious notion of her accusing Tom of murder. Piper floated on the periphery of the conversation inserting snippets of information when applicable. It was obvious she didn't want to interfere with the siblings' reconciliation. Naturally, the exchange circled back to the fire at Peeps & Petals. Whether it was connected to Gus's murder or not had yet to be determined.

When it appeared as if the men had exhausted all avenues, Piper suggested they part for the day. Each had a full agenda needing to be accomplished. Max seemed disappointed when it was time to leave, but Piper assured the dog with a tender scratch behind the ears that they'd meet again soon. Just as they were making their way to the door, her cell phone rang. Piper waved the men off saying it was probably Penelope checking up on her and that she better take the call. She promised to touch base with Rusty later on as the brothers scooted out the door.

As she checked her called id, she was surprised to see it was not her sister after all. "Tanya," she said. "I'm so glad you called. Rusty feels so badly about bailing on Johnny today. I hope he understands. It's been such a disastrous morning. Did you hear about the fire?"

Tanya knew that was not a direct question, rather simply an invitation to sit back and listen to Piper ramble. As expected, she did not interfere with Piper's meticulous retelling of the day's events despite knowing full well what had already happened and then some. With just the right amount of *oohs* and *aahs* inserted at the appropriate times, she proffered much needed support for her cherished friend. When she sensed Piper was finally wrapping up, Tanya warily interrupted in order to address the reason for her call. Being the bearer of bad news was never any fun, especially when Piper was concerned.

"So you were saying that you opened up without Chad being there this morning, correct?" Tanya needed to clarify exactly what had happened in order to make sure she had her facts straight.

"Right. He was supposed to meet me there, but he never showed up." Piper made her way to the laundry room and began throwing some clothes into the washing machine as she continued to talk. "Correction. He did show up when the fire broke out, but by then it was too late. I can only imagine how distraught he is. I hope he had plenty of insurance on the place."

"What did you do while you were waiting for him?" she inquired.

"Oh, I turned on the coffee maker like he'd instructed. Chad's diet consists of coffee, coffee, and more coffee. He's quite the caffeinated person. Doesn't eat much either. I guess that's how he stays so slim."

Tanya cringed when she heard Piper's response, and then said, "What kind of coffee maker does he have?"

"The cheap kind, for sure. First, I had to insert some flimsy white paper liner into the filter. Next, I had to guesstimate the amount of coffee grinds to use. I had no idea, so I just eye-balled it. Then, I clicked it into place. Voila! It was good to go. I'm sad to say I never got to taste the final product. By the time I had returned from Penelope's, the building had disappeared into a puff of smoke."

For a moment, Tanya said nothing. She needed to choose her words carefully before proceeding.

"Tanya? Are you there?" Piper must have thought the call had been dropped.

"Sure am," she chirped in return.

"Why do you ask? Do you know something that I don't?" Piper twisted a lock of hair as she paced back and forth. Ding! Ding! Ding! Finally the alarm went off in her head. "Oh, Tanya! I forgot to add water!" she shouted. "I forgot to put water in the coffee pot!"

"Yes, honey. We all know." Tanya tried her best to console her friend. "Have you seen the recent Carpool Chatter blog?"

Piper sighed. "I have a feeling I don't want to."

After some prudent words of encouragement, Tanya cut short their conversation. She hated to leave Piper hanging at such a vulnerable moment, but excused herself due to previous plans with her husband Johnny.

Piper turned off her cell phone as she stood at the kitchen counter. She surmised it was better to see what was being said about her from the comfort of her own home. She clicked the mouse attached to her laptop. Within seconds, she'd located the blog. Bracing herself, she read...

Carpool Chatter
Interested in remodeling your current home or business? Looking for a quick way to cash in on an insurance policy with no money down? Just ask for the name of Peeps & Petals' star employee. All it takes is just a flip of a switch. No water or common sense is needed. Rates are very reasonable and include the removal of murderous deeds. References are available upon request from ex-lovers and those who

have dared to cross her path. Prices are
subject to change depending on the severity
of the crime. All work guaranteed.

Hole 13

Of all things the Carpool Chatter blogger could have posted, why did I have to be the target once again? thought Piper. *Did someone put a red bull's eye on my back and neglect to tell me?* Frustrated by the latest jab, Piper decided to blow off some steam by taking a much needed walk. The morning drizzle had cleared up, leaving behind picturesque blue skies. *Perfect weather for listening to a book on tape on my MP3 player from the library.* Speaking of which, she had heard the Board of Trustees of the Woodlawn Public Library was searching for a couple of new members. Carolyn was toying with the idea of filling out an application. Since the likelihood Piper was ever going to work at Peeps & Petals again was nil, she took it as a sign that she was destined to apply for the position. What did she have to lose? She was unemployed, an accused arsonist, and a potential murderer. Who better than she to stir things up among the blue-haired librarians? As an added bonus, she could volunteer her services as a fashion consultant to the staff. Even librarians loved a good make-over. Her favorite Aunt Karen whom she immensely admired was a retired librarian from New Jersey. She was quite the fashionista in her heyday.

Pairing her gray cheetah yoga pants with an off-the-shoulder sweatshirt, she felt fashionably fit to engage in some light exercise. With earphones firmly in place, she clicked on her MP3 player and set out for a walk. The library was only a few blocks away making it easy to get to from there.

Within minutes, Piper was fully engrossed in her recorded book so much so that she tripped on a crack in the sidewalk. A quick look around confirmed no one had witnessed her blunder. After rewinding her MP3 player back to the correct chapter, Piper continued on her way. When she reached the intersection, Piper suddenly altered her route and headed down Elm Street towards Helen's house instead. It was no secret the woman didn't approve of Piper's relationship with her son. Hoping to curry her favor, Piper decided to pop in for an impromptu visit.

Piper couldn't blame Helen's reluctance to accept her relationship with Rusty. It had been a volatile one from the start. True, Piper came with a lot of baggage. Having been burned once, she was very reluctant to start over again. Oftentimes, she felt as though she were living in a fishbowl. Their relationship was front and center for all to see due to the unfortunate circumstances fate had dealt. This added stress caused her to react to situations a tad differently than she might have done had their relationship been not so public. Ironically, Piper was back in a relationship with core trust issues. This repeatedly kept her awake at night. At some point, she'd have to decide whether this relationship was worth fighting for, but not now. Too much was going on in her life to allow her to devote the energy into sorting it out. For now, she'd play nice with Helen in order to keep the peace.

When the house came in full view, Piper spotted Helen sitting in her wheelchair by the side door. From the way she was positioned, it looked as if she were waiting on someone. As Piper got closer, she noticed a police car parked by the curb. Piper's heart started beating faster. She immediately thought the worse.

Something awful must have happened. As she quickened her pace, she watched as Captain Morgan exited the house and placed his hand gently on Helen's back. Piper came to an abrupt halt. Suspecting she was witnessing something she shouldn't, she dodged behind some bushes and peeped out.

"Oh! No!" Piper couldn't believe her eyes. Captain Morgan leaned over and kissed Helen squarely on the lips and then tweaked her boob. "That jerk is sleeping with Rusty's mother!" Piper grabbed her purse and began rooting inside for her cell phone. "I have to take a picture. Rusty has to see this for himself!" Sure enough, she snapped a couple of candid embraces worth sharing. As she was readying herself to message them to Rusty, she thought better of it. Instead, she rustled out from behind the shrubbery and announced loud and clear, "Well, hello you two!"

The looks on their faces was priceless. Piper was certain she was the last person in the world they wanted to see. "I'm not interrupting anything, am I?" She couldn't help but snicker. She had them both exactly where she wanted them...on her side.

"Piper?! What are you doing here?" asked Captain Morgan. He looked sheepishly at Helen who returned the same expression.

"I was going to ask you the same question." Piper waited for him to respond as she eyed them both suspiciously.

"Um, I was, um, just asking Mrs. O'Brien if she knew the whereabouts of her son Tom. I need to bring him in for questioning concerning the murder of Gus Barnes." Captain Morgan seemed satisfied with his response.

"And I guess fondling her bosom is your way of getting her to talk, huh? I didn't realize Woodlawn's police force had sanctioned that as an acceptable form of interrogation." Piper winked at him.

Capt. Morgan's face turned beet red while Helen appeared white as a ghost.

"Are you going to tell Rusty?" Captain Morgan cut to the chase. He knew better than anyone in this town. Piper had an agenda.

Piper smiled. "Maybe. Depends on if you two give me what I want."

"I warned Rusty about her. She's evil," Helen said to him.

"I'm not evil," Piper maintained. "That's far from the truth. I think I love your son, Helen, but I'm not sure. I have so much crap going on in my life right now that I can't think straight. Excuse my language, by the way."

"Yes, I heard you forgot to add the water." Helen shook her head in disdain.

Piper groaned.

"So, what's it going to cost us?" Captain Morgan wanted to clear this up as fast as he could.

"Helen, I want you to stay out of my relationship with Rusty. I don't need you adding your two cents every chance you get. I'm a nice person. I am. I think if you'd give me a chance, you'd actually like me," Piper insisted.

Helen uh hummed.

"And, you!" she directed at Captain Morgan. "Leave Tom alone. He had nothing to do with Gus's murder. Danielle is the person you need to track down. That woman is evil."

"And, I'm supposed to believe you because why?" Captain Morgan asked.

"Because. That's all you need to know." Piper was adamant.

"Doesn't look like we have a choice, dear," Helen said as she patted him on the hand.

"I'm not going to be told how to run my investigation by some..." he stammered.

"Then, fine. Let me just text these photos of you two lovebirds to Rusty." Piper held up her phone for them to see.

"No!" they shouted in unison.

"So, we have ourselves a deal?" Piper held her hand out.

"With the devil," Captain Morgan mumbled under his breath as he sealed the deal with a firm handshake.

Piper didn't wait for them to kick her off of Helen's property. Her impromptu visit had certainly paid off.

Strategically placed in the middle of town, the library served as a meeting place for any number of clientele. Solidly built with rust-colored brick, the two-story structure was situated on a well-manicured lot adorned with attractive landscaping for each season. A gathering place for senior citizens, the programming and special events made it a hot spot for socialization. During the day, young moms congregated with their babes in the story time room engrossed in the latest tale. At night, the adults gathered for book club meetings and author chats. The local teens used it as a hang out due to the overabundance of blockbuster movies and video games available for circulation. The librarians set up various gaming centers in each of the branches in the county enticing the teens to congregate there after school. Believe it or not, it was cool to be seen hanging out in the library. The parents appreciated the staff's willingness to put up with the adolescent crowds despite the occasional nonsense that inevitably would occur. Whenever the county's officials threatened to cut the library's funds, it was the parents of these teenagers who rallied the community in support. In an election year, no one dared mention cut backs in relation to the library's budget. As one incumbent sorely learned, it would turn out be political suicide.

By the time Piper had reached the library, she was exhausted. Blackmailing in the name of love had turned out to be a strenuous task. All she could think about was finding an iced cold drink to satiate her thirst. As the sliding doors parted, she was met by a welcome swoosh of cool air. Breathing in the familiar smell of the library brought her much solace, especially during a difficult time like the present. Her happiest memories from childhood took place at the library among the big, comfy chairs reading Beatrix Potter's books alongside Penelope. Lots had changed since those innocent days, except for the fact that reading continued to play an important part in her life. Her taste in books was slightly more sophisticated these days. *Fifty Shades of Beige* had certainly proved to be an eye opener.

Just then, Piper's cell phone went off. The librarian at the circulation desk raised a disapproving eyebrow. Cell phone usage was prohibited. Piper signaled she was going to take the call outside. The lady nodded her approval.

"Hello," Piper whispered as she stepped back outside.

"Where are you?" It was Rusty trying to hunt her down.

"I'm at the library. I wanted to pick up an application for the board of trustees." She stepped aside to allow a mother with a blue and white baby stroller pass by.

"Good for you. I think you'd make an excellent addition to the board. Just be careful you don't send any of the old-timers into cardiac arrest with your voluptuous décolleté," he teased.

Piper giggled. "Thanks for your words of wisdom."

"Anytime. Listen. I'm on my way to my mother's house…"

"No!" she interrupted him.

"What do you mean no?" Rusty paused.

"I mean, no. Don't go to your mother's. She's taking a nap." *With Capt. Morgan,* she thought.

"How would you know?" Rusty sounded suspicious.

"Because, I was just there." *Which is true,* she thought.

"Oh, okay. Thanks for the letting me know. I'll be real quiet. I dropped my jeans off to have them hemmed, and there's a receipt in the back pocket that I need."

"No, you can't go," she pleaded with bated breath. "I miss you too much. You have to come get me at the library. I want to experiment with some things I've learned from Mr. Beige."

Piper couldn't believe she'd just suggested having sex, but her choices were limited. She couldn't think of anything else besides the obvious that would have grabbed his attention. Clearly, she'd buckled under pressure. Saving Helen from being exposed came with a hefty price tag. She'd be sure to let Helen know next time she saw her. Shocker! Rusty said he'd be over in five minutes or less. It was amazing how available he could be when it involved unzipping his pants.

"Um, okay. If you insist..." Rusty was not one to question unsolicited sex. An open invitation as such could not be ignored.

Before Piper left for the afternoon rendezvous, she headed over to the information desk to pick up an application. Seated in the middle chair was her least favorite employee, Mrs. Johnson. The cranky old woman had served as maid of honor in Mrs. Haigley's wedding. When Mrs. Haigley was carted off to prison, no one took it harder than Mrs. Johnson. To make her feelings known, Mrs. Johnson lashed out at Piper as only a shrewd librarian could do. Returned books mysteriously were lost. Requested materials never seemed to be available when Piper stopped by the drive-thru. Wrestling a mere piece of paper from her grasp was going to be a Herculean feat, to say the least.

Piper dreaded the thought of engaging in a war of unspoken words with this woman, but it had to be done. If she wanted to be appointed to the board by the County Executive Jack Conway, she had to first complete the application. Next on her agenda would be an impromptu meeting with Jack where the mentioning of her desired position would be casually inserted into the conversation. For an ex-trophy wife, Piper was making tremendous strides.

"May I help you?" Despite Mrs. Johnson's distaste for her present customer, Piper could tell she was making an effort to be on her best behavior. Word on the street was she'd recently posted for the vacant branch manager's job. Mrs. Johnson would have big shoes to fill if she were lucky enough to land the position. The prior manager, JT Cantrell, was a beloved member of the community. The patrons took it very hard when he announced his retirement.

"Well, hello, Mrs. Johnson. So good to see you, as always. I absolutely love your new hairdo." When it doubt, resort to flattery.

Mrs. Johnson said nothing. She didn't even react to Piper's attempt to sweet talk her.

"Okay, then." Piper was short on time. "I'd like an application for the board of trustees, please." There, she'd said it.

Still no reaction.

"The piece of paper that is needed in order to be considered for the board," Piper insisted.

"Why?" Mrs. Johnson was not making this easy.

"You know I asked myself that very same question. And, you know what I said? Why not?" Piper fake laughed in an attempt to lighten things up.

Mrs. Johnson was not amused.

"Okay, so if you wouldn't mind just looking maybe in your desk or perhaps somewhere in your file cabinet, I'd really appreciate it." Piper didn't know what else to say. It took everything in her not to lean over that desk and wipe the annoying grin right off of Mrs. Johnson's face. The mean librarian was enjoying this way too much.

Just then, Piper's cell phone buzzed. She glanced down and saw that it was Rusty.

"Well?" Piper was fed up. Rusty was waiting outside and she needed to go. "May I have one or not?"

Mrs. Johnson took a moment and then pointed to the other side of the room near the self-check-out station.

Piper followed her finger. There on the corner of the desk was a petite sign with neon lettering: Board of Trustees Applications.

Mrs. Johnson replied, "No need to thank me."

Piper didn't bother to answer her.

As soon as she got in the car, Piper read aloud the application, asking Rusty his opinion as to what he thought she should say. The right of censorship and intellectual freedom were not topics in which he felt well-versed, yet he did his best to offer an educated response. Rusty had no clue whether she stood a chance of getting appointed to the board. His only concern was getting her home and between the sheets.

When Rusty pulled up to the house, he noticed the front storm door was ajar. He asked Piper if she'd left it open, but she insisted she had not. Parked in front of the house was an unfamiliar car. Rusty was not in the mood for any uninvited guests. He had spent the good part of the ride over fantasizing about potentially new sexual positions. Most likely, it was Penelope and a girlfriend of hers just dropping by for some gossip. If Rusty played his cards right, he might get her to leave in ten minutes or less. All he needed to do was mention her not-so-secret relationship with the nefarious Dr. King. For some reason, she didn't like discussing it openly with Piper.

The two eagerly entered the house, curious as to who would be there. Each had their own agenda in mind. Neither was in the mood for idle chit-chat. Upon entering the kitchen, they were greeted by the most unlikely of pairs seated at the table.

"Penelope? Marc? What are you two doing here?" Piper exclaimed.

"Hi, sis!" Penelope replied. She got up from her chair and leaned over to give her sister a kiss on the cheek. She acknowledged Rusty with an air kiss.

"Well, hello, Marc," said Rusty. For the life of him, he couldn't figure out what Marc was doing there.

Marc stood up and the two men shook hands. "How's it going?"

"Fine, fine," Rusty replied.

Well this is awkward, thought Piper. *I thought she was dating Dr. King.*

"So, I stopped by to see how you were doing after that horrible fire and found Marc here on your doorstep," Penelope explained. She exchanged questioning glances with her sister as Piper and Rusty joined them seated at the table.

The foursome just stared at one another waiting for someone to start talking. Not one to let an opportunity to take center stage pass by, Piper fired away, "What's up with you and Candy? I had no idea you two were so close."

Rusty and Penelope's wide-eyed expressions were hard to miss. They both were taken off-guard by Piper's bluntness yet chose to remain silent.

"Um, well, we are friends," Marc said. "We have a lot in common."

"Really? How do you figure?" Piper asked. "A most unlikely pair, if you ask me. C'mon. A county council president and a …."

"Not sure what you'd call her," Penelope offered sotto voce.

Piper nodded in agreement. "Let's be honest here, Marc," Piper continued. "With Candy, you can't dig too deep. It's a given…you're gonna hit rock." She wasn't buying it for one second. Something just wasn't right.

Marc looked a bit uncomfortable but explained, "We've had our own issues with Gus. When he passed away…"

"You mean when he was clubbed to death?" Piper clarified.

"Piper!" reprimanded Rusty. "Be nice."

"It's the truth." She did have a valid point.

"Go on," insisted Rusty. He shook his head in deference to Piper's insensitivity.

"I heard you two were investigating Gus's murder. Is that true?" He looked at Rusty and then Piper.

The couple didn't confirm nor deny the accusation.

"They are," Penelope acknowledged. "Rusty is opening his own P.I. firm." She couldn't help but volunteer the information.

Rusty took the lead and asked Marc, "Who told you that?"

"Word travels fast in town." Marc chose to keep his sources anonymous.

"Why do you need to know?" Penelope interjected into their conversation.

Marc pressed on. "I have some information you might find useful."

"Yeah? What's that?" Rusty was definitely intrigued.

"I know for a fact that Janie was at the club the night before Gus was murdered," Marc offered.

"Why would that be important?" asked Piper. She glanced over at Rusty and raised her eyebrows in doubt.

"She was forced to return the next day because she had left something behind." Marc didn't flinch.

Rusty looked skeptical. "Do you have any proof? I mean I just can't take your word for it without having some kind of evidence."

Penelope butted in, "Have you told the police yet?"

"Nope. I can't." Marc shifted from side to side in his seat.

Rusty could sense there was more to this story than Marc was letting on, but getting him to fess up without having Piper interfere would take some doing.

"I highly doubt…" Piper began.

"That Captain Morgan would appreciate the validity of what you have to say without accusing you of somehow being involved." Rusty took a stab at trying to win him over by proving they were on his side.

"Exactly. A bunch of us were there for a business meeting of sorts. That's all I can say. What I can tell you is that Janie was there to meet Gus." Marc checked his watch.

"Gus?" queried Penelope. "Why was she meeting Gus? Did it have something to do with his daughter Willow?"

Marc shrugged his shoulders. "Maybe. Can't be sure."

Rusty frowned. Marc's vagueness irked him. "So what is it that you thought was so important that you had to come here and tell us?" So much for the gentle approach.

Marc paused for a moment and then said, "Gus and Janie were having an affair."

"Hot damn. Gus certainly made the rounds with the ladies." Rusty seemed quite impressed with the representative's sexual prowess.

"I warned Tanya that Janie was up to no good when she hired Willow as her nanny! For heaven's sakes! She's sleeping with the father of her nanny!" Piper was disgusted.

"That certainly is a new spin on the typical cheating scenario," observed Rusty.

"Who knew about them besides you?" Piper demanded. "Who knew he was screwing around on Danielle?"

Penelope nudged closer to her sister. Stories pertaining to cheating spouses infuriated Piper to the point of uncontrollable emotions. Penelope knew this could get out of hand if they weren't careful.

"It was common knowledge among a few of us who belonged to Gus's inner circle. We never really spoke about it." He ran his fingers through his hair.

"Of course not!" shouted Piper. "Why would you? You all are probably sleeping with each other's wives!" She slammed her fists on the table causing it to shudder.

"I'm not married," Marc clarified.

"That's a complicated story from what I've heard," Piper quipped back at him. "Just sayin'."

All signs pointed to Piper being on the verge of a breakdown leading Rusty to press on.

"I'm guessing Ed was not privy to this information," probed Rusty.

Marc snickered. "He had his suspicions that she might be screwing around, but after Gus passed away the topic became a non-issue. I highly doubt he knew it was Gus."

"May I interrupt for a minute?" It wasn't really a question but a demand. Penelope wanted in.

The men stopped talking and looked at her.

"You said that it was common knowledge among those in your little bromance club, but you never admitted from whom you obtained this information. Who told you Janie and Gus were having an affair? Did Gus himself tell you slimy creeps? Did he give you a play by play?"

"Penelope," pleaded Rusty. "Behave."

Marc seemed to be weighing his options before speaking.

"Yeah, who told you?" Piper insisted on knowing the truth. She jumped up from the table and began pacing back and forth.

Penelope added, "I'd think the representative would have been well versed on the art of discretion. It would have been too dangerous to divulge that kind of information to a handful of guys. You all are worse than a cackle of hens when it comes to keeping secrets. How did you find out about their affair? You had to have an inside source."

Marc clasped his hands together and gazed right into Penelope's eyes. Leaning forward and with conviction he whispered, "Candy. I learned everything from Candy."

Hole 14

The threesome were blindsided by Marc's bombshell of news implicating Candy in the cover-up. This startling revelation certainly put an unexpected twist on Gus's murder case. Much to their dismay, they never got the chance to question Marc further. As soon as he delivered his information his ears reddened, his mouth clamped shut, and he made for the door. Piper pleaded for him to stay, but to no avail. Some excuse about having to meet some fellow councilmen at a last minute meeting provided him with the perfect escape route. Piper's last ditch effort of inviting him over later for drinks fell flat. Marc hastily declined as he said his good-byes and bolted out the door.

The clock revealed the necessity for wrapping up quickly since the afternoon had slipped away. The girls would be leaving for book club while Rusty needed to make good on his promise to take his mother to mass. All thoughts of afternoon delight were forgotten. As soon as the door clicked shut, the trio converged on the living room, each with his or her own theory on the identity of Gus's possible murderer.

"I think it's pretty obvious that Candy is the guilty one. C'mon. She's the mother of his lovechild. She probably flipped when she realized Gus was playing hide the banana with Janie," insisted Penelope as she sat down in the leather chair.

"No way!" responded Piper as she joined Rusty on the couch. "That bloody golf club has Danielle's name written all over it, wherever it may be. I betcha ten bucks she planted that fake one in Penelope's trunk. Lest you forget; she thanked me for killing him. She knew darn well Gus couldn't keep his pants zipped up. The woman hit her breaking point and snapped. Plain and simple. You're reading too much into this, Penelope. Speaking from personal experience, hell has no fury like a woman scorned. Knowing Danielle, she had someone feed the information about Janie to Candy. None of us truly knows to what extremes Danielle was willing to go in order to punish Gus for his philandering ways. Throwing Candy under the bus is an easy way out."

"I think you both are wrong." Rusty wasn't jumping on either bandwagon as he put his feet up on the ottoman.

"How do you figure?" Piper asked. She rested her feet on the ottoman.

"I think Marc is the guilty one. He and Jack Conway have been vying for Gus's seat for years. Now that he's dead, it's ripe for the picking. If truth be told, Marc probably had some dirt on Gus. Remember, he was at the club the night of the big pow-wow, as well as the next morning. I bet he confronted Gus and things got out of hand. I doubt he had any intention of actually killing him. Now he needs someone to take the rap. Who better than Candy? She already has a history with Gus. It's a no brainer."

"Yes, but Jim Wagner was at the club that very same night. Did you ever think maybe he was somehow involved?" Piper knew she was stepping into the lion's den with her farcical notion but couldn't resist voicing it aloud.

"No," shrugged Rusty. "Let's not even go there."

"Just saying…" Piper gave him a little love tap on the belly.

The three contemplated their options in silence. Each possible suspect had a motive and opportunity. Finding the one who actually pulled the trigger, so to speak, was going to be the real challenge. Despite the convincing arguments, none was 100% sold on who killed Gus. Further probing was needed in order to catch the killer.

"So, how do you want to proceed? We need to find some evidence, real proof that we can take to Captain Morgan. Should we divide up and interrogate each potential suspect? Isn't that how they do it on the cop shows? Separate them to see if the stories match?" Penelope chirped.

Her enthusiasm for the investigation was duly noted by Rusty.

"Hold on there, partner. Let's take it one step at a time. Piper, why don't you try to corner Danielle tonight at book club, preferably after she's had a couple of drinks. See if you can find out if she knew about Janie and Gus." He draped his arm around her shoulder.

"But Janie is going to be there, too. That might be a tad bit difficult to maneuver," said Piper. She weaved her fingers threw his hand.

Penelope butted in, "Not if I entertain Janie while you're questioning her."

"There's a thought. I like your positive attitude." Rusty winked at Penelope.

"Fine. What's next?" Piper tried to hurry them along. "This investigating stuff is cutting into my hair and make-up time. I need to primp before book club." Keeping up her image was and always would be high on her priority list despite any circumstances.

"Candy is a walking time bomb for numerous reasons, so I think you'd better leave her alone for now. I think mom snookered Tom into coming to mass as well. So after church, we'll drop her off and then he and

I will swing by Jack's favorite watering hole, Beers to You. If we're lucky, we might be able to find him. Tom knows him way better than I do, so maybe he can pry some information out of him. After a few rounds, Jack is always a good source for what's going on in the county. Maybe he can shed some light on a few things. It's worth a try. Do you two need a ride to Danielle's? I can drop you off on my way." He started to get up.

"Thanks anyway, but Tanya volunteered to pick us up," Piper said, following his lead.

"Good. Then I won't have to worry about you two making it home safely." Rusty smiled. He said his goodbyes and promised to call Piper later with an update.

As soon as he left, the sisters headed upstairs in search of the perfect outfit to wear. Like usual, Penelope planned on shopping in Piper's closet. Within minutes, clothes were haphazardly strewn across the bed. Stripes, patterns, polka dots…everything imaginable was laid out for review. Between the excitement of attending their first book club meeting and the prospect of finding a potential killer, the girls were revved up.

"Have there been any updates on the Carpool Chatter blog?" asked Penelope as she glanced at the rows of shoes in the closet. "It's a hot topic at Dr. King's office. Everyone talks about it."

"Not that I know of," replied Piper. She was stationed front and center at the bathroom sink applying her make-up primer. "I know Janie is the ghost writer. I just have to find a way to prove it."

"Ya think?" Penelope didn't seem to buy her sister's theory.

"I do. But for the life of me, I just can't figure out her source. Someone has to be feeding her the information on me, but who? You need to help me, sis.

Ask around at work and see what you can find out."
Piper added the finishing touches on her foundation and
then moved on to her eye make-up. With a quick touch
of the brush, she transformed her drab eyes into
sparkling jewels.

Joining her in the bathroom, Penelope continued,
"I'm not so sure that's a good idea. Maybe you should
just let her be for now. We have too much on our plates
as it is. Have you talked to Jay lately? I saw him at the
grocery store the other day. He's a little strange if you
ask me."

Piper combed her drawer in search of some lipstick.
"I highly doubt Jay is in cahoots with Janie."

"I never said he was." Penelope snapped. She
yanked the chair out from under the bathroom vanity
and plopped down. Pulling the drawers open in search
of make-up, she began the process of transforming her
face into party glam ready.

"Whatever!" Her sister's snarky attitude put a
sudden damper on what had been a festive, light-
hearted mood. Changing the subject, Piper said, "Do
you know who's coming tonight?"

"You, me, Tanya, Danielle, Carolyn, Candy, Janie,
Laura...," Penelope counted on her fingers.

"Laura! Why?" Piper huffed. She threw her hand on
her hip in protest.

Penelope glossed over her comment. "I think your
future mother-in-law might be coming, too. Oh, and Liz
Monroe and Kat Conway are going to grace us with
their presence. It's going to be a who's who of
Woodlawn tonight. I heard your favorite librarian is
even showing up. Good times! I can't wait!" She
clapped her hands together.

Just like that, Penelope adjusted her attitude.
Hoping for a pleasant evening, Piper decided to
overlook her sister's peculiar hissy fit and move on.

"Well, we better look our very best then. Tanya should be here any minute. Are you about done in here?" Piper flipped the light off in the closet and then grabbed her lip gloss from the counter. "I'm ready when you are. By the way, who invited the mean librarian?"

"It must have been Helen. I doubt Mrs. Johnson and Danielle are friends," Penelope replied.

"Why am I not surprised?" she sighed.

While the sisters made their way to the book club meeting, across town Rusty was headed to his mother's. He was a bit apprehensive about seeing his brother again. They hadn't spoken since Tom's surprise visit to Piper's house. Rusty wanted to further discuss his involvement with Danielle, but it would have to wait until they were alone. Having Helen involved in the discussion would make matters worse. The need to express her own biased opinions surpassed her sense of logic when it came to moderating a discussion between her sons. Rusty usually found himself with the short end of the stick. For now, he was focusing all of his energies on facilitating a stress-free gathering. Celebrating mass was going to be a family affair with no drama. Afterwards…well, that was yet to be seen.

Rusty noticed Tom's car parked in front of the house. His brother's punctuality was as customary as Rusty's tardiness. Upon entering the house, he wasn't the least bit surprised to find them waiting right inside the door. Rusty tried to engage them in idle chatter but his mother's incessant tapping of her watch signaled the need to hurry along. Tom asked Rusty to lock up as he wheeled his mother outside towards the truck. As he made his final sweep, Rusty noticed a NY Yankees baseball cap lying on the floor behind the recliner. He leaned over, picked it up, and then placed it on the coffee table. Rusty assumed Tom must have dropped it although he was surprised by his brother's choice of teams. The O'Brien brothers had always been Cincinnati Reds fans. Rusty made a mental note to rib his brother about it later.

Tom took care of helping Helen get buckled up and then proceeded to load the wheelchair into the bed of the truck. Of course, she criticized his handling of her apparatus pointing out how expensive the cost would be if it needed to be replaced. Tom was less than overjoyed with her attitude and mumbled some inaudible comment under his breath. When Rusty approached the truck, he could tell his mother was in one of her moods, so he decided to zip it in order to keep the peace. With the threesome all snuggled in tight, they were off.

The church was located not far from Helen's house. For each of them, it served as a reminder of happier times when things were far less complicated. The boys had made their First Communions and Confirmations in this very church. The youth group minister filled a void for the fatherless boys. Other kids in similar single-parent families congregated here, making it a safe place to go to discuss fears and boyhood problems. Nowadays, finding time to worship together presented its challenges. Of the two sons, Rusty took his faith the more seriously. Lately, Helen had been urging both to find their inner peace by returning to the place that served as their home away from home. Making mass a priority was a step in the right direction.

As soon as they entered the sanctuary, they were greeted by a pleasant usher who inquired if the brothers would be interested in taking up the gifts before communion. Helen's magnanimous smile indicated her happiness at the offer, so Rusty readily accepted on their behalf. The usher briefly reviewed what it would entail and then thanked them for their willingness to serve. With only five minutes to spare until mass started, they quickly made their way up the aisle. Rusty was surprised to see Captain Morgan kneeling in prayer all by himself. He'd never seen the police officer in church before. It was strange seeing him in this environment due to his rough and tough persona. *Good thing Piper's not here,* he thought. She would have been less than thrilled to see him.

For an ordinary Saturday evening mass, the church was packed. For some odd reason, Helen chose to sit in the same pew as Capt. Morgan. Granted, it was one of the few rows left available that could seat three people, but why with him? Rusty gave his brother a quizzical look, but went ahead and seated her next to Captain Morgan anyway. Tom shrugged his shoulders and mouthed 'whatever' and then sat beside them. Rusty wheeled the chair to the side and slipped in on the end. If he didn't know any better, it looked as if his mother and Captain Morgan might even be friends. *How odd,* he thought.

Helen's wish for a swift mass was granted. Father John sped through the liturgy in record time. Her sons carried the gifts to the altar as requested, and the Eucharistic minister kindly came to the pew after everyone had been served to administer the wafer to Helen. Captain Morgan fled right after communion leaving his empty seat quite noticeable. As soon as the final verse was sung, Tom left in search of Helen's wheelchair. Mistakenly, it had been moved by one of the ushers. Rusty seized the chance to speak with his mother in private.

"I had no idea you were friends with Captain Morgan. When did this happen?" he said in a quiet, non-accusatory voice.

Helen adjusted her sweater and then brushed an imaginary piece of lint off of her pant leg. "Oh, I don't know. We've known each other for some time now. I don't keep track of things like that."

Rusty made an annoying clicking noise with his tongue. "With my involvement in Gus's murder case and the launching of my private investigating firm, you'd think maybe, just maybe, that would be something important to mention."

"Dear...since when has it become obligatory for me to report in with whom I speak? I think your hanging out with Piper has made you a bit overly dramatic. I am friendly with Captain Morgan. Period. That's all you need to know. Chief Derbyshire is also an acquaintance. Add that to your notebook so I don't get in trouble next time we bump into either one of them. Geesh. Lighten up, Rusty." She gave him a perturbed look.

Rusty was taken aback by her condescending tone. It wasn't like his mother to be so testy. He was about to push further when Tom interrupted their conversation.

"Some old lady was trying to hightail it to the parking lot with your wheels, mom. Good thing I showed up when I did. I bumped her right out of the seat and took off." Tom smirked.

"Tom O'Brien, you did no such thing!" Helen insisted. She was in no mood for senseless chatter.

Tom chuckled, "Okay, maybe it didn't go down exactly as I had reported. But you should be thankful I intervened on your behalf. It may not have ended so well."

Helen just shook her head. Her youngest son had a knack for making up stories. Helen often wondered how much his involvement with Danielle was true, or if their supposed relationship was merely a figment of his imagination. It was a fine line when it came to Tom's skewed version of the truth.

By the time they left the parking lot, Helen had finagled them into agreeing to a quick bite at the diner.

The boys seemed to be forgiving of her fickle attitude for which she was grateful. Capitalizing on the harmonious vibes, she engaged them in a light conversation on what was happening in their lives. Her overzealous concern was simply a ploy to avoid any mentioning of Captain Morgan. Her intentions were greeted wholeheartedly as her sons took turns filling her in on their news. Rusty skirted any sensitive topics such as Piper and Gus's murder while Tom took the easy way out by rambling on about nothing.

When they reached the diner, Rusty dropped Tom off at the door in order for him to secure a table. The diner was a popular gathering place after mass for the older generation. Portions were generous and liquor was served; the perfect combination for a Saturday night out. Tom greeted the hostess, who promptly added his name to the waiting list. Her name tag read Susie. A perky blond with a bob haircut, her attempt to catch his eye went unnoticed by Tom. He was too concerned with the two men seated at the counter.

It came as no surprise that Captain Morgan and Chief Derbyshire were chums. Both men held important positions in town and often crossed paths professionally as well as socially. With a killer on the loose, no wonder the two were conferring over a meal. So far, Captain Morgan had come up empty-handed. The townsfolk were starting to doubt his ability to get the job done. The editor at the local paper took no mercy when it came to publishing derogatory comments about the case. He blatantly chose to print editorials in favor of replacing Captain Morgan as the lead investigator. His slanted view had caused much friction between the police department and the newspaper. The only way for Captain Morgan to redeem his reputation and restore his credibility was to find the killer, and fast.

Having just spent the last hour praying beside the man, Tom felt as if he'd earned the right to interrupt the men's conversation. He made his way through the diner in search of some news.

"Hey, Captain Morgan!" Tom said as he approached the counter. "I thought that was you." He jockeyed himself into position by squeezing into the tiny gap between the captain and the chief.

With food in his mouth, Captain Morgan grunted hello as he tried to swallow what he was chewing.

"Chief Derbyshire," Tom said. "Good to see you as well." He patted him on the back.

Chief Derbyshire was not one to mince words. "Can we help you with something?" It was quite obvious he was annoyed by the interruption. He shook his head in disgust.

"No, just waiting on a table," responded Tom. "I saw you two masterminds over here and thought I'd take the time to say hello." Turning towards Captain Morgan, he continued, "Any leads in Gus's murder case?" Tom couldn't help but ask.

"None that I'd feel compelled to share with you," Captain Morgan retorted. "I take it you and that brother of yours are keeping your noses clean? I warned you both about interfering with my case." He picked up his fork and took another bite of his chicken pot pie. The chief just chose to ignore Tom and went back to eating his meatloaf and mashed potatoes.

As Tom prattled on, Rusty entered the restaurant. Wheeling his mother around the crowded space presented its challenges, but most people seemed more than willing to accommodate them. Helen scanned the place in search of her son. His tall, broad stature made him easy to find. Not realizing with whom he was speaking, she ordered Rusty to wheel her over towards him. As soon as they neared the space, Helen heard

Captain Morgan's voice. Panicking, she blurted, "Let's go see where we are on the list. I'm hungry."

Confused, Rusty said, "You said to wheel you over here. Let's just ask Tom. He probably knows."

"He never knows anything. I want to see for myself," she insisted.

By then, Tom had noticed them. "I'm over here," he waved hello.

"I'm not blind," Helen snapped. She adjusted her purse on her lap.

Judging by her cantankerous mood, Rusty chose to remain silent rather than take a chance by saying something inane to irritate her further. Fed up with her unpredictable demeanor, he pushed her chair right next to Tom and then took a step back.

"Hey, mom. Look who I bumped into! Twice in one night," Tom tapped Capt. Morgan on the back.

Rusty watched as his mother and Capt. Morgan exchanged furtive glances.

"I was surprised to see you at mass," Rusty began. "I wouldn't have taken you as the religious type."

"Can't a man just eat his meal in peace?" mumbled Chief Derbyshire.

"We apologize for bothering you, Grant. I told Rusty to check in with the hostess but he insisted on wheeling me over here," Helen fumed.

"Really?" said Rusty. It wasn't like his mother to blatantly lie.

"I apologize, Helen. Long day. The missus is out of town." The chief said bashfully.

"No offense taken. Let's go boys." According to Helen, the party was over.

As luck would have it, the hostess called Tom's name. Thankful for the interruption, Helen snarled at Rusty demanding she be taken directly to the table. Cutesy Susie seated them on the far opposite side of the diner which pleased everyone. She gave it one last try to snare Tom's attention as she handed him the menu, but sadly came up empty-handed. As soon as she stepped away, Rusty began firing questions at his mother.

"What is with you and Captain Morgan? First, we go to church and just *happen* to sit by him. Really? Like that was purely coincidental? C'mon, mom! And, don't think I didn't notice that little look you two exchanged in mass. It creeped me out! Then, you bald-faced lied about me insisting on wheeling you over to the counter. You gave him that same weird look again here at the diner. Lest you forget, that man tried to put your youngest son here behind bars for a murder he didn't commit. If I didn't know any better, I'd think you are keeping something from us. So, what is it, mom? What's going on?" He demanded some answers.

Helen closed her menu and carefully placed it on the table. She looked at Tom and then Rusty. Drawing in a deep breath she brazenly revealed, "Captain Morgan and I are seeing each other."

Rusty could barely spit out the words, "As in dating?"

"Keep your voice down!" demanded Helen. "You act as if I told you something horrific."

"You kinda did," explained Tom. "Who woulda thought?"

"I'm surprised Piper didn't tell you," Helen commented. Two could play at this game. If she was going down, she might as well take Piper right along for the ride.

Rusty couldn't believe his ears. "She knew?"

"Of course, she knew. I told you from day one that girl is not to be trusted. I hate to say it but...I told you so. Now are you boys ready to order? I'm absolutely famished." She flashed them her notorious mother-knows-best smile.

As the O'Briens were busy sorting out their own personal issues at the diner, the book club meeting was just getting started at Danielle's McMansion on the other side of town. Piper and Penelope were among the first to arrive due to a last minute change in their plans. Tanya's ill-fated car trouble led to Laura's volunteering to drive the group. Not surprisingly, Piper quickly passed on the offer. It was a well-known fact in Woodlawn that Laura liked her booze. Having to monitor Laura's alcohol consumption plus investigating a murder would have pushed her over the edge.

Opening the door, Danielle cautiously greeted the sisters. Not knowing if Tom had shared their not so rosy encounter, she'd previously rehearsed her side of the story should a confrontation arisen. By all accounts, the sisters' behavior seemed as friendly and jovial as normal, so she immediately put them to work to avoid any unforeseen issues. Danielle readily explained that there was no hired help for the night due to a sudden death in her private caterer's family, so she needed the sisters to assist with the finishing touches. With the guests about to arrive, she never gave them a chance to object.

First, Danielle led them into the great room and enlisted their help with moving the furniture into clusters around the fireplace. After much hemming and hawing, the seating arrangements were set. Danielle tossed pillows around and scattered extra coasters on the various tables as the girls tidied up the magazines and books. Pleased with how the room looked, she politely instructed the sisters to go in the kitchen to prepare the food to be served. Danielle suggested Piper take out the veggies and fruit platters from the refrigerator while Penelope fill the coffee maker. Her reference to the coffeemaker was duly noted by Piper. When the doorbell rang, Danielle scurried away in order to greet her guests saving herself from hearing Piper's snide remark. Penelope hushed her sister and sent Piper into the living room to investigate the liquor situation.

Just then Helen and her librarian friend Mrs. Johnson entered the room. Feeling rather haughty, Piper said, "Well, hello ladies. Welcome to book club." She threw her hands in the air as if she were the tour director welcoming them onto a cruise ship.

Since Helen now held the upper hand, unbeknownst to Piper, she decided to toy with her a bit. "Oh, Piper dear. I didn't know you were working this event. Here's my coat. I'd like a white cranberry cosmo, please." Turning towards her friend, "Judy, would you like one, too?"

Before Piper had a chance to explain, Liz Monroe and Kat Conway waltzed into the room followed by Laura and Tanya. "Ladies! The party may now begin. Kat and I have arrived," giggled Liz as she walked towards Piper blowing air kisses to her friend. Liz never failed to mention her place on the social ladder nor her connections, unlike Tanya and Laura who just waved a quick hello and then headed over to speak with Danielle.

Piper welcomed the reprieve and guided Liz and Kat to the kitchen under the guise of locating her sister. Realizing she still had Helen's coat in her hands, she discreetly stuffed it in a chair in the corner. As soon as the ladies spotted Penelope, they enveloped her in big hugs commenting on her chic and stylish outfit. Hoping to score some points with her friends, Piper made sure to tell them she had a hand in the preparation for the evening's festivities. The polite compliments bestowed upon Piper for her generous spirit were like music to her ears. Penelope didn't bother to mention her own involvement, simply allowing her sister to bask in her self-induced adulation.

Over the next twenty minutes, the invited guests trickled in, each with their own stories to share among the group. The house was bubbling over with excitement fully aided by the flowing pitchers of white sangrias and flavorful cosmos. Danielle made the rounds welcoming her friends to her glorious home, as she referred to it, making sure to highlight expensive works of art and knick-knacks of note. Whispers concerning the absence of photos of her deceased husband Gus monopolized the snippets of conversation behind Danielle's back. Some chalked it up to intense grief. Others snickered that Danielle had already moved on. Candy and Carolyn were unusually quiet, choosing to remain in the corner sequestered in a deep conversation with Janie. Piper joked with the others that Candy was probably explaining the book to her sister and friend. Her comment sent a bellow of laughter around the room.

After Danielle was certain the girls had had enough gossip peppered with cocktails, she shepherded them into the great room. Acting as the perfect hostess, she purposely seated certain cliques together and separated those with conflicts. Right as she was finishing arranging the guests, the doorbell rang. Annoyed by the interruption, she begged Piper to answer the door. Liking the attention, Piper agreed and made a concerted effort to draw all eyes upon her as she sashayed to the front hallway. Upon opening the door, she was greeted by a chirpy hello.

"Beth?" Piper was puzzled. "What are you doing here?" Piper was a bit surprised to see the club's barmaid in attendance. Last time she remembered meeting, Beth was calling 911 to report Gus's murder. My how times had changed!

Walking through the entrance, Beth answered, "I'm here for book club. The meeting is tonight, right?" The woman pulled a copy of the book from her purse as proof that she was in the right place.

"Um, sure. Whatever!" replied Piper. It wasn't her party so why argue. Piper led her into the house being careful not to become too chummy lest Beth should be asked to find her way back out the door.

When they entered the great room, the conversation among the ladies abruptly ceased. Piper paused for a brief moment taking pity on poor Beth and then scooted back to her seat alongside her sister. Beth stood there awkwardly, waiting for Danielle to acknowledge her presence. At first, Danielle just stared at her as if not quite sure what to say. Beth gazed around the room looking for a familiar face to rescue her from this embarrassing situation. No one dared to break the silence. Sensing the need to take charge, Helen piped up, "Come join us, dear. We were waiting for your arrival. We all can't wait to get started."

The sheer sigh of relief expelled from Beth's lungs was deafening. If it weren't for Helen's kindness, the situation would have gone from bad to worse. Perhaps it was the alcohol that delayed Danielle's reaction to Beth's arrival, or merely her outright disdain for the woman. Whatever the reasoning, Danielle pointedly chose not to acknowledge Beth for the entire evening. Piper and Penelope thought it was quite odd for Danielle to be acting this way. Piper did recall that indeed Danielle had extended an invitation at the Member-Member party; however, Danielle had been notably intoxicated at the time. Piper whispered in Beth's ear that she did remember that being so, which made Beth feel a tad bit better. Sweet Beth assumed this gathering marked her entrée into the members' social circle when really it was just a slap in the face. It appeared as if Beth had a pleasant time with the ladies. Yet when the circle of friends wrapped up the book discussion, she was one of the first to leave.

Candy and Carolyn were anti-social the whole evening, making it rather difficult for Piper or Penelope to mingle with the sisters. Janie had been a sour puss most of the night, causing Penelope to pass on the opportunity to dig for dirt. Helen and Judy departed under the pretense of meeting up with some friends at the diner. Piper surmised after grabbing a bite to eat, Helen would be shagging Captain Morgan at her place as usual. Kat and Liz babbled on about another commitment and made as grand an exit as their earlier entrance.

By the time the crowd had thinned, Danielle was beyond inebriated. Her attempt to tidy up was comical to watch as she staggered in and out of rooms in pursuit of cleanliness. Laura and Tanya were the only guests who chose to linger. Piper welcomed the chance to catch up with her good friend Tanya and made a concerted effort not to brood over past transgressions involving Laura. Since she couldn't rewrite the story of her life, it was high time she learned to just deal with it. Serving as the temporary hostess, Piper invited the ladies to gather at the kitchen table to rehash the night's events. The leftover crème puffs were passed around as Penelope poured hot cups of decaf coffee.

On one of her frequent trips to the kitchen, Danielle seemed rather surprised the girls were assembled at the table.

"Whatcha doing?" she slurred.

The ladies held onto their coffee cups as Danielle literally slammed into the table. Evidently her spatial judgment was way off.

"Why don't you sit down right here?" suggested Tanya. She patted the seat next to her. "You've done enough cleaning for one night. Come sit with your friends and relax a bit." The ladies nodded in agreement.

Danielle took a moment to look at each person as if she was taking attendance.

"Where's Beth? Is she still here?" She peered around the room.

Penelope placed a cup of piping hot coffee in front of her and patted Danielle gently on the back.

"She left," Tanya informed her. "Come sit next to me." Tanya motioned to Piper to push her along in the right direction.

Danielle finally acquiesced and parked herself next to Tanya as instructed. "She never should have been here in the first place. I sure as hell didn't invite her!" Danielle insisted. She slammed her fist on the table. The mugs of java quaked.

"Easy there," Tanya answered as she settled the table. "No need to worry about it now. Everyone had a wonderful time despite the raunchy book selection. Next time, I'm picking the book, not Piper." Tanya was doing her best to make light of the situation.

Until then, Piper had been unceremoniously quiet. Hearing her name mentioned, she spoke right up. "Why don't you like Beth?"

Penelope raised her eyebrows at her sister. Leave it to Piper to stir up trouble.

Danielle slurped her coffee and then babbled, "She can have him. He's a damn murderer anyway. Let her figure out how to keep his ass out of jail." She stuffed an oozing crème puff into her mouth.

"Oh! No!" shouted Laura. "We really don't want to go there tonight. Let's talk about something else."

"What did you just say?" asked Piper. "Who's a murderer?" She blatantly disregarded Laura's warning.

Danielle swallowed her sweet dessert and then slurred, "Tom!" She licked her lips. "Beth is screwing around with Tom again."

"Again? When was the first time? And, how do you know?" asked Piper.

"I just do." Danielle was having a hard time staying awake. She laid her head down on the table.

"Did you catch them in the act? Did Beth tell you?" Piper gave her some plausible explanations.

"Piper! Enough already. Can't you see she is totally wasted? Let's put her to bed and leave." Laura's seething tone signaled to Piper that there was more to this story than just an unsubstantiated claim.

"I don't need to go to bed. I want another drink." Like a jack-in-the-box, Danielle popped right back up.

"That's the last thing you need, dear," said Tanya.

Piper interrupted, "How do you know that those two are together?" She wasn't giving up without a fight. Her pseudo brother-in-law was proving to be quite the man around town.

"We had an argument in the parking lot after the Member-Member party. We ran into Beth when we were trying to leave. She told him either put a ring on it or he could go…," Danielle slurred.

"We get the picture. Are you sure that's what you heard? Maybe she was referring to something else," suggested Tanya.

"Hell, no!" maintained Danielle. "I heard every word of it. She wants to be his wife. Like that would ever happen." Danielle laughed followed by a loud hiccup.

"That's an interesting story. You'd have thought Rusty would have mentioned their relationship before now. Why the big secret?" Penelope gave her sister a quizzical look.

"There are lots of things Rusty doesn't know about his brother," Danielle said as matter-of-factly as a drunken person possibly could.

The women just looked at each other.

"If you don't believe me, just ask your friend Laura. She and her hubby Jim were standing right there. Right, girlfriend?" Danielle gave Laura two thumbs up with half-closed eyelids.

"I think it's time we leave," Laura insisted. "Look at her! She's a mess, and it's almost midnight." Laura started to stand up but was pushed right back down by Piper's strong hand.

"Oh, not so fast," Piper cautioned. "Take a seat and buckle up, *girlfriend*. It's going to be a very long night."

Hole 15

By the time Piper finished grilling Laura, it was well past midnight. Laura made a concerted effort to plead her case; however, Piper wasn't buying it. Her gut instincts told her Laura could never be trusted. As far as Piper was concerned, Laura had just become a person of interest. Keeping such valuable information hidden from Rusty was a big No-No in her book. Piper could only imagine what his reaction was going to be once he learned his supposed best friend and wife were not being truthful.

Before leaving the house, the ladies made sure Danielle was tucked securely into bed with a garbage pail at her bedside. Penelope placed the phone on the nightstand alongside a glass of water and two aspirin. The ladies turned everything off except for the recessed lighting in the kitchen just in case Danielle ventured out of bed in search of something to eat. On their way out, Tanya turned the lock from the inside and closed the door behind them. Danielle was safe and sound in the comfort of her own home. For that, she should be thankful.

There were no air kisses or assurances of future get-togethers promised when they departed. The sisters quietly drove away in Piper's car followed closely by Laura and Tanya in Laura's vehicle. On the way home, neither pair entertained the notion of further discussing the night's goings-on. All were equally exhausted from the mixture of alcohol and drama. Penelope opted to stay with Piper for the night. She reasoned there was no sense going home to an empty house at such a late hour. Like sisters often do, they crawled into bed together and fell fast asleep.

Sunday morning snuck up on them. It was nearly eleven when the sisters finally opened their eyes. Penelope reluctantly dragged her tired body out of bed. She had a long week ahead of her, so she decided to skip brunch and head home. She promised to catch up with her sister later on in the day.

Piper stared at the ceiling contemplating her next move. A phone call to Rusty was in order, but she really didn't feel up to it. No matter how much she sugarcoated the story, it wasn't going to be an easy conversation to have. She briefly considered showering and going to mass, but opted to say a couple prayers in bed instead. As she lay there weighing her options, her kitty Ralph jumped right in and began rubbing up against her leg. The poor cat was feeling neglected. He hadn't dared try to sleep with them last night, since it was no secret Penelope despised the little fur ball. Ralph was no dummy, though. He made sure she knew the feeling was mutual by leaving little presents wrapped up in her clothing.

The decision of what to do next was made for her when the phone rang. Checking caller ID she recognized the number immediately. It was Chad Freedom. The man held the fate of her job, and her life for that matter, in his hands. If only she could hit rewind and play that day all over again. Piper reasoned it was the coffeemaker's fault for the fire. There should have been a warning on the front clearly spelling out the need for adding water. Piper was worried Chad's insurance company wouldn't cover the damage. If that were the case, she'd have to kiss her future good-bye. Piper knew she didn't have enough money in the bank to cover the costs. *Why me?* she wondered.

"Hello?" Her voice did little to hide her apprehension. As if she was a fugitive running from the law, her demeanor revealed her belief of a guilty conscience.

"Piper? Is that you?" Chad didn't recognize her dulcet voice.

Piper braced herself for the inevitable. "Hi, Chad. Yes, it's me. Late night. I'm still in bed."

He laughed. "Good for you. I was concerned you might be taking the fire incident a little too personally. Accidents happen."

"They sure do," agreed Piper. She liked the way this conversation was heading.

"Sorry to bother you on a Sunday, but I heard back from my insurance agent."

Piper braced herself. "You did?"

"Nice guy. He said all the paperwork is in order. The fire has been ruled accidental. Everything is covered."

"Hallelujah!" sang Piper.

"My thoughts exactly," he concurred. "I just need for you to give my agent a call to arrange a meeting time. He needs you to sign off on the paperwork."

"That's it?" She bolted up in bed.

"That's it!" he said.

Piper sighed with relief.

"I'll send you a text with his contact information. If you wouldn't mind taking care of it ASAP, I would greatly appreciate it."

"Of course," agreed Piper. She couldn't wait to share the good news with Rusty. A celebratory feast was in order. Maybe even a little something more to make up for lost time.

"So what were you doing last night that caused you to stay out so late?" he inquired.

"Book club. Danielle Barnes hosted a book club meeting. It turned out to be quite a doozy." Piper chortled.

"Danielle Barnes, huh?" his voice signaled displeasure.

"Not her biggest fan?" Piper suggested.

Chad took a moment to formulate a politically correct response. "Let's just say she's not my favorite person. She screwed over a good friend of mine long ago. It's hard for me to look past it. Know what I mean?"

Do I ever! she thought. "Mmm hmm." Piper preferred not to rehash the obvious.

"Was there a big crowd?" he asked.

"The usual suspects. Liz, Kat, Tanya, Laura..." Piper read off the list.

"Any surprises?" he inquired.

Chad's interest in the latest gossip piqued Piper's curiosity. "Funny you should ask. Beth, the barmaid from the club, showed up. Threw Danielle for a loop."

"Really? How so?" Chad was not letting up.

Piper did her best to rehash the night's events skimming over the non-important moments and highlighting those of circumstance. She glossed over the fact that Danielle never even acknowledged her husband's passing, which had caused quite the stir among the ladies. Rather she focused purely on Danielle's gauche behavior towards Beth. Hoping to score some points with her boss, Piper boldly emphasized how she swooped in and came to poor Beth's rescue by publicly acknowledging that indeed, she had been invited. Of course, Piper's version was not exactly accurate, but that didn't matter. The point was well taken. Just when she was about to divulge the shocking revelation concerning Laura's duplicity, she was interrupted by the clicking of her call waiting.

"Oh, darn. Can you hold on for a minute?" she implored. Piper swung her feet to the floor.

"Sure," he agreed.

"Great! I have no idea who this is. I don't recognize the number." She got up and walked towards the bathroom.

"No worries. Take your time." Chad obliged.

"Hello?" Piper paused for a second. "Hello? Anyone there?"

"Shh! Not so loud. I heard you the first time," a familiar voice said.

"Danielle?" Piper inquired. She checked her appearance in the mirror.

"Who else would be calling you this early on a Sunday morning?"

Piper ignored her question. "I'm on the other line with Chad. Can you hold a minute?"

"Chad? Why are you talking with him? Just hang up. He's not worthy of your time," Danielle ordered.

Danielle's hostility did nothing to alter Piper's mood. "I'll take that as a yes. Hold on."

Piper clicked back over to Chad. "Hey, Chad. I gotta run. That's Danielle on the other line."

"Why are you talking with her? Just hang up," he said.

Okay, I feel like I'm having the same conversation but with two people, she thought.

"She's nothing but trouble," he continued.

"Um, okay. Chad, thanks for being so understanding about the fire. I really appreciate it. Please text me your agent's info and I'll give him a call as soon as I hang up with Danielle. And if you need me for anything else, please don't hesitate to call. Okay?" *This is what I get for skipping mass*, she thought.

"Sure," he replied. "I'd still hang up though, if I were you. Nothing ever good comes from associating with that woman. Believe me. I know firsthand."

Piper winced. "Okay, thanks for the advice. I'll talk with you later."

She then clicked over to Danielle. "Hello, Danielle?"

"What took you so long? My time is valuable, you know." Danielle wasn't budging.

Catering to her incessant need to be coddled, she replied, "Of course, Danielle. My apologies. What can I do for you?"

"That's more like it. I need your help."

Piper had no clue where the conversation was heading. "With what?" Piper meandered back to the bedroom and climbed into bed.

"Well, I'm extremely frustrated. I'm sure you know that Gus had a stellar military career before politics," she began.

Piper did not, but she decided to be nice and play along. "Yes." She tugged the bedding up to her chin.

"Due to the unfortunate circumstances surrounding his death, which I thanked you dearly for providing that service," she continued.

"I..." Piper blurted. She kicked the covers off in frustration and jumped out of bed.

"I've already thanked you once. I'm not thanking you again. Just be quiet and listen," she ordered.

Piper's inability to get a word in edgewise was misinterpreted as agreement. She fiddled with the drawstring on her pajama pants as she listened to Danielle rattle on.

"Since he really didn't go out the way we all had expected, I've decided to honor Gus's last wishes and have him interred at Arlington Cemetery."

"Really? How nice." What she really was thinking was... *What a farce!*

"So, seeing as how you have much experience writing eulogies for dead husbands, I was wondering if you could do me a huge favor and whip up something spectacular for Gus? Now, I don't want anything as mushy as Charles's. From what I hear, it was a bit over the top. Just the facts. Something simple, but tasteful. Maybe a thousand words or so?" Danielle requested.

"A thousand words?" Piper mumbled.

"Yes, I thought that might be over your limit, so if you need to cut it back to eight hundred, I guess that will do," Danielle conceded.

"Eight hundred?" Piper babbled.

"You have plenty of time," she insisted. "I don't need it right away. You see, I haven't received the actual date of the ceremony yet. It could be six months from now, for all I know. And, yes. You *will* be invited. I know that question was on the tip of your tongue. No worries!" she chuckled. "Now, I can't guarantee a front row seat, but you *may* tell all your friends you made the cut. We'll talk more on Tuesday at the ladies' nine hole about particulars. Oh, and remember. it's our little secret. Naturally, I plan on taking full credit for your well-crafted words. Au revoir!" And with that, the line went dead.

Piper stared at her phone in pure amazement. Even she had a hard time recapping what had transpired. Surely Danielle was not serious about Piper completing the task. Writing Gus's eulogy should be completed by someone who actually cared, and that would not be Piper. Danielle had a lot of nerve even suggesting she would do it. Just then, an idea popped into her head. Janie seemed to be quite the wordsmith these days. Immediately, she began texting Danielle with her brilliant suggestion. The smile on her face said it all. It was about time Janie got what she justly deserved. *Let her deal with Danielle's insanity,* she thought. Piper had her own problems to solve, like hunting down her man.

Meanwhile, all was not well in the Wagner home. Jim had booked an early tee-time with Tanya's husband Johnny in anticipation of his wife sleeping in late. Unlike in the Wagner marriage, Tanya had dutifully filled her husband in on all the details of the previous evening leaving nothing out. Imagine Jim's surprise when he heard the news of Laura's slip of the tongue. It angered him so much so that his game severely suffered. By the time he made it to the last hole, it was necessary to order a beer from the cart girl for some liquid courage. He could only image how Rusty was going to take the news. Not surprisingly, he passed on playing an emergency nine. His feeble excuse caused Johnny to roll his eyes in disgust. After leaving the course, his first stop was home. Even the neighbors on the next block could hear the screeching of his tires when he slammed the car in park in the driveway. By the time he made it in the house, Laura was wide awake. She knew all too well what had caused this sudden outburst of anger.

Having grown up in a verbally abusive household, Jim was well-versed in the tricks of the trade. Luckily for him, Laura had been instrumental in getting him the help he needed to move forward. Occasional lapses occurred from time to time, today being one, but in general, he'd learned how to properly deal with his anger management issues. As soon as he entered their bedroom, Laura knew exactly what was on his mind.

"Danielle is the one who spilled the beans. I had no choice but to tell the girls our side of the story. And, you know what Piper's reaction was without me even telling you. I can only imagine the spin she put on this whole episode when she filled Rusty in. Have you tried calling him?" Laura did her best to keep him on an even-keel. She encouraging him to take a seat.

Frustrated, he said, "No. I wanted to hear your side of the story first. Why didn't you just keep quiet? According to Johnny, Danielle was drunk out of her mind. You should have passed her comments off as nonsensical gibberish." He slipped his shoes off and placed them on the floor, and then lay down next to her.

"Believe me, Jim. I tried. You should have seen Piper. She had that crazed look in her eyes, just like when she's at a Lilly Pulitzer sample sale. There's no stopping her," she insisted.

"Well, when you put it that way, then I guess you tried your best." Jim sat up and ran his fingers through his hair. "Time to shower, my dear. We need to go find Rusty."

Laura paused for a moment and then said, "I think you're better off going by yourself. He's never been too fond of me. I have some errands to do anyway. Try the man-to-man approach. Better yet, throw Tom under the bus. I betcha Rusty has no clue that Tom has been messing around with both Danielle and Beth."

In an effort to smooth things over, Laura seduced her husband by offering an impromptu strip tease. Jim was taken off-guard, yet embraced the invitation with open arms, and legs. After some skillful tongue exploration, all was forgotten. Twenty minutes later, Jim left the house a very happy man. As for Laura, despite her precarious situation she once again managed to come out on top.

After Piper's harrowing morning, she decided to put off talking with Rusty for a little while longer and instead take the rest of the day off. To lighten things up a bit, she arranged to meet Jay at the park for an afternoon walk. It had been a while since she'd

connected with her partner in crime. So much had
happened in such a short amount of time. She couldn't
wait to bring him up to speed.

While Piper sat leisurely on the park bench awaiting
his arrival, she couldn't help but notice the children
playing in the sandbox. With all the turmoil in her life,
she hadn't given much thought to her future. Becoming
a mom had always been high on her priority list. With
her birthday quickly approaching, she'd come to realize
her window of opportunity was slowly closing.
Growing up, she'd clearly envisioned being married at
this point in her life with two tow-headed children
nestled in her arms. Nowadays, her idealistic picture of
familial harmony seemed a bit unclear. Yes, she longed
to have children; however, she wasn't convinced she
needed a man by her side in order to fulfill her dream.

"Solving world peace?" Jay interrupted her thoughts.

"Hardly," she replied with a lopsided smile.

"Hi, pretty lady." He leaned over and gave her a
peck on the cheek, and then took a seat.

"Not so sure about that, either. I apologize for my
attractive bedhead look. I needed to escape." Piper
made a failed attempt to tame her golden locks.

"What's got you all out of sorts?" Jay wasn't used to
seeing his friend so flustered.

"It's not what, it's who." Piper took an elastic from
her wrist and twisted her hair into a sloppy half
ponytail.

"Let me take a guess. You read the latest Carpool
Chatter." Jay was known for being a techno geek. He
habitually checked his iPhone for breaking news and
updates. In his skewed version of the world, Carpool
Chatter ranked right up there with *USA Today* in terms
of importance.

Piper whipped her head around and gave him a
wide-eyed stare.

"Oh," he cowered. "Guess you haven't. Probably shouldn't have mentioned that, huh?" He inconspicuously slipped his phone into his pant pocket.

"I don't even care what it says. Wait 'til you hear what's been going on around here." Piper sucked in a walloping breath of air.

"From the way you look and sound, I can only imagine," Jay replied.

Over the next ten minutes, Piper filled him in on the latest developments, freely embellishing the stories as she saw fit. From Helen's secretive affair with Captain Morgan to Marc's scandalous accusations concerning Candy, Piper's gift of gab was quite contagious. As expected, Jay's responses were shockingly animated, causing Piper to hush him more than once or twice due to the gawking stares from inquisitive moms. By the time she finally brought him up to speed, the two were doubled over in laughter by the absurdity of it all.

"So like I said, where the heck does Danielle get off asking me to write her husband's eulogy? And then, she turns around and insults my intelligence. Like I can't write over 1,000 words! Really? Who does that?" Her hands mimicked her comments.

"Evidently Danielle Barnes!" he howled.

"Sh!" she scolded him. "Enough about her. The bottom line is we need to make some headway with this case. Evidently Captain Morgan is spending too much time playing peek-a-boo under the covers with Rusty's mom."

"The visual is enough to make me sick to my stomach," he replied.

"Tell me about. I've witnessed the fondling part, and it wasn't pretty." Piper stuck her finger down her throat in a pretend gagging motion. "So, what's next? Who are we going after?" She perked up.

"Here's the thing. We can't catch what doesn't want to be caught. We need to set up the killer by luring him or her out into the open," said Jay.

"Okay…" Piper responded.

Jay looked her straight in the eyes and said, "What's your favorite subject?"

"Me," she answered without skipping a beat. She flashed her perfect white teeth.

Jay laughed. "Exactly, my dear Watson."

"Who's Watson?" she asked him with a quizzical look in her eyes.

He shook his head. "Don't worry about it. Listen. The easiest way to get anyone talking is to encourage them to talk about themselves."

"That sounds logical enough. How do you propose we go about doing that?" It was obvious Piper was depending on him for all of the answers.

"From what you've said, it's Marc, Candy, or Danielle. Personally, I have a hard time believing it could be Danielle, but that's just me. She may be a nut job, but she's no murderer."

"You don't know that, Jay. She was probably over the moon when she figured out he was messing around with Janie. Maybe she left the tennis courts and confronted him at the club. It's plausible." Piper pleaded her case.

"Yes, maybe. But if I were a betting man, I'd place all my chips on Marc's number. He wants Gus's seat. Wasn't he an investor at Peeps & Petals?"

"No clue. I only had access to the day-to-day goings-on."

"Doesn't matter," he replied. "I think he's willing to sacrifice Candy. It's up to us to prove it." Jay was adamant about his position.

The pair was interrupted by the sound of Piper's phone ringing.

"I can only imagine who's after me now." She tapped the screen and said hello. Piper's voice became deeper and more professional sounding as she marched back and forth. Nodding her head up and down, she assured the caller of her availability and thanked the person at least twice. By the time she hung up, she was bouncing up and down.

"I take it that was good news?" He couldn't help but smile at his friend.

"Indeed, it is. I've been asked to interview for the vacant position on the library's board of trustees!" She was brimming over with enthusiasm.

"Wow!" He stood up and gave her a congratulatory hug. "I had no idea you were such a booklover."

"I am now, boyfriend!" She wagged her finger back and forth. "The secretary scheduled my appointment for tomorrow night at six o'clock. That works out perfectly! I have the ladies nine hole on Tuesday. I can brag to all of the ladies about my new position. What do you think I should wear for the interview? Dress or suit? I know! I'll wear my fake leopard print glasses to look more studious. They have reading lights built right in. How cool is that?" Piper was obviously pumped.

Jay paused a second and then said, "Hold on there, amigo. First of all, don't go broadcasting it around town until you have been officially offered the position. Take it from me. That never ends well. And, as for your wardrobe, that's the least of your worries."

Piper scrunched up her little nose. "What do you mean?"

"Well, did the lady tell you what kind of questions the panel may be asking? I assume it will be a panel of board members and not just one person."

"Oh, yes! She did say something about being prepared to respond to questions concerning my stance on intellectual freedom and my views on censorship.

Any clue what that means?" Piper placed her hand under her chin in thought.

"Nope. We probably should look that up on Wikipedia," he suggested. Rocket scientists they were not.

"And no, there won't be a panel. Just some woman named Denise Halbreath," Piper confirmed.

"Ouch! You mean Dragon Lady Halbreath?" Jay cringed.

"Am I supposed to know who she is?" Piper asked.

Jay nodded his head yes.

"Remind me, please. You know I'm not good at remembering names, unless of course I've read about them in *People* magazine." She folded her arms across her chest.

If it were anyone else, Jay would have thought they were kidding. With Piper, he knew she was completely serious. "She's the shrewd lawyer who sits at the end of the bar by herself. No one dares to try to approach her. She usually comes in after court proceedings on Tuesdays and Wednesdays."

Piper had a blank stare. "Not ringing a bell."

"She likes whiskey with her water," Jay crooned.

"Oh, I know her!" Piper pointed at him. "As a matter of fact, Beth was singing that country song in the locker room one day. Said it reminded her of the Dragon Lady. I never made the connection."

Jay smiled. "Well, that's her! She earned the name Dragon Lady due to her ferocity in the courtroom. Like a dragon, her fiery verdicts seek vengeance for their victims."

"So what you're insinuating is that I'm toast?" she pouted.

"Not necessarily. As long as you come prepared, you should be fine. Kill her with kindness, my friend," he suggested.

"Must you use the *k* word?" she couldn't help but chide.

"Call me tomorrow sometime and we'll rehearse what you should say. In the meantime, you might want to Google "board of trustee interview questions and answers" and see what you can find."

"Aren't you just Mr. Helpful," she complimented him.

"At your service," he said while bowing. Jay took a quick peek at his watch. "Oops! It's almost dinnertime. I need to get going."

"Before you leave, mind showing me the latest Carpool Chatter blog?" Piper couldn't resist the temptation.

Jay turned his head to the side, "I thought you said you didn't care."

"Just be quiet and show it to me," she pleaded.

Jay fetched his iPhone from his pocket. With a few touches to the screen, he was able to locate the entry. Handing the phone over to her, he warned, "Whoever this person is, he or she is dead on."

Carpool Chatter
Mirror, mirror on the wall.
Who's the guiltiest of them all?
Could it be Woodlawn's leading
man? Or perhaps he's just
covering for the woman who has
his hand. The answer is kept
close to the vest. Maybe Mr.
Private-Eye himself will try to
lure them into his nest. Have no
fear…he will have no such luck.
His so-called girlfriend will run
it amok. Keep a watchful eye on
the quiet ingénue. Nothing's

stopping her from murdering
you, too.

With her mouth gaping open wide, Piper handed his
phone back to him and then said, "From what this
blogger is saying, Candy is out for blood."

"Sounds like it. But remember, you can't always
believe what you read," said Jay as the voice of reason.

Piper nodded her head in agreement. "True. What's-
her-name married to the basketball player is not having
marital problems despite what the tabloids are saying."

Leave it to Piper to try to equate her celebrity
fantasy land with true reality. "So, what's next?" Jay
tried his best to reel her back into the task at hand.

"I think we need to keep an eye on Candy. Let me
talk to Rusty and see if he has a better handle on things.
I'm hoping he and Tom bumped into Jack Conway last
night at the bar. If anyone knows what Marc is up to,
it's Jack. The two keep close tabs on each other for
obvious reasons."

After a quick run-down of what needed to be done
before they reconvened, Piper and Jay hugged good-bye
and decided to go their separate ways. As they both
realized, coming up with a plan to corner Gus's
murderer was easier said than done. There were many
potential clues that still needed investigating. Jay took
off in his Volkswagen Jetta while Piper took a leisurely
stroll back to her house. The birds were singing, and
there wasn't a cloud in the sky. By the time Piper
reached home, she was revved up and ready to go. The
sheer prospect of becoming a board member got the
adrenaline pumping through her veins. As a child, she
often found solace within the pages of library books.
Having the opportunity to give back to Woodlawn, her
newly adopted hometown, would be like a dream come
true. Now if only she could figure out how to snowball

this Dragon Lady person into believing that Piper was the best person for the job. Getting by on her charm alone would not be enough.

Over the next hour or so, Piper dallied around the house catching up on her chores. When she finally stepped into the shower, it was refreshing and restorative. The hot beads of water massaging her back felt invigorating, yet soothing. As she adjusted the setting on the shower head, she lingered a few minutes longer under the cascade of water washing away her anxieties from the past few days. Unfortunately, her private oasis of pleasure was interrupted by the change in water temperature. Piper begrudgingly made a mental note to research the cost of replacing her water heater with something more substantial. This was not the first time she'd been interrupted by the lack of hot water. As soon as she finished drying off, she slipped into her king size bed and snuggled under the soft, down comforter. The crisp, cold white sheets sent a tingle down her spine. Closing her eyes, she took a deep breath and slowly exhaled. Now all she needed was her favorite bare skin rug to come keep her warm.

A quick text sent to her lover produced the desired results. Less than fifteen minutes later, she was covered by the skin of a hot naked man. There were no talks of strategies or comparisons of investigative notes. The only audible sounds were moans of pleasure from both parties present. The glow from the moonlight signaled the day had ended. Neither had any place to be, so their lovemaking continued into the wee hours of the morning. Their impromptu rendezvous was well overdue. Finally, they were able to get their relationship back on track.

Meanwhile across town, Candy lay awake bothered by the illuminating rays of moonlight shining through her window pane. Fear kept her tossing and turning as she did her best to avoid what seemed to be staring her right in the face. Piper was not the only one who had read the Carpool Chatter blog. Whoever was behind it knew exactly what was going on in Woodlawn, and that person needed to be stopped before it was too late. Only Candy knew how far Marc would go to get what he wanted. What had her deathly afraid that eerie spring night was what she knew all too well he was capable of doing in order to make it happen.

Hole 16

Not everyone was pleased by the couple's all night love fest. Ralph the cat spent the better part of the morning walking up and down Rusty's back piercing his claws into Rusty's skin whenever the mood struck him. Just when it seemed the cat had finally settled down, Ralph decided to clean himself right next to Rusty's head just to accentuate his displeasure with the unwanted houseguest. The constant licking sound irritated Rusty to no end causing him to quietly leave Piper's house in utter frustration before she awoke. As soon as he was gone, Ralph curled up in the crook of Piper's legs and enjoyed a peaceful nap. Mission accomplished. Like his owner, Ralph always got his way.

When Piper finally opened her eyes, she was disappointed by Rusty's choice to leave without saying good-bye. Patting Ralph's head she said, "You're the only man I can count on these days." Ralph purred in agreement, and then returned to a quiet slumber.

Grabbing her phone, she fired off a text questioning his whereabouts. Immediately, her phone rang.

"Looking for me?" Rusty asked.

"Evidently. I thought we were going to spend the day together." It wasn't like Piper to seem so needy, but there was much that needed to be accomplished. Piper was beginning to wonder if they ever would solve this case.

"That cat of yours is my worst nightmare. You should see the claw marks on my back," he protested.

Feeling a bit playful she teased, "Are you sure they're from him?"

He laughed. "So, what's on tap for you today?"

Piper began, "Well, I need to prepare for my board interview. That's tonight at 6 p.m. Jay said he'd help me rehearse over the phone. I'm bummed he has to go into work today."

"So basically he'll be helping you on company time," Rusty clarified.

"Something like that," she concurred. "It's really important that he does. Like I told you last night, these questions are not easy."

"Are you sure you want to go through with this?" Rusty voiced his concern.

"Why? You don't think I can handle it?" Piper snapped.

"Whoa! Don't go putting words in my mouth. I never said that." Rusty heard the sassiness in her voice.

"Sorry. I shouldn't have said that. I'm really nervous about this whole thing. I've never wanted anything so badly. I want to prove to this town that what I think matters." He heard the fiery spark in her voice.

"You're really passionate about this, aren't you, babe?"

"Yes. This is just what I need to help me move forward in my life," Piper said with conviction.

"I have no doubt you'll land the seat. Just be yourself. How could they not love you? I do," he assured her.

His tender words of encouragement melted her heart. "Thanks, Rusty. I needed that."

"So, do you have plans for the morning?" Rusty was masterful at changing the subject when emotions ran high. No one could accuse him of being the touchy-feely type.

"Why? What are you up to?" Piper inquired.

"I had a phone message from Jim. For some reason, he wants to meet at ten o'clock at the diner. Maybe he has something to report involving Gus. Care to join us?" Rusty suggested.

His not knowing the motive behind Jim's call caused Piper to hesitate. In her head, she debated whether or not to tell him about Laura and Jim's involvement with Danielle, Tom, and Beth the night of the party. Also, she wasn't certain if he knew about Tom and Beth's relationship. Personally, she'd dealt with many trust issues in the past and frowned upon people deliberately not divulging the whole truth. Here was her chance to set the record straight, but instead, she opted to take the easy way out. She wasn't taking the fall for the Wagners' negligence in reporting the facts.

"Why don't you text Tom and ask him to come along as well? You said we needed to all come together and compare notes anyway. It's been a while since I've seen him. Better yet, I'll text my sister right now and ask her to join us. She doesn't go into work today until three o'clock. It would be nice to get her perspective on the case, too." Piper stopped before she incriminated herself any further.

"Great idea! I'll text Jim and ask him to get us a table for five. You're always thinking ahead," he insisted.

"Don't you mean six?" she clarified.

"Oh, no. Laura has some place to be this morning," he said

I'm sure she does. That little weasel, she thought. Suddenly Piper felt much better about her decision to be partly open and honest. *Let Jim take the fall for his disloyalty. Even his wife bailed on him.*

"So, I'll meet you there around ten. Sound good?" Piper asked.

"Sure," he replied. "That'll work. I need to go by the liquor store and open up. I hired a college kid part-time. He's been real helpful so far, but I don't trust him with the keys."

"I don't blame you," she said. "That would be a recipe for disaster. Anyway, I want to swing by the library before I head over and look some stuff up. I'm hoping maybe one of the librarians can shed some light on all of these fancy terms. I just need to figure out a way to ask without looking so conspicuous."

Rusty couldn't help but laugh. "Babe, blending in has never been your strong suit. Try not to mention your interview. Be nonchalant about it."

"I'll try. Once I figure out what my position is on these issues, then I'll jot down some key phrases to memorize. I think I have some extra index cards stuffed in a drawer somewhere around here. I'll throw them in my purse with a pen and a highlighter. Gotta be prepared! Jay said to call him around four o'clock. The pro shop is usually dead at that time." Piper got up out of bed and headed towards the kitchen in search of the materials.

"That sounds like a good plan." Rusty was trying his hardest to be a supportive boyfriend.

"See you at ten," Piper replied.

Rusty wished her good luck with her mission.

Once Piper located what she needed, she went upstairs and raided her closet for something comfy to wear. Immediately, her eyes were drawn to her gray owl sweater. For some reason, that silly pullover always put her in a hooting and hollering mood. Grabbing some wide-leg faded jeans and worn-out cowboy boots, her outfit was complete. A quick application of make-up followed by a few swipes to her hair with the flat-iron, and Piper was on her way.

The parking lot at the library was nearly empty which made it easy to park. As Piper neared the front door, she was greeted by a huge red sign reading, 'Library closed until noon for cleaning. Sorry for the inconvenience.' Piper rolled her eyes. "Of all times to clean the library, they had to pick today!"

Piper marched back to her car and sat down. Her brain spun into overdrive as she tried to figure out what to do next. Her options were limited, as was her timeframe. She desperately needed to talk with someone who had personal knowledge about the inner workings of boards...someone who had rubbed elbows with the likes of Denise Halbreath...someone who would be privy to some inside information about the library. It didn't take Piper but a minute to come up with her answer. Hurriedly, she turned the key in the ignition and put the car in drive.

As Piper rolled into Helen's driveway, she was pleased to see the storm door ajar. Piper took that as a sign that Mr. Loverboy had just left. One less variable in the equation would help solve her problem more efficiently. Rather than knock on the door, Piper dashed right in tossing her purse on the kitchen countertop. "Hello? Anybody home?" she shouted. Like usual, Helen's house was picture postcard perfect. She stopped for a second to admire the shiny red apples nicely arranged in an exquisite crystal bowl on the kitchen table. Her grumbly tummy beckoned her to snatch one up. Seeing as Helen was nowhere to be found, Piper helped herself. Taking a bite, she savored the sweet taste of goodness.

"Didn't your mother ever teach you to knock?" Helen snarled.

Caught off-guard, Piper turned around and garbled a weak retort. "Oh! I didn't hear you come in."

"How do you know those apples are edible?" Helen asked as she rolled her wheelchair closer to Piper.

"Right," she answered. "Forgot where I was. I should have checked them for razorblades." Piper stopped chewing and pretended to carefully examine the half-eaten apple.

"I don't have time for such nonsense. What are you doing here?" she demanded.

"I need your help." Piper got right to the point..

Helen sneered, "You're too late. The cat is out of the bag. Rusty knows all about Captain Morgan and me."

Piper was taken aback by the news. "I'm sure that didn't go over well." She tossed the core into the trashcan.

Helen smirked. "You're right. He was less than pleased when I told him you already knew. He couldn't believe you hadn't shared the news with him. Tsk! Tsk!"

Piper was stunned. Clearly she'd been beaten at her own game.

"Still want to ask me for help?" Helen chided.

"I have no choice. You're my last resort," Piper's usual perky voice sounded deflated. She washed her hands in the kitchen sink and then wiped them dry with a paper towel.

Helen's interest was piqued. "Okay, I'll bite. I've got nothing better to do today anyway."

Pacing back and forth in the kitchen, Piper did her best to relay the information. Halfway through her commentary, she changed gears and pretended as if she was prepping for the actual interview. Her colorful rendition caused Helen to respond with irritating facial expressions. By the time Piper was done, Helen just shook her head.

"Did my son tell you this was a good idea?" Helen did little to hide her disapproving tone.

"I don't need his approval, but since you asked, he did." Piper stood her ground.

"He's an idiot," she stated rather matter-of-factly.

By the look on Piper's face, it wasn't hard for Helen to decipher that Piper indeed was serious.

"I think it's a great idea!" Piper maintained.

Maybe it was the sound of conviction in Piper's voice that convinced Helen to take pity on her. Or perhaps it was the cry of hopelessness that hit a nerve. Whatever it was, at that very moment, their relationship took a turn for the better. "Thinking is not your friend right now. If you insist on going through with this ludicrous charade, then sit down, be quiet, and listen. Take out a pen and start taking notes, dear. Let me show you how it's done. If you bungle this interview, you'll have only yourself to blame."

By the time Piper finished Helen's crash course on the public library system, she was exhausted. Her thick stack of notecards was filled with terms and catch phrases used among the librarians and board members. Piper took full advantage of Helen's generosity by asking her to role play what she might expect to be asked in a typical interview. At first, Piper sensed Helen was a bit wary of the whole thing, but by the time they were done, Helen was really getting into it. Piper couldn't believe her ears when Helen went as far as to suggest that she should take advantage of her widow status. When they were all said and done, Piper felt confident with her newly acquired wealth of knowledge.

Looking at her watch, Piper said, "Oh! No! It's quarter to ten. I'm supposed to be meeting Rusty and the gang at the diner." She tossed her notecards and such into her mammoth purse and stood up. "Helen, I just can't thank you enough."

"You'll do fine. Just remember what I taught you. Denise Halbreath will be duly impressed with your wisdom." Helen couldn't help but smile.

Piper stood there in awe.

"Go, on! Don't keep my son waiting." Helen shooed her away.

Then Piper did what neither woman expected. She leaned over and gave Helen a hug and a kiss.

Meanwhile, the group was assembled at the Fat Owl Diner anxiously waiting for Piper's arrival. Each was hiding behind a menu for various reasons. The usual banter among friends was replaced by a forced exchange of pleasantries. Jim did his best to engage Rusty in neutral topics, making a concerted effort to avoid mentioning Danielle's name. Tom passed the time trying to play nicey-nice with Penelope in spite of their mutual dislike for one another. All four kept glancing at the door as if they could magically make Piper appear. It was a welcomed reprieve when their favorite waitress Susie came around and took their drink orders. Much to her dismay, Tom continued to be indifferent towards her grandiose flirtations. As soon as Piper entered the restaurant, each breathed a sigh of relief.

"Sorry I'm late," she said while scooting next to Rusty in the booth. She gave him a peck on the cheek and then dropped her purse on the floor. "What did I miss?" She picked up the glass of water in front of her and took a big sip.

"Um, nothing," replied her sister. "We were waiting on you, like usual."

Susie came over to the table. "Are you ready to order?"

The friends nodded in agreement.

"Go ahead. I just need a minute." Piper scanned the menu in search of some lighter fare.

Jim pointed to Penelope and said, "Ladies first."

Piper glanced over the top of her menu and smirked. His attempt at civility was long overdue.

"I'll have two scrambled egg whites and rye toast with a cup of coffee. Thanks." Penelope handed Susie the menu.

"And for you?" Suzie batted her eyelashes at Tom.

He kept his head down and read directly from the menu. "I'll have this #2 breakfast special with sausage."

"Anything to drink?" Suzie tried one more time to make eye contact.

"Coffee, black, please." He tilted his head and politely smiled at her. Much to Susie's dismay, the moment was short lived. He then proceeded to check his phone for emails.

Both Jim and Rusty ordered pancakes with bacon. Nothing healthy for the macho guys. As for Piper, after much hemming and hawing, she chose the same thing as her sister.

Now that brunch had been ordered, it was time to get down to business. Rusty decided to take the lead.

"Piper and I appreciate you all coming this morning," he began. "We really need to put our heads together and come up with a way to catch the murderer. According to the papers, Captain Morgan has absolutely no clue who that could be. Glad our taxpayers' money is being well spent."

They all snickered.

"So, I guess the logical place to start would be with Jim since it was his idea to meet today." Rusty paused for a moment, "Enlighten us, my friend."

Jim was suddenly overcome with a violent coughing fit making it impossible for him to speak. Rusty swooped right in and patted him on the back.

"Take a sip of water," Piper suggested. "It'll help wash all your fears away."

Penelope shot her sister an amused look. Her comment was a dead giveaway. Piper was heading straight down the rabbit hole, and there was no heading back.

When Jim had gained control of himself, he suggested Rusty start with someone else.

Piper took it as her cue to let the games begin. "So, I'm assuming y'all read the latest edition of Carpool Chatter?"

"Yes, indeed," answered Tom. "Have we come up with any more clues as to who is behind that? It's gotta be someone with total access to either you, Rusty, or Piper."

All eyes were upon Penelope as the most plausible suspect.

"Like I'd waste my time blogging about you two," she chortled. "Give me a break. Not to mention, I can't rhyme. You know I failed poetry in eighth grade, sis." Penelope threw her hands up in the air.

Piper nodded her head. "That would be true."

Feeling as if the topic was a safe one, Jim joined the discussion. "So how do we go about finding this person's identity?"

"Maybe we plant something," suggested Penelope hoping to remove all suspicions from herself.

Rusty disagreed. "That's too complicated. I think once we lure the killer out into the open, the blogger will follow closely behind."

Susie interrupted their conversation. "Brunch is served. Be careful, please. These plates are hot." The waitress handed everyone their meal except for Tom. His was a special delivery complete with visual aids. Leaning clear across the table, her bosom attempted to overflow from the top of her low cut shirt. Finally, she had grabbed his attention. Licking her lips she proceeded to say, "'If you need anything else, just call me." As she made her way to the next table, all three men were mesmerized by the swaying of her curvaceous hips.

"Okay, are we all done with the peep show?" Piper said to no one in particular.

The guys lowered their heads as if they were concentrating on their meals.

Piper rolled her eyes at her sister, and then went in for the kill. She was tired of all the pussyfooting around. "Jim, Tom, have you seen Danielle lately? I can only imagine what trouble she's been stirring up."

Both men looked at one another. Neither dared to take the bait.

"Oh, for heaven's sakes. Why do I always have to be the bad guy? Rusty, your brother here is not involved with Danielle as we previously were led to believe. He's screwing around with Beth from the club."

Penelope gasped.

"Hold on, sis. It gets better. And, Rusty, your BFF right here has known that tidbit of info all along and just neglected to tell you. Seems Jim and his lovely wife Laura did find Danielle and Tom the night of the Member-Member having a little powwow with Beth. Apparently, they forgot to tell you about that, too. Why, you ask? I have no clue. Maybe that's not the only thing they're hiding. Come to think of it, Jay mentioned yesterday that Laura had perfected her golf swing. Hell, with all the lessons she's been taking, I would certainly hope so. Remind me, Penelope. How was Gus killed?"

"With a ladies' golf club," she answered without skipping a beat.

"Oh, that's right. I plum forgot. Tom, would you mind passing the salt?" Piper innocently requested.

The men sat there in disbelief. Only Piper could get away with such chutzpah. As for Jim and Tom, they spent the next twenty minutes clamoring for Rusty's attention.

"Let me explain...," Jim offered.

"I was going to tell you about Beth and me..." Tom butted in.

"I told Laura we should have said something to you, but she thought it would have complicated things by..." Jim droned on in a desperate attempt to plead his innocence.

Tom cut him off. "So, the thing is Beth and I just want to keep things casual..."

That comment made Piper raise her eyebrows in disbelief. Tom noticed her reaction and adjusted his plea accordingly.

The running commentary between the guilty parties monopolized the remainder of the gathering. It came as no surprise that by the time Susie brought the check, nothing had been accomplished. Rather, more questions had been raised concerning the potential involvement in Gus's murder case by those present. Once each threw in their share of the bill, like thieves in the night, the group parted ways. Only Rusty and Piper stayed behind to mull over the loose ends.

"Some brunch," Rusty commented.

"That's putting it mildly. Sorry you had to find out this way. I can only imagine how you feel." Piper rubbed his back.

"My brother is an idiot!" said Rusty.

Piper was quick to respond, "No, he's not. He's just your typical thirty-something guy looking for the next best thing. Cut him some slack. He's not the one you need to be worried about. It's Jim."

"Nah, Jim was just trying to spare my feelings. He knew I'd be really upset if I found out Tom was involved in a twisted love triangle. I'm glad to hear he nixed his relationship with Danielle. That was long overdue. As for Beth, she seems nice enough. Not sure why he didn't just tell me about her. Maybe he thought I wouldn't approve," Rusty reasoned.

Unable to stifle her anger, Piper exploded, "When are you going to finally admit that Jim is not who you think he is? That man is a liar. The hell with your theory! I'm telling you…Jim is up to no good. He doesn't have your back. I do! Wake up and open your eyes, Rusty! Mark my words. You need to distance yourself from him. If you don't, it's going to come back to bite you. Too much is at stake right now."

Rusty picked up his glass of water and took a sip. His stalling technique played right into Piper's hands. It was time to move on before acrid words tarnished their relationship any further.

"I have a plan. I know who killed Gus, and I can prove it." Piper boldly stated.

"Mind sharing it with me?" he raised his eyebrows.

Piper grabbed her purse and then stood up. "Later. Let's get out of here. Too many gossiping hens. Why don't you walk me to my car and I'll fill you in."

Rusty removed his wallet from the back pocket of his jeans and threw some bills on the table. "That should cover it." Placing his arm around Piper's bony shoulders, he leaned over and gave her a kiss on the lips. "I love you."

Piper smiled, "I know."

The two headed towards the door with every intention of sticking to the case. Yet once outside, all roads seemed to lead to a lazy afternoon cozying up under the sheets.

Sitting at a table in a sunny kitchen across town, Candy and Carolyn were busy addressing their own set of issues. Unfortunately, theirs weren't nearly as pleasing as Piper and Rusty's. Carolyn had planned on working out at the gym while the kids were in school, but a frantic phone call from her sister caused her to put off exercising for yet another day. Evidently, the recent Carpool Chatter blog hit too close to home. According to Candy's message, she was afraid of the potential fallout and was in desperate need of reassurance.

"Now tell me again why you're so upset? The blogger didn't mention you by name," Carolyn asked between bites. She had served a scrumptious chicken Caesar salad for lunch upon Candy's arrival.

Rolling her eyes, Candy blurted, "Duh! It's obvious the blogger is talking about me. I had nothing to do with Gus's murder. Why would I kill Gus? He's Willow's father."

Carolyn nixed her usual condescending tone, and resorted to one more sympathetic. She could tell something was definitely off-kilter with her sister. "Of course you didn't. Have you spoken to Marc? Has he read it?"

Candy's eyes opened wide, "No! I'm staying far away from him. If he calls looking for me, tell him you haven't seen me for days. Would you mind passing the pepper mill?"

Carolyn did as she was asked and then proceeded to say, "I can't help you if you don't tell me what's wrong. What has Marc done that has spooked you so much?" She looked Candy straight in the eyes.

Candy placed her fork on the table and then took a deep breath. "I think he killed Gus."

"You don't know that!" insisted Carolyn. "Candy, you can't go around accusing people of crimes they haven't committed." Carolyn had a proclivity for assuming Candy would be misinformed, which caused much angst in their fickle relationship.

Shaking her head in frustration, Candy said, "Before you go climb up on your soapbox, you might want to listen to what I have to say."

"By all means, please tell," she encouraged her sister.

As requested, Candy filled Carolyn in concerning her lack of judgment in sharing the news of Gus and Janie's affair with Marc. She also mentioned her impromptu meeting with Captain Morgan at the grocery store which led to her hinting about Marc's desire to run for Gus's seat prior to his death. The icing on the cake involved Chief Derbyshire. The morning of the fire at Peeps & Petals, she'd spotted Marc's car parked a street over but hadn't given it a second thought. When she bumped into the Chief at the dry cleaners a few days later, she'd offered up this information thinking it could be important. After some inconsequential comments pertaining to Marc, Candy asked Carolyn for her take on the situation.

"Why?" was the sole word Carolyn uttered.

Candy looked confused. "Why what?"

Carolyn hesitated, and then said, "Why are you still involved with him? I told you a year ago, walk away. There is nothing good that can come out of this relationship. It's water under the bridge. You don't owe him anything, sis."

"I've tried, but I can't. I'm in too deep. I love him." Candy hung her head.

"I can help you. Don has connections. We can make it look as if Marc acted all alone. You said yourself. He looks guilty as hell." Carolyn ached as she watched her sister crumble in defeat.

Candy ran her fingers through her hair. "Don't tell Don, sis. I don't want to involve your family in this mess. I've done nothing that would implicate me in Gus's murder except of course being guilty by association. What I am going to do? I'm not taking the fall for a crime I didn't commit. I swear. I didn't kill Gus. You've gotta help me," she begged.

All that could be heard was the ticking of the grandfather clock from the hallway marking the passing of precious time. Neither sister said a word. The table was cleared, and the dishwasher was filled. Both concentrated on the problem at hand trying desperately to come up with a viable solution. It was nearly two o'clock. Carolyn had to leave immediately in order to make it in time for carpool line to avoid having her children be embarrassed again by her tardiness. Candy thanked her sister for hearing her out. After a tender moment peppered with encouraging words from Carolyn, the two parted ways.

Hole 17

The afternoon zipped by, and now it was finally time for Rusty to depart. He knew Piper wanted to rehearse her spiel with Jay before leaving for the interview. He made sure to wish his girlfriend good luck, and promised to call her later for a complete recap of the interview process. After some playful kisses, Rusty scooted out the door on a mission of his own. There were too many unanswered questions concerning the financial backstory of the club. Since he'd had no luck locating Marc the other night, Rusty intended to stop by his county office unannounced under the pretense of conducting other business in the building. If asked, Rusty thought about mentioning Piper's work permits for the addition as a plausible excuse. He was banking on Marc not knowing that the work had been completed nearly a year ago.

Upon his arrival, Rusty noticed Jim's truck parked in the municipal lot. It was common for him to be there due to his construction business, yet Rusty was less than pleased by his presence. Rusty wasn't nearly as hot and bothered about Jim's culpability as Piper, but then again, there was a reason for his undemonstrative response at the diner. Someone had to know exactly how the permits for Peeps & Petals passed over the zoning director's desk without any hint of it finding its way in the press. Despite being a newcomer in town, Jim certainly had made up for lost time. No one knew better than his dear old friend how to work the system to his advantage. Jim had bragged about this on more than one occasion. The thought previously crossed Rusty's mind concerning the possible notion of a connection between Marc and Jim in relation to Gus's murder, but he brushed it off as totally absurd. Now, he seemed to think that maybe he'd been right.

Access into the building was easy despite the security measures that had been put into place after 9/11. The guard at the desk buzzed Rusty right in without showing any signs of hesitation. It turned out the old man was a regular customer at Rusty's liquor store who enjoyed trading jabs with him over rival sports teams. After exchanging brief hellos, Rusty made sure to promise him a discount the next time he came in for his weekly libations. He figured it was a small price to pay for not having to explain the reason for his visit. The smile on the guard's face indicated Rusty's gesture was well received. A quick trip on the elevator landed him on the second floor right outside Marc's office door. His secretary was nowhere to be seen giving Rusty a green light to enter the area without permission.

Seated with his back to the door was Marc dressed in his usual business attire. Rusty paused for a moment taking in the grandeur of his friend's office. Trophies and plaques lined the shelves. Noticeably absent were family photos. The telltale sign of a confirmed bachelor.

"Dreaming this was all yours?" The question seemed to materialize from thin air.

Rusty coughed.

Marc swiveled his chair around and beamed his pearly whites at his friend. "How are ya, Rusty? This is unexpected." He stood up and firmly shook Rusty's hand. "Not much going on today, so I sent Libby home early. Hard worker she is."

"That's good to hear. You better hang on to her, man," Rusty said.

Marc pointed to the empty seat in front of his desk. "What brings you by today?"

Rusty wished he could skip all the formalities and just ask him about the financial machinations for Peeps & Petals, but no such luck. His calculated moves were deemed necessary in order for him to achieve his desired results. "As a matter of fact, I just happened to be in the building so I thought I'd drop by and say hello."

Always receptive to visitors, Marc replied, "Glad you did. I need a break. See this pile of papers? I'm filling out my petition for candidacy for Gus's seat."

There was no better segue than what was just handed to him. Rusty made the split second decision to dive in head first. "Wow! I had no idea you'd be interested. I thought Jack was the logical replacement for his old friend."

Marc's face reddened. "I don't know why you'd have thought that, Rusty. I have much political support here on the local level. Woodlawn is a much better place since I became president of the County Council." He fiddled with a couple of paper clips as if he were warding off a bout of aggression.

"Oh, don't get me wrong. I think you've done a great job, except for allowing the opening of that strip club, Peeps & Petals. Not sure how the zoning board allowed that kind of establishment to slip through the cracks unnoticed. Many folks around here see that business as a significant threat to our wholesome town. Quite unfortunate that it burned to the ground, huh? You think it will be rebuilt?" Rusty kept a watchful eye on Marc to gauge his reaction.

"Don't go blaming that on me, man. I tried my best to block it, but Jack Conway did what he pleased. My so-called fellow politician disregarded whatever I had to say and pushed the permits right through without blinking an eye. Gus had them all wrapped around his finger so tightly. He and Jack were quite the team, but no more. I'm in charge now. Good 'ol Gus will be rolling over in his grave when I fill his seat. Just you watch! My time is coming!"

Rusty was taken aback by Marc's forthrightness. From what Marc had just revealed, he had a sure motive for wanting Gus dead. Rusty's stunned expression said everything.

"No, I didn't," said Marc emphatically.

Rusty tilted his head to the side, "You didn't what?"

"I didn't kill him, if that's what you're thinking. I'm not keeping any secrets from the cops. My history with Gus, and Danielle for that matter, is like an open book," he snickered. "I can't say the same for everyone I know."

His furtive glance made Rusty squirm in his chair. Their amiable conversation had taken a sudden nosedive into dangerous territory. It certainly wasn't public knowledge that Danielle and Rusty had been engaged. It was hard to tell if Marc was making a blanket statement, or if he was privy to that confidential information. If volunteered to the police by a third party, Rusty would certainly look guilty. Weighing his options, Rusty decided to focus on something a little less volatile in hopes of gaining favor with Marc.

"Have you picked a campaign manager yet?" Rusty asked.

Marc replied, "Um, no. I hadn't thought about it. Have any suggestions?"

"How about Ed VanHorst? He's very active at the club. I bet he could garner some votes for you with the club members." Rusty was pleased with his suggestion.

Marc seemed amused. "I appreciate your input, but I'd be leery of trusting Ed with my political future. He and Jack are thick as thieves. If given the chance, he'd sabotage my campaign in a heartbeat." He paused for a moment and then continued, "I have to give Gus credit. Not only was he sleeping with the wife of his biggest nemesis, but also he was making a fool out of him behind his own back. This is exactly why I'm never getting married. It's way too complicated for me."

Rusty was blown away by Marc's lack of discretion. "So, do you think Jack is the killer?" It seemed only logical to ask.

"Hell, no," Marc replied without skipping a beat. "He's not that dumb. If I were a betting man, I'd place all my chips on Candy. I can't say for sure she's guilty, but the two of them were like oil and water. Quite frankly, I'm surprised she didn't off him sooner."

Rusty wasn't buying it. Sure, Candy had her issues with Gus, but solving them by committing such a ghastly murder just didn't fit. Instead, Rusty tried a different approach. "What about Jim Wagner?"

Marc laughed. "I'm surprised you're even asking that question. I would think that you of all people would know about his relationship with Gus. He was part of that trio...Gus, Jack, and Jim. How do you think Jim was able to grow his company so quickly? It surely wasn't by happenstance. Gus took care of Jim and vice versa. Heck, Jim covered for Gus on many occasions when he was screwing around with Janie, even bragged about it. Isn't that what friends are for, man?"

Rusty had a hard time digesting this information. His so-called best friend was living a double life of sorts. It pained him to admit it, but Piper was right. Jim could not be trusted. Not to mention, Rusty was surprised Jim would openly condone a cheating spouse after his own personal woes. Why Rusty was not privy to Gus and Jim's secret alliance troubled him. The thought did cross his mind that Jim might be in cahoots with Marc, but he shrugged it off as nonsensical. Even he thought that was unlikely. The nagging voice in his head begged him to walk away before it was too late. Marc's willingness to divulge such vital information without the slightest hesitation made Rusty question his motives. His gut instincts were telling him that Marc was covering for someone, but he couldn't pinpoint exactly who or why. Being associated with Marc could prove to be a deadly mistake, especially due to his past history with Danielle. It was definitely time to leave.

"I hate to cut my visit short, but I need to get going." Rusty stood up.

"Let me walk you to the elevator," Marc offered.

There was no time to decline his offer. Marc was right by Rusty's side matching him step by step. His suggestion for meeting up for drinks sometime in the near future was met with a polite smile. Rusty neither confirmed nor denied his availability. As soon as the elevator arrived, the men shook hands and said their good-byes. When the doors opened, they both were caught off-guard by its unexpected passenger. Leaning against the wall directly opposite from them stood Jim Wagner.

"Well, hey Rusty! What are you doing here?" Jim shouted from inside the elevator car.

Rusty had absolutely nothing to say.

Across town, tension was also high due to Piper's impending meeting. She couldn't help but feel confident about her readiness for the board interview. She and Jay had rehearsed so much that Helen's prepared responses were assuredly committed to memory. All the fancy library terms had been written on separate notecards with catch phrases underlined in pink. Piper was as ready as she was ever going to be. The hardest part was selecting her outfit. Her stunning pink suit jacket paired with flared black pants made a bold statement. Classy, yet fashionable. Simple diamond stud earrings and a strand of pearls complemented her look. Her pièce de résistance was her snakeskin pumps. In order to make her six o'clock appointment, she needed to leave promptly or risk being late.

Piper drove straight to the library. There wasn't much time to gather her thoughts for one last pep talk. Upon her arrival, she was surprised by the number of cars in the lot. If this was any indication of the number of patrons passing through the library's doors each day, then the taxpayers' money was being well spent. Evidently, this was the place to be these days. The building appeared to be shipshape and the grounds were impeccable. Piper made a mental note to praise that aspect if given the chance. Her eye was drawn to the hand painted bench under a maple tree—a perfect spot for reading a book to a youngster. Secretly, Piper was hoping Rusty would show up in order to wish her good luck. From a quick look around, it didn't appear as if his truck was parked in the lot.

As Piper walked through the front doors, she pushed her shoulders back and held her head up high. She was brimming over with novel ideas. Soon this would be the place where she'd leave her mark on the town. She had heard from her Aunt Karen that in New Jersey, libraries, patrons had the capability of downloading free magazines and music to their personal devices. If appointed to the board, she'd make it her first initiative to bring the same to Woodlawn.

Seated primly at the information desk was her not-so-favorite librarian, Mrs. Johnson. Piper took her mere presence as a challenge. If she was to serve on the board, maintaining cordial relationships with the library's employees would be expected. What better time than now to adhere to this protocol. Earning Mrs.

Johnson's respect would certainly be a feather in her cap.

"Good evening," Piper said as she approached the desk.

Mrs. Johnson looked up from her desk and responded, "We've been expecting you. I'm rather surprised you arrived twenty minutes early. I'll be sure to mention it to Ms. Halbreath later on. That's a definite plus in your column. She just started her interview with another candidate. I doubt he's in contention for the position, but Ms. Halbreath is required to proceed with the interview nonetheless. At least you have the necessary pocketbook for future contributions. That's another plus in your column. You even look the part. Triple check. Maybe you have a chance after all. Please take a seat over there by the conference room door. I'll let you know when she's ready for you. Good luck."

Piper smiled. "Thank you, Mrs. Johnson." She was amazed by the librarian's kind words.

The librarian grumbled, "Helen said she wouldn't bring her famous apple pie to cards next week if she heard I wasn't nice to you tonight. Make sure you mention my amiability."

So Mrs. Johnson was coerced into being pleasant, Piper thought. She just shrugged her shoulders. *Whatever it takes.* "Will do!" she replied.

While she waited patiently in her appointed chair, Piper reviewed her notecards and rehearsed her responses one more time. She was so engrossed in what she was doing that she never saw Rusty enter the building.

Mrs. Johnson pointed him in the right direction while blowing him an air kiss. Her affection for the rugged guy was blatantly obvious. Rusty was like a second son to her. Mrs. Johnson smiled as his high-pitched whistle startled Piper causing her notecards to become airborne.

"Shhh!" She put her index finger to her lips. "You're supposed to be quiet in here. Look what you made me do! Piper couldn't help but smile. Her man came by after all.

Rusty leaned over to kiss her lips, but was met with a cold cheek instead.

"Don't mess up my lipstick, babe. I won't have time to reapply." She puckered her lips. "Later. I promise."

Rusty slid into the unoccupied seat next to her. "I'm going to hold you to that! Are you all set?"

"I think so." Piper adjusted her blouse. "How do I look? Do you like my outfit?"

He smiled. "You look like a million bucks. You're going to kill this interview."

"Ugh. Must you use the *K* word?" Piper joked.

"Speaking of which, I stopped by Marc's office. You're not going to believe what I found out." He looked anxious.

Over the next five minutes, he filled her in on the latest developments concerning Jim's duplicity. He made sure to point out that, yes, Piper had been right all along even though it pained him to do so. Together, they both voiced concerns over the actual degree of Jim's culpability, as well as the possibility that Marc was setting Rusty up to take the blame for Gus's death. Piper agreed to broach the subject with Laura at tomorrow's nine hole gathering. Their foursome would consist of Danielle, Janie, Carolyn, and Piper. Tanya had paired herself with Laura and added Penelope and Candy to the mix. With everything going on lately, it was sure to be an eventful morning.

The opening of the conference room door interrupted their exchange. A pale looking man exited in a hurry. "Are you next?" he asked Piper.

"Yes. Yes, I am," she boldly stated.

"You might want to reconsider and leave now. That woman is ferocious!" he exclaimed. The frightened gentleman didn't wait for Piper's response. He marched straight out of the building without even looking back.

"Not the ringing endorsement you hoped for, huh?" kidded Rusty.

Piper wasn't fazed a bit. "It's just par for the course from what I understand. The key is to beat her at her own game. Just watch how it's done, baby." She stood up and then straightened her suit jacket.

Rusty patted her derriere. "That's my girl."

"Piper," Mrs. Johnson called. "You may go in now. Good luck, dear."

Rusty gave Piper a quick hug and then whispered in her ear. Whatever he said brought a huge smile to her face.

The conference room in use was normally reserved for children's programs and book club gatherings. Paintings on the wall reflected famous children's authors and notable characters from classic literature. Piper was in awe of the magnitude of space. She was picturing more of a closed-in room rather than such an expansive area. There was a single table positioned in the middle of the room accompanied by two chairs. Dragon Lady Halbreath occupied one. The other sat empty. The clicking of her heels made for a loud entrance. Immediately, Ms. Halbreath looked up. Instead of acknowledging Piper with a greeting of sorts, she simply waved her over. Piper took that as a sign that formal introductions were unnecessary. If her subdued demeanor was any indication of what lay ahead, Piper felt confident she could handle this woman.

"I don't believe we've ever met," Ms. Halbreath began, "which really doesn't matter since I highly doubt we'll ever speak again after tonight."

So, perhaps Piper's fairytale rendition of how this was going to go down was completely off-base. Obviously, the rumors swirling around town about Dragon Lady were true. The woman did not mince words. Piper approached the table with a spark of renewed energy. Evidently, Ms. Halbreath had no idea with whom she was dealing. No one messed with Piper O'Donnell and got away with it. As far as Piper was concerned, game on bitch!

Capitalizing on her strengths, Piper replied, "Is that a Rachel Zoe scarf you're wearing? I love the intricacies of the pattern. Black and white is oh so chic."

Dragon Lady tilted her head down and then looked at Piper over the top of her reading glasses, "Why, yes. As a matter of fact it is. I bought it as a daily special on one of those television shopping channels."

"QVC?" Piper tilted her head to one side.

"I think so," Dragon Lady said. She fondled her scarf.

Piper thrilled, "I just love that channel. Such classy and intelligent hosts and their products are top of the line. Here's a little known secret. I was a runner-up for a program host position on a similar network back in the day. Not sure why I didn't get the job. My five minute segment lasted more than twenty minutes. Everyone else could only talk for five or less. I just nailed that presentation."

Dragon Lady demurred, "Such a shame you weren't selected."

Piper continued, "I can talk about anything for hours on end. I've been told that all my life."

"Somehow, that doesn't surprise me," Dragon Lady conceded.

Piper took that as a sign to press further, "Actually, it's a very useful trait that would sure come in handy when dealing with the press over controversial topics such as budget cuts and the right of intellectual freedom." *Score one for me*, she thought.

Dragon Lady chose to ignore her pointed references. Instead, she shuffled the papers in her grasp and then said, "Speaking of which, let's get down to business. I have three more interviews after yours. Please tell me why you are applying for this position."

Piper cleared her throat. "I believe everyone has a civic duty to give back to their community. With the passing of my husband last year, I have realized that time is precious. It seemed only logical to want to represent the organization that has had the most impact on my life over the years. My family has always avidly supported the library."

Mrs. Halbreath took a moment to scribble some notes on her paper. "I verified your account before you arrived. A fan of romance novels and gossip magazines. Why am I not surprised?"

"I take it you haven't read *Fifty Shades of Beige*?" Piper tried to impress the woman by throwing out the name of a current bestseller.

"You mean *Grey*," she corrected her.

"*Beige*," insisted Piper. She was taken aback that this so-called important trustee didn't know the exact name of such a controversial book. Evidently, Mrs. Halbreath needed to be briefed on current hot topics. A job perfectly suited for Piper.

"Whatever," Mrs. Halbreath conceded. "Let's move on. What experience do you have that would help with capital projects or financial concerns?"

This subject would prove to be the most difficult for Piper to spin since she'd had minimal job experience.

"My position at Peeps & Petals has been vital to the growth of the business."

"Was this before or after you scorched it to the ground?" Mrs. Halbreath rested her chin on her hand.

"Before," she answered.

"Duly noted." Dragon Lady took a red pen and marked an obvious X on her paper. "So moving on, are you familiar with our data bases and computer services?"

Piper perked right up. This area of the library she was well-versed in. "I believe the library needs to change its tune when it comes to addressing the needs of today's consumer. I'm sure you agree that actual books are overrated."

Mrs. Halbreath cringed.

Piper didn't even notice her negative reaction. "Personally, I download eBooks to my tablet from online retailers all the time. We need to jump on the digital craze and offer eBooks and even eMagazines to our patrons. In New Jersey, that's the norm. We're kinda behind the times here in the cornfields, don't cha think? I'm just the person to bring Woodlawn into the twenty-first century."

"And from where do you presume we're going to come up with that kind of money to fund these so-called grandiose projects?" Mrs. Halbreath demanded.

"Let's throw a library ball! We can get local businesses to donate items for an auction, and maybe we can get Chef Henri Samuel to cater it. Carolyn DeWitt is very tight with him. I'm sure she wouldn't mind speaking with him on our behalf. Just think of the possibilities!" Piper's enthusiasm was infectious.

Mrs. Halbreath cracked a tiny smile. "As a matter of fact, Carolyn is my next interview candidate. I'll make a note to mention it to her."

"On second thought, scratch that idea." Piper popped up from her chair and threw her hands on top of Ms. Halbreath's papers in an attempt to stop her from writing. "I heard he uses imitation crab in his soup." Realizing her gross error of judgment, she withdrew her hands and sat back down. "Next question?" she inquired with a plastered smile across her face.

"One usually remains seated for this type of dialogue." Ms. Halbreath admonished her with a blatant evil eye.

"I have to draw the line somewhere when it comes to the use of inferior products in my food." Piper's weak comeback did little to help the situation.

Dragon Lady sighed. "So besides party planning skills, is there anything else of note you wish to share?"

"The library's blog. I could contribute a weekly piece," Piper volunteered.

"Oh, let me guess. You want to write something along the lines of the Carpool Chatter Blog," Dragon Lady proposed. "Here we go again. There's no room for idle gossip on the library's website. How many times do I have to repeat myself? I said the same thing to that woman when she first pitched the idea to me. Why she'd think I'd change my opinion now is beyond me."

"What woman?" shrieked Piper.

"Shh! We don't raise our voices in the library." Ms. Halbreath scolded her.

Piper shrugged her shoulders in frustration. "Fine," she whispered. "What woman?"

Ms. Halbreath answered, "The blogger."

Piper tried a more direct approach. "Would you happen to know the name of this Carpool Chatter Blogger?" Being so close to discovering the identity of the person who'd caused such angst in her life caused Piper to become jittery.

"No," Dragon Lady replied.

"Dadgumit!" Piper exclaimed.

"But Beth does," Ms. Halbreath volunteered.

"Barmaid Beth from the club?" Piper chimed in.

Ms. Halbreath shook her head in agreement. "Yes. She and Beth are good friends. Beth is the fool who gave her my unlisted phone number."

"Really?" Piper wished she'd known this before sticking her neck out for Beth the night of Danielle's book club debacle. Things might have turned out much differently. "Isn't that against the club's policies? I could talk to Jay for you. I'm sure he could get her fired. He's got a lot of clout up there."

"I recommend you stay clear of such nonsense. Nothing good can come from it," Ms. Halbreath warned.

"Believe me, Dragon Lady. I wish I could." Piper gasped. The slip of the tongue should have been the cause of her dismissal from the interview. Instead, it produced the most unanticipated results.

Ms. Halbreath appeared rather unscathed by the comment. "Finally someone has the gall to call me that to my face."

"I'm sorry," Piper said.

"Don't be. I've earned that nickname through many years of hard work and dedication to my job," she said quite proudly.

Piper's quizzical look led to her second faux pas for the night. "I thought it was in reference to your bourbon swigging ways?"

"I should think not! And anyway, I don't drink bourbon," Ms. Halbreath countered.

"That's right. You like whiskey!" Piper corrected herself.

Ms. Halbreath was smitten by the bubblehead blonde with the absence of common sense. "Oh, Piper. What am I going to do with you?"

"That's easy," she retorted. "Appoint me to the board of trustees!"

"I'll see what I can do." Ms. Halbreath stood up.

Piper proceeded to round the table and embraced the woman in a hug.

Taken by surprise, Ms. Halbreath said, "It was nice to meet you, Piper O'Donnell."

"Likewise. I'm sure we'll be seeing each other again soon." Piper flashed her best beauty queen smile.

Ms. Halbreath concurred, "I have no doubt."

And with that, Piper sauntered out of the conference room in search of her man.

Entrenched on the couch by the magazine racks, Rusty was doing his best to stay awake. With all of the stress he'd been under lately, he was finding it hard to concentrate. After scanning a few articles in a car magazine, he finally gave up. Instead, he had used the past twenty minutes trying to come up with plausible theories concerning Gus's murder. Narrowing down the list was harder than he had imagined. He kept circling back to Jim and Marc. Piper's sudden appearance took his breath away. Despite having known her for two years now, he couldn't help but be attracted to her model-like body. As she strutted in his direction, he envisioned her totally naked accessorized with just her snakeskin heels and bright pink lipstick. He took her come hither grin as an indication that all had gone well. If he played his cards right, perhaps he could participate in the bonus round. Unfortunately Rusty's dream world was rudely interrupted by Carolyn.

"Poor soul! She looks like she just swallowed a canary. There's no way Denise Halbreath will recommend her to fill Mary Kay Getz's vacant seat.

Mary Kay was a pillar in our community. Piper couldn't find her way out of a paper bag," sneered Carolyn.

Before Rusty got a chance to defend his woman, Piper joined them. A quick kiss to Rusty's cheek and then she said, "You're next. Ms. Halbreath is taking a restroom break which gives us a few minutes to catch up."

Carolyn couldn't resist asking, "How did your interview go?"

Not wanting to sound too overconfident Piper replied, "I gave it my best shot. We'll just have to wait and see."

Carolyn snickered, "What took so long? Did you need help understanding the questions?"

Piper didn't take the bait. This was her opportunity to question Carolyn about Marc and Candy. She wasn't going to allow some petty comments to distract her. "Are Candy and Marc still an item?"

"No!" Carolyn emphatically replied. "They're nothing but friends. Who told you they were together?"

Piper and Rusty exchanged knowing glances. His slight nod was all the encouragement she needed to push the envelope a bit further.

"I just assumed so since they were rather cozy at the Member-Member party," Piper offered.

Carolyn lowered her voice. "Leave my sister alone. She has enough issues without you sticking your nose into her business."

"Funny. That's exactly what Marc said when he unexpectedly dropped by my house for a chat." Piper's mischievous smile caused Carolyn to lose her temper.

"That lying son-of-a-bitch," she growled. "My sister had nothing to do with Gus's murder. Marc has no business discussing my sister with you of all people. Read my lips. Stay clear of that man or else."

Over the intercom, Mrs. Johnson requested Carolyn to proceed to the conference room. Before Carolyn left, she said, "We'll continue this conversation tomorrow at the club. I'm not done with you, Piper."

Piper wasn't fazed by her menacing stare, "I look forward to it. Good luck!"

Rusty didn't even wait until Carolyn was out of earshot before clamoring, "What the hell was that all about?"

Piper tugged on his shirt, "Let's get out of here."

The two headed into the parking lot in silence. Upon entering Piper's car, the conversation exploded into a frenzy of questions.

"So, do you think she knows who killed Gus?" Rusty asked.

Piper shook her head no, as she rolled down the windows. "Wait a second. It's hotter than hell in here. I need some air."

"Shouldn't we just put the air conditioning on in case someone overhears us?" Rusty asked. As a detective, it was in his blood to be ever cautious.

"Nah. The only people in the parking lot are library patrons. All they care about is library books. Listen. During my interview, I learned some fascinating information. Evidently, Beth the barmaid at the club knows the identity of the Carpool Chatter blogger."

"Really?" Rusty was stunned by the news.

"Long story, but the gist is she has access to that person. Dragon Lady is my source. You can't get better than that, right?" she shrugged.

"True," Rusty acknowledged.

"So, all we need to do now is feed Beth some false information. If the killer thinks the police are closing in, he or she will panic. Then, we set a trap. Easy-peasy. Catch a Killer 101," she snickered.

"I don't think it's going to be as simple as you claim it to be, babe," he lamented. "I'm afraid to ask. Do you have a plan?"

"I do!" insisted Piper. "But first, you need to help me set up the framework. Any chance we could get your mom to occupy Captain Morgan tomorrow morning?"

"Ugh. Must we encourage them?" Rusty groaned.

"I feel your pain, but unfortunately, if we want to find Gus's killer, we'll need Captain Morgan out of the way." She gave him a pleading look.

Rusty sighed. "I'll see what I can do."

Piper clapped her hands in approval. "Great! Next, we need for Marc, Jack, and Jim to be at the club. I'll call Jay and ask him to set up some phony card game."

"For the morning?" Rusty protested.

Piper replied, "Yeah. You're right. Maybe an emergency stockholders' meeting instead?"

"That's more like it. What are you going to do about the ladies?" Rusty rested his arm on the back of her seat.

"The women should already be there for the Nine Hole weekly match, so I think we're set. I just need to confirm with Jay that Beth will be working. The hard part will be coming up with some erroneous tip about the murder case. Think you're up for the challenge, big man?" Piper winked at him.

Rusty disregarded her flirty gesture and proceeded to say, "Piper, what if the blogger is the murderer?"

"What do you mean? You think Janie is the blogger and the killer?" She was confused.

"No, babe. Forget about Janie. There's no way she could have done it. Sure, she was having an affair with the guy, but the last thing she'd want to do is kill him. It doesn't make any sense. She needed him alive to continue their affair. No, it's definitely someone else," he insisted.

Piper shook her head no. "I don't buy the blogger/murderer combo theory either. I think the blogger is covering for someone, but whom?"

Rusty leaned back against the passenger side door. "Okay, then what if Candy is covering for Marc? That would explain why Carolyn flipped out when you suggested their connection. Maybe Candy knows that Marc is guilty and she's in way too deep. Exposing the identity of the blogger is the key to solving this crime. All roads are leading in one direction, babe."

Piper turned the key in the ignition. "So, I guess it's up to us to follow the signs."

Rusty leaned over for a quick kiss and then exited the vehicle. "I'll follow you. My truck is parked around the side of the building," he said through the car's window.

"Sounds good," Piper smiled.

As the two slowly pulled out of the parking lot in anticipation of what lay ahead the next day, inside the library sat the blogger busily composing one final post. With a brush of the keys, the devious writer, safely ensconced in the corner of the room, would forever be remembered as Woodlawn's most notorious literary genius.

Hole 18

Carolyn's interview took less than fifteen minutes.

There wasn't much to discuss considering they'd known each other for years, yet they weren't what you would call bosom buddies either. For a small town such as Woodlawn, social circles overlapped on a regular basis. Carolyn tried to pry information out of Ms. Halbreath concerning Piper's interview. She was gravely disappointed when the topic was noticeably skirted. When asked the timeframe for notification, Carolyn was annoyed by Dragon Lady's ambiguous response. The only positive outcome from their meeting was Ms. Halbreath's promise to officiate a mock trial day at the local elementary school come spring. Besides that, not much information had been exchanged.

Once the meeting ended, Carolyn decided to peruse the library's bookshelves. For almost seven o'clock at night, the place was hopping. Nothing appealing caught her eye on the bestseller display, so she decided to look in the stacks for an old favorite. As Carolyn turned the corner of the far bookcase, she ran smack into Laura. A pile of books flew right out of Laura's hands landing haphazardly on the floor.

"I am so sorry!" exclaimed Carolyn.

Laura quickly bent over and gathered her materials. "Don't worry about it, Carolyn." Pressing the books to her chest, she said, "I wish I could stay and talk, but I'm in a hurry. See you tomorrow at the club?" she asked without waiting for a response. Laura waved good-bye, and then darted straight towards the exit.

"What was that all about?" Carolyn said to no one in particular. "I hope she at least used the self-checkout station before leaving." All of a sudden, her day caught up with her. Sighing, she grabbed a couple of random books from a display and decided to call it a night. With a swipe of her library card at the kiosk, she was all set.

As for Piper and Rusty, after leaving the library, they stopped for a quick meal at a sandwich shop. While sharing a Philly cheesesteak sub and fries, neither mentioned a word pertaining to Gus's murder. Overanalyzing the situation would do little to help solve the case. It was in fate's hands as to what the future would hold for Gus's killer. The pressure was on for Piper to remain calm and collected while the plan unfolded. The desired results would be well worth the aggravation. Once they were through, the two parted ways despite Rusty's protest. The last thing Piper needed was a sleepless night to add to her already nervous energy.

Rusty decided to swing by the store on his way home to check on sales. This time of year was usually hit or miss. As soon as the summer holidays rolled around, business would pick up and remain steady until the end of the year. For now, the store's income relied solely on special events such as the Member-Member party. Tom was manning the store for the night. Fortunately, the brothers were getting along much better lately. Rusty was hoping to capitalize on the good vibes by pawning off Piper's rendezvous assignment for Helen and Captain Morgan on his little brother. The thought of voluntarily trying to get them together made his stomach sick.

When Rusty entered the shop, he found Tom at the counter engaged in a lively conversation with Jim. Of all people to have to run into at this late hour, Jim was the last person on his list. He briefly considered skipping out, but Tom had already waved hello upon his arrival. Mustering up his best smile, Rusty greeted the men with a welcoming hello. After a bit of innocent banter, Tom said he was leaving. He wanted to work-out before the gym closed. Rusty shot him a *don't leave me* look, but Tom either missed the mark completely or chose to ignore the signal in an attempt to get out the door. Rusty tried one last time to keep him around by saying he needed to talk with him. Yet, Tom insisted he'd call Rusty as soon as he returned home. The store was empty save the two men. The eerie silence did little to help alleviate the awkward situation.

"Twice in one day!" Jim commented.

"Yes," agreed Rusty. "It's good to see you again."

"So, what were you doing with Marc?" Jim's shaky voice betrayed his obvious nervousness.

Rusty was less than prepared for this spur-of-the-moment confrontation; however, Jim gave him no choice but to reply, "Nothing, really. I just happened to be in the building on business, and I thought I'd stop by and say hello." From what he could tell, Jim seemed to accept his response as truthful.

"Oh," he said. "Listen, I want to clear the air about something."

Rusty raised his eyebrows in concern.

"I should have told you that I saw Tom, Danielle, and Beth that night, but Laura insisted I keep my mouth shut," Jim explained.

"Why's that?" Rusty wasn't letting him off the hook that easily.

Jim sighed, "Who knows why? Why do *you* listen to Piper when she tells you to do stupid things? Looking back now, I probably should have kept my mouth shut about a lot of things, especially Gus's murder case. Usually, Laura gives sound advice. Just not this time, huh?"

Rusty just stared blankly at him.

Jim continued. "She's had such a hard time adjusting to Woodlawn with the mistress label attached to her name."

"But," Rusty interjected.

"I know we supposedly cleared the air, but I think she still resents Piper for everything that happened in the past. I mean c'mon. They can't even be in the same room without complaining."

The two men politely laughed in agreement.

Jim seemed to relax a bit. "I have to say. Lately, she's been in a better frame of mind now that she's become close friends with Beth."

"Beth the barmaid from the club?" blurted Rusty.

Jim looked at him with a rather exasperated look on his face. "Um, yeah. Why? Is that a problem? Don't tell me Piper is best friends with her or something. That's all I need to hear."

Warning bells went off in his head. "No. Piper's not. But, how often would you say they talk? Once a day? A couple of times a week?" Rusty seemed restless.

Jim took a moment and then answered, "At least once day."

That was all Rusty needed to hear to confirm his suspicions. "I hate to cut this short, but I need to be closing up shop for the night." He grabbed the keys from the drawer.

"Oh, my bad. No problem, man. Let me get some wine for Laura, and I'll be on my way," he said.

Rusty grabbed the closest bottle and handed it to him. "Here you go! My treat. Enjoy."

"Are you sure?" Jim pulled out his wallet from the back pocket of his jeans.

Rusty held up his hand, "I insist. Put away your money, and get on home. Your wife is probably wondering where you are."

Jim shook his hand. "Thanks. I'll see you soon."

The door hadn't been shut two seconds before Rusty was calling Piper. The obvious connection between Laura and Beth could not be ignored. Rusty paced impatiently back and forth as her phone rang, and rang, and rang. As soon as it clicked over to voicemail, he hung up. Instead, he sent her an urgent text asking her to call him. Afterwards, he slipped his phone into his pocket and proceeded to lock up. Five minutes later he was in his car on his way home. At a red light, he was about to check for messages, but then thought better of texting and driving. By the time he made it home, he was beyond antsy. A quick look at his phone confirmed Piper had yet to respond. Once again, he messaged her, and then decided to call it a night. He surmised she was probably fast asleep. What he needed to tell her would have to wait until morning. He wouldn't dare risk waking his sleeping beauty from a peaceful slumber. Instead, he collapsed on his comfy leather couch, and eventually fell fast asleep watching reruns of his favorite television show.

Around five o'clock in the morning, Piper opened her eyes to a darkened room. Her anxiousness for what lay ahead had resulted in a fitful night of sleep. Tucked under her warm covers, she allowed the gentle pitter patter of raindrops to temporarily lull her back to sleep. Her much desired rest was interrupted two hours later by the kneading of two insistent paws on her chest. Opening her eyes, she was greeted by a soft, "Mew."

Ralph the cat summoned her presence. It was time for him to eat.

Out of habit, Piper reached for her mobile phone on the bedside table only to come up empty-handed. Then it dawned on her. She'd lost it somewhere in her travels the previous night. Whether it happened at the library or the sandwich shop, she wasn't certain. When she checked the library's website for hours of operation before going to bed, she had learned that on Tuesdays, the branch didn't open until one o'clock. This didn't help her cause. With no other option, she'd have to go to the club without her trusty phone which meant no e-mail alerts and no access to texts.

On her way to the kitchen with a hungry feline mewing at her heels, she thought about giving Rusty a call to ask him for help in locating her phone. A quick glance at the clock made her think better of it. Realizing how early it was, she decided to touch base with him later on once she arrived at the club. After indulging Ralphie with a special morning treat of canned food, she helped herself to a Greek yogurt and a glass of orange juice. On her iPad, she was able to make a quick scroll through her inbox while finishing her quick breakfast. Luckily, no messages warranted an urgent reply. She decided to send Rusty a brief e-mail just in case he checked his account. She knew he preferred texting, but that wasn't an option for her.

Her morning beauty routine normally took over an hour, but due to the inclement weather, Piper opted for a sleek ponytail hidden underneath a cute pink baseball cap. Peering out the bedroom window she surmised the rain had stopped for now, although the forecast on the local news channel was for mid-morning showers. *Humidity is not my friend*, she thought. To be prepared, she threw some straightening serum and a flatiron in her bucket purse for the après-match luncheon. With a kiss good-bye to Ralph, she was off to the club. Along the way, she tried to come up with some feasible excuses for engaging Beth in a conversation. There were only so many drinks she could order at the bar at nine o'clock in the morning. She had to somehow trick Beth into divulging the identity of the blogger without becoming totally inebriated.

Upon her arrival, she spotted Danielle's convertible in its usual spot. Parked two cars from hers was Carolyn's sports car. Most likely she and Candy had carpooled for the event. It was a known fact that Carolyn's penchant for going green only came into play when it involved saving her money. Across the aisle, Piper noticed Tanya's pick-up truck. A quick view of the area confirmed Laura, Penelope, and Janie in attendance. *Let the games begin,* she thought as she lugged her clubs from the trunk of her car.

It was impossible to ignore the looming black clouds hovering low over the clubhouse as if they were an omen of bad things to come. If it weren't for the picturesque view of the course's glistening greens, Piper might have turned right around and driven back home. While walking towards the pro shop, Piper struggled to balance the clubs on one shoulder with the monstrosity of a purse on her other.

"Looks like you could use a hand," said a voice from behind.

Piper tilted her head to the right just enough to catch a glimpse of Marc. His sudden presence caused her to stumble.

"Wow! Let me grab those clubs for you, Piper," he insisted.

In this case, she wasn't in a position to refuse. "Thank you." She handed them over.

Marc adjusted the strap accordingly and then hoisted the clubs on his shoulder. "Think the weather is going to hold out for you today?"

"Hope so," is all she said in response. Since his presence was summoned under false pretenses, Piper decided to forego any lengthy conversation for fear of compromising her plan. Instead, Piper kept pace with his stride as they swiftly neared the pro shop. Jay must have been on high alert because as soon as he spotted them, he scurried inside to assume his assigned position. Once they arrived, Marc graciously set her clubs down in the rack outside the shop's door. Before he had a chance to speak, Piper politely thanked him and then scooted in the opposite direction leaving him standing alone. Piper slyly glanced back and witnessed him shrugging his shoulders in confusion. She didn't wait to see if he entered the building. She just assumed he would. Her sigh of relief said it all. One potential glitch had been avoided.

Convened around the tee box was a gaggle of golfing groupies waiting for the start of the competition. The inclement weather kept the old-timers at home leaving the younger crowd to brave the elements. Each lady dressed in rain appropriate gear adding her own signature flair to the outfit. Of course, Danielle's addition of a designer scarf looked oh so chic compared to Tanya's frumpy oversized waterproof jacket; however, if the skies opened up as predicted, the jacket would prove to be the better choice.

Piper said hello en masse preferring not to dole out any individualized greetings to the group assembled. She wanted the option to follow-up with a one-on-one later on, if need be, without drawing undue attention. She noticed Laura shying away from her which seemed rather odd. Most times, Laura clung to her like a lost puppy in search of a home. Piper nudged herself between Danielle and Carolyn who were debating whether the rain would hold off. This topic would most likely monopolize the majority of conversations that morning. Luckily, Piper was saved from listening to the chances of stormy weather when Gabe the assistant golf pro suddenly appeared.

"Ladies," he began. "The forecast doesn't look too good for this morning."

"As if that was news," mocked Danielle. A few ladies giggled at her snide comment.

"With that said," Gabe shot Danielle a disapproving glare, "we're going to tee-off ahead of schedule. If everyone could please man your carts, and then proceed to your designated hole as quickly as possible, we can begin play. Cart path only please due to last night's rain. The greens are too soft to be driven on today. We don't want any damage done to the course. *If* for some reason you don't know where you should be going, please come see me. I have the list right here. If you don't like which hole you have been assigned, take it up with Jay later on. I had nothing to do with it. Please pay attention while playing. If I sound the horn, you must seek shelter immediately. We don't want anyone getting hurt. Any questions?"

The ladies shook their heads no, and then meandered to the carts amid complaints regarding the cart path only rule. Having to leave the cart parked on the path meant they'd have to walk extra steps to each hole. Extra steps equated to more energy exerted throughout the day. On paper, they belonged to the Ladies Nine Hole group for the love of the game. In actuality, they were really only interested in gossip and lunch. Sure, burning a few bonus calories was always a plus; however, not when it involved the possibility of ruining a perfectly fresh face of makeup.

Danielle and Piper chose to ride together simply because Carolyn and Janie had already commandeered the lead cart. The foursome was assigned the fourth hole. Its close proximity to the restrooms on the fifth hole was essential should the rain begin to fall. The ladies buzzed around the cart path and landed at the tee box in good time. Piper volunteered to keep score in spite of the obvious displeasure of the other three. To make things easier, they decided to play in alphabetical order. Carolyn strutted her way to the green swinging her driver haphazardly in the air.

"That's a mighty swing you have there," Danielle commented. "You could cause a lot of damage with that club of yours."

Oh, you did not just say that, Piper thought.

A sinister smile crept across Carolyn's face. "Don't you know it, my dear friend." Carolyn leaned over and inserted her tee into the plush grass. Gently she placed her yellow golf ball atop the white tee.

Piper watched as the two eyed one another. Something was definitely going on between these childhood schoolmates, yet Piper couldn't figure out exactly what.

The thick clouds appeared to be closing in as Carolyn beamed a straight shot into the fairway. Picking up her tee, she said to no one in particular, "It must be hard for you without Gus in your life anymore. So much has changed."

Janie looked nervously at Danielle.

"Are you speaking to me?" Danielle asked as she approached the green with her club in hand.

The two friends were face-to-face. "Who else would I be talking to?" asked Carolyn.

Piper held her breath as the two women simultaneously turned around and stared at Janie.

"Am I up?" Janie placed a trembling hand on her golf bag in search of a club.

"Not yet, dear. Be patient. You wouldn't want to step on Danielle's toes," Carolyn retorted as she walked to the cart to return the club to her bag.

Janie's arm dropped to her side.

Carolyn continued. "What do you miss the most about him? His smile? His laughter?"

Danielle set her tee in the ground and then situated her white gold ball firmly on top. "It's hard to say. Janie, what do you miss most about Gus?" She stood with her hand on her hip waiting for Janie to speak.

Piper moved closer to Janie for fear of missing her response.

Janie fidgeted with her skort. "I, um...well, I...." was all she could say.

"Why him?" Danielle demanded. She slammed her club in the ground.

"What do you mean?" Being coy didn't suit Janie one bit.

Danielle walked right up to her with the club held firmly in hand. "It was bad enough that my husband was cheating on me, but with my own friend? You humiliated me!"

As if on cue, the skies opened up and the rain began to fall.

Janie tried to back away. "I never meant for it to happen."

Danielle inched closer to her. "Why did you ask Piper to kill him?"

"What?" Piper shouted. "I did *not* kill Gus!" she bellowed.

"Be quiet," Carolyn insisted, "Let her continue."

Janie threw the hood of her jacket over her head. "You're insane. I had nothing to do with Gus's murder. How dare you insinuate that I did!" Janie looked hurt.

Carolyn came up beside Danielle in show of support. "Then who did?"

All three ladies looked at Piper.

"Oh, for crying out loud." Piper shook her head. The raucous sound of the bullhorn interrupted their conversation. "Time to take cover!"

All four ladies hurriedly put away their clubs and then zipped up their golf bags. Carolyn went ahead and flipped up the windshields on both carts to help deflect the pelting raindrops. As soon as they were seated in the carts, they took off for the clubhouse. It was a given they weren't going to wait out the storm on the greens. At that point, golf was the last thing on their mind. Evidently, they weren't the only ones who called it a day. Tanya's foursome was already parked under the awning. As they scrambled to collect their belongings, the intensity of the rain picked up.

"Just leave your clubs where they are and get inside," Gabe shouted. The man was completely drenched. "There's a terrible storm heading our way."

While the ladies clamored to make it through the doors, tempers were already flaring inside. Assembled on the opposite end of the building was an eclectic group of men: Marc, Tom, Jim, Jack, Ed, Don, and Chad. Each was questioning Jay as to the reason for their presence in the board room. Jay's ability to keep them occupied was waning. First, he told them the board had requested they come. Next, he said there was an issue with their memberships. Tom did his best to help the cause, but he couldn't be too cooperative or it would blow his cover. Luckily, the sudden hailstorm pounding on the windows produced a much-needed reprieve from the business at hand. Like men do, they checked their weather apps only to discover that a tornado watch was in effect. *How appropriate,* Jay thought.

Since Jay was the manager-on-duty, it was his responsibility to secure the building and make sure everyone was safe, a daunting task for a nervous Nellie like him. He opted to take the easy way out by literally calling for reinforcements. "I'll be right back," he explained to the men. He rushed out of the room before they could object. Hidden in a storage closet, he dialed Rusty's number. "There's a tornado watch," Jay swore under his breath over the phone.

"I know," Rusty answered. "I've been trying to call Piper all morning to warn her."

"Oh, she told me to tell you that she lost her phone, but I didn't have time to call you. All hell is breaking loose here at the club," Jay informed him.

"Thanks for the heads-up about the phone," Rusty replied sarcastically.

"No problem." His sardonic tone went undetected by Jay. "Where are you? I need help." The high pitch of his voice betrayed his apprehension.

"I just finished breaking my mother's toilet," Rusty said. "It's a mess. If I do say so myself, I did a helluva job."

Jay was confused by his commentary. "Oh, okay. I guess that's a good thing. Congrats, man on trashing your mom's john."

Rusty considered reminding Jay that it was all part of the plan to lure Captain Morgan over to her house in order to keep him away from the club, but chose not to waste his breath on such details. Instead, he had bigger issues to deal with right now.

"So what's going on?" Rusty needed the facts.

Jay said, "Well, I'm hiding in a storage closet so no one hears me."

"I know, you idiot! Where's Piper? And, have you seen Laura?" Rusty's curtness spurred Jay back to action.

"Oh, right. Piper and the ladies are making their way from the pro shop to the bar area. It's my job to make sure everyone is safe and secure seeing as *I am* the MOD today. Remind me. For a tornado warning, we're supposed to go to the second floor and fill the bathtubs with water, right? Since we don't have a second floor or bathtubs, should I just fill the bathroom sinks? We have lots of them. Should we sandbag the building? On second thought, probably not. I don't want to pull my back again. Do you think we'll lose power? I may have some flashlights around here somewhere. The grounds crew was playing flashlight tag after hours last week. They let me join in on the fun. Have you ever played? Rusty? Rusty, are you still there?" Jay shouted into the phone.

Rusty's lack of patience led him to explode, "Are you kidding me? It's not a hurricane, Jay. It's a freaking tornado. Check your manual. There's a big difference. We live out in the middle of nowhere surrounded by cornfields. I know you're from the East Coast, but somewhere along the line you must've heard of a tornado. There's no flooding involved here, man. Just lots of rain and wind. Get everyone away from the windows now! Maybe put them in the bathrooms and the storerooms since those are the most inner rooms of the building. There's no time to lose. The tornado might be headed straight for the club. And, whatever you do, keep an eye on Piper. I'm on my way!"

"Sir, yes sir!" Jay saluted even though Rusty was not there.

"Whatever," Rusty groaned, and then ended the call.

A double knock on the door startled Jay as he was securing his phone in his pants pocket. Jay cracked it open just wide enough to find Piper's quizzical face staring right back at him.

"Answer me something. Whatcha doing?" Piper twitched her lips. "You do know there's a tornado watch, right? The rain has stopped, and there's an eerie calm outside."

Jay laughed it off as purely nonsensical. "Well, duh! That's why I'm in the closet. Checking for supplies."

"Open the door, you ninny!" she yelled.

Jay did as he was told.

"Okay. So if you insist on sticking to that kooky story, I'll just leave you be. I have a criminal to catch." Piper turned to walk away.

Jay clutched her jacket in desperation, "Don't go! I have no clue what I'm doing!"

Piper tilted her head to the side, "Shocker!"

Jay threw his hands up in the air in a frantic plea for help.

Piper took pity on her chum. "First off, get the heck out of the closet." She tugged him forward causing him to spill into her arms. Stepping back from her embrace, Jay smoothed down the material on his shirt.

"You look fine," Piper insisted as she fixed his collar. Nice shirt, by the way."

Jay boasted, "Forty percent off online *and* free shipping."

"Score," Piper expressed approval of his thrifty purchase. "Anyway, you need to get everyone in an inside room and far away from the windows. Pronto."

Jay's voice squealed, "That's exactly what Rusty said, minus the pronto."

"You spoke to Rusty? When?" Piper questioned.

"Uh, yeah. He's on his way. I told him about you losing the phone." Leaving out the timeframe of that said conversation was a deliberate move to avoid another scolding from a friend.

"Oh, thanks, Jay. I can always count on you." Piper gave him a big hug.

Jay breathed a sigh of relief.

"By the way, whatever happened to that supposed mystery package for Gus?" Piper inquired. The severity of the weather took a backseat for the moment.

Jay raised his eyebrows. "Good question. I've scoured this place, but no luck finding it. Maybe there never was an actual package after all. Perhaps the killer just made it up."

"You may be right. He or she could have used that ploy to lure him here," Piper conceded.

"Lure who?" asked Danielle.

Piper and Jay twirled around.

"How long have you been standing there?" Piper barked.

"Whoa, calm down," insisted Danielle, "long enough to know that you two are up to no good. Perhaps you could put aside your sleuthing activities for the time being and come help with the others before a tornado blows this building to smithereens."

"Of course." Piper nudged Jay.

"I'm assuming you read the latest Carpool Chatter, and now you two are trying to decipher that cryptic message," Danielle declared.

Piper and Jay just looked at each other.

"By the way, how did your interview go with Denise Halbreath?" Danielle couldn't help but ask. "Carolyn told me it was quite the busy night at the library. First, she bumped into you. Always a pleasure is what she said. Then, she had her brief interview. I hate to be the one to tell you, but Carolyn says she's a shoo-in for the position. Then, on her way out the door she practically knocked Laura over."

"Excuse me," interrupted Piper. "Think of it this way. At least you tried. You didn't really think Denise Halbreath would recommend you, did you, dear?" Danielle empathized with her.

"Oh, hush, Danielle. I could care less about that position right now. What do you mean she practically knocked Laura over?" Piper wanted to know.

"Exactly that. Carolyn accidentally bumped into Laura, and her stack of books went flying out of her hands. Who knew reading could be so dangerous?" Danielle joked.

"What kind of books?" Piper persisted.

"Funny you should ask. Carolyn did think it was rather odd that Laura would be reading up on websites and blogging. She doesn't strike us as the intelligent type. Maybe she's thinking of starting a new career or something," Danielle surmised.

All of a sudden, everything clicked. "What time did you say the Carpool Chatter posted?"

Danielle looked confused. "Why are you asking me? I thought you two were discussing it when I interrupted your conversation."

"Right, that's right," established Jay. "But do you remember what time it posted? I forget."

Piper whispered, "He's not the sharpest tack."

Jay nodded his head in agreement.

"See what I mean?" Piper pointed to him.

At that moment, the tornado siren sounded.

"We need to take cover. Now!" Danielle panicked as she ran in the opposite direction.

Then it dawned on Piper. "It's Laura. How could I have missed that?"

"Of course, she's the blogger," Jay confirmed. "She hates your guts."

"Thanks for pointing that out," Piper scoffed.

"And, that husband of hers has been feeding her the information straight from Rusty's mouth. You told him to stay clear of Jim. He's nothing but…"

It all clicked. Piper gasped. "…a killer. Jim killed Gus. She's covering for her husband."

The shrill of the siren was deafening.

"Ya think?" Jay shouted. He wasn't so sure.

"It makes perfect sense. Gus and Jim probably had a disagreement over something with the opening of Peeps & Petals. Things got heated. Then, wham! Jim slugged him with a golf club."

The two paused for a moment to look outside. A green hue covered the sky, and then all stood still.

"C'mon." Jay grabbed hold of her. "We have to find Rusty and tell him before we all blow away!"

The crowd inside the clubhouse was scurrying in search of a safe place to bunker down. The direction of the wind changed, signaling ripe conditions for a tornado. As predicted by Jay, the power did go out leaving everyone in the dark. As Piper and Jay made their way towards the barroom, they were separated by the pushing and pulling of the crowd. Despite the spooky calm outdoors, inside it was a scene of pure mayhem. Out of nowhere, a hand grabbed Piper's arm dragging her along for the ride. Piper clenched her purse as she passed through an obvious doorway and entered another room. From the smell of the air, she surmised it was the women's locker room. The poor ventilation led to an overpowering scent of baby powder and perfume.

"What's going on?" Piper demanded.

"I'm trying to save your life," Danielle claimed. "Why? I'm not so sure myself. Just go with it."

Piper jerked her arm from Danielle's firm grasp. "I appreciate your generosity, but must you cut off my circulation in the process?" She vigorously rubbed her arm to restore the blood flow.

Danielle led Piper deeper into the locker room. Insulated from the noise, they were able to hear themselves think. Thoughts of the potential tornado wreaking havoc on the club sent chills up their spines.

"It pains me to say so, but I think it's best if we brace ourselves against the shower stall walls," Danielle suggested. The distinctive sound of the door swooshing open and then being bolted shut caused her to pause.

"Hello?" asked a familiar voice. "Anyone in here?"

"Beth?" Piper asked.

"Oh, shoot me now," Danielle grumbled. "I'd rather take my chances with the tornado than hunker down with Beth, of all people. I'm outta here." Danielle tried to leave but was thwarted by Piper's refusal to get out of her way.

"Not so fast," Piper countered. The two were standing face-to-face in the unnerving dark. "You brought me in here. You're staying put. Just be quiet and play nice."

The ladies could hear the click of Beth's heels on the tile floor as she made her way towards their direction.

"I mean it. I have no idea what your problem is with Beth but frankly right now I don't give a damn, excuse my language. We have bigger problems to deal with than personality conflicts." Piper spun Danielle around and pushed her towards the shower stalls. Taking a few steps in the opposite direction, she called out to Beth, "Danielle and I are near the back. Follow the sound of my voice. Watch your step. Is the tornado headed our way? Is Rusty in the building? What's going on?"

"Sorry, Piper, but I have no clue if he's here. It's pitch black in the hallways," Beth offered as she approached the two. "Where are we?" She grabbed hold of Piper's arm.

Piper volunteered, "The sinks are to our left. If we take about four steps to the right, we'll be in the shower area."

"Let's do that," Beth insisted. "We'll be safer in there. We probably don't have much time left." She didn't wait for a response. Leading them in that direction, the ladies found themselves brushing up against a shower curtain. Danielle gave Beth one extra push, just because she could.

"Ouch! Not so hard," Beth whined.

"Easy does it." Piper was doing her best to play peacemaker between the frenemies. She hoped safety in numbers would bring a feeling of calm to the room.

"Which stall is this?" Danielle needed to know. Her husband had met his maker in this very spot.

"Why would it matter?" Beth quipped back.

An eerie feeling suddenly came over Piper similar to that haunting moment when she had discovered Gus's body. Something just wasn't right.

"I think it's the third one. Too bad you can't see it, Piper. The curtain is drawn shut just like last time you were here," Beth volunteered.

Piper gasped. The only reason Beth would know that the curtain had been drawn was if she had killed Gus herself. But, why? This made no sense.

"What's the matter? What happened?" Danielle's voice quivered.

"Oh, shut up, Danielle. I'm sick and tired of listening to that grating voice of yours," Beth hissed.

Piper chimed in, "Let's just stay calm, ladies. No need to get testy with one another." Piper was frantically grasping for ideas on how to avert a potentially deadly situation with an irrational killer on her hands paired with a dangerous tornado mere moments away. It was safe to say this scenario was not one she and Rusty, or Jay for that matter, had rehearsed. From the tone of Beth's voice, the woman was a loose cannon just waiting to fire. Piper had to come up with an escape plan quickly without letting Beth know she was on to her.

Piper secured her purse against her body and gently took hold of Danielle's arm while whispering, "Shh! Follow me."

"Praise, Jesus, we're getting out of here. I couldn't take another minute with her!" Danielle announced.

So much for the quiet approach.

"You two are going nowhere!" Beth announced. She took hold of the shower curtain and whipped it to one side. "Sit down on the cold floor. I'm in charge now."

By that point, Danielle had had enough. "I'll do no such thing. Who do you think you are?"

Beth's sinister gurgle sent shivers down Piper's spine. "Finally, you ask. I'm Lacey Barnes' sister. Name rings a bell?"

Then it was Danielle's turn to gasp.

Piper butted in, "Who's Lacey Barnes?"

"Was," corrected Beth. "Who *was* Lacey Barnes?"

Piper sensed an opportunity to wiggle towards direction of the exit. She pulled Danielle along for the ride while she engaged Beth in a conversation. "Fine. Dare I ask? Who was Lacey Barnes?"

"Gus's second wife," Danielle stated rather sheepishly.

"Oh, no," declared Piper.

Beth took a step closer. "I'm surprised you remembered her name."

Piper was in the middle of scooting a few more inches when suddenly the lights came on. The crazed look in Beth's eyes caused the ladies to panic. Time was not their friend.

"Sit back down," she yelled. "The only person leaving this room alive is me."

Piper and Danielle exchanged worried glances. With nothing to lose, Piper said, "Why did you kill him?"

Danielle sat by listening as she fumbled with something in her pocket.

Beth shook her head. "Why wouldn't I? He destroyed my sister's life. When Gus found out she had cancer, he was out the door and hopping right into her bed." She pointed at Danielle.

In her defense, Danielle replied, "That's not entirely true. Gus was there for Lacey, but she turned him away. You don't know all the facts, Beth. Her last wish was for Gus to be happy."

"Yeah, right." Beth protested.

"The press portrayed Gus as a mean, cruel man when in actuality, Lacey could have set the record straight had she so desired. I know this is hard for you to hear, but Lacey wanted him to move on with his life," Danielle claimed. "She was a selfless person, unlike you."

Piper rolled her eyes. Clearly those were not the words she would have used.

"Shut up! Don't you even breathe my sister's name, you home wrecker! My sister suffered, and now you're going to pay for Gus's sins!" Beth leaned into the second shower stall and pulled out a familiar golf club.

Piper took it as her cue to intervene. "But I don't understand, Beth. How does Laura fit into this picture? Was she your accomplice?"

Beth began pacing back and forth as she tapped the head of the club in palm of her hand. "I knew you'd ask, Piper. You can't stand her, can you?" she snickered.

Not one for mincing words, Piper replied, "Nope."

"The feeling is mutual. That's why she was the perfect choice to pen the Carpool Chatter." Beth rubbed it in.

This piqued Danielle's interest. "Really? I didn't peg her as being that intelligent or witty. I'm kinda impressed with her literary skills."

Once again, Piper rolled her eyes.

"I'll be sure to tell her so," Beth offered. "Piper, your so-called boyfriend was the perfect source for news. You should have told him to keep his mouth shut rather than sharing your business with Jim."

"He always was a big gossiper," Danielle added.

Beth nodded her head, "No doubt."

"Well, at least you two can agree on something, even if it is at my expense," Piper huffed. "So, does Laura know you killed Gus?"

Beth smirked, "Hell no. She's not that smart. I just told her I had an easy way to make you look like the town fool without anyone knowing. She jumped right on it."

"How kind of you," Piper sneered.

Beth's voluntary admission of guilt was interrupted by a rapid knock on the locker room door. The loud sound reverberated in the confined area causing Danielle to jump to her feet.

"Maybe someone has come to find us," shouted Danielle. Piper moved close to her side.

"What part of sit down and shut up don't you two understand?" Beth's threatening tone did little to deter them as they shuffled closer to the door.

"See this golf club?" Beth waved it in the air like a crazy woman. "I'm gonna crash your skulls in just like I did to Gus, except this time I'll get two for the price of one."

Feeling brazen, Danielle pulled her iPhone out from her pocket and held it up in front of Beth's face. "Would you mind repeating that one more time? You kind of garbled your words."

"What the hell?" Beth shouted.

Piper took a step back. For once, she had no problem not being the center of attention.

"Piper's not the only one who knows how to play detective. I recorded our entire conversation including *your* heartfelt confession. Totally illegal, I know, but quite effective. Perhaps you should have heeded your own advice and kept your mouth *fermez*. That means closed in French by the way. Captain Morgan is going to be thrilled when he hears it," she declared. "Just give me a moment while I figure out how to forward it to him." Danielle's Cheshire smile caused Beth to react. Armed with the golf club, she whipped it back behind her head in an attempt to strike.

Suddenly, the locker room door flew open and in ran Jay. "The tornado has passed," he announced oblivious as to what was going on. "What's with the golf club?" he pointed at Beth who had the club poised to swing.

With only seconds to react, Piper reached into her mammoth purse and withdrew her concealed weapon. In one fell swoop, she knocked Beth out cold with a blow to her head. Collapsed in a heap on the cold tile floor, the three of them stood there staring at Beth's motionless body.

"Piper! What did you just do?" Jay shook his head in disbelief with his hands up in the air.

"Believe it or not, here lies Gus's murderer," Piper proudly declared.

Jay glanced at Beth in total disarray. "Really?"

"Yes, really!" Piper clapped her hands in delight. "She totally confessed!"

"You did it!" Jay leaned over and gave Piper a big congratulatory hug. Then naturally, the two quirky friends grasped hands and jumped up and down in pure joy.

"Excuse me." Danielle tapped Piper on the shoulder. "Correction. *We* did it."

"Oh, right. I forgot about that," Piper grinned.

"Um, Piper. Is that a flatiron you're holding in your hand?" Danielle looked totally confused.

Piper couldn't help but laugh. "Yes, Danielle. Indeed it is. I'm always armed with protection. From frizzy hair to crazy kooks, you never know when a flatiron might come in handy."

"Only you," chuckled Jay. "Only you, Piper O'Donnell."

Hole 19

The Bar

It took some time before Captain. Morgan made his way to the club. Between the toilet fiasco at Helen's and the destruction from the near-miss tornado, he was overwhelmed with responsibilities. Rusty commandeered the situation and moved Beth away from the mob amid curious stares from gossiping housewives. Danielle resumed her role as the mournful widow savoring the attention from friends and even foes as she recounted the series of events that brought her husband's killer to justice. Upon Captain Morgan's arrival, Piper was more than happy to fill him in concerning Beth's voluntary confession while making a point to mention Laura's indirect involvement. Yet his refusal to arrest Laura on the spot caused Piper much disappointment. Being a class act, Captain Morgan opted to have one of his junior officers escort Beth out the back exit while reading her rights. He was trying his best to prevent the scene from turning into a three-ring circus.

At the bar, Jay recounted Piper's heroic rescue to a modest assemblage. Since he wasn't privy to all the details, Jay slightly embellished here and there to give his version a more dramatic flair. Piper neither confirmed nor denied his colorful interpretation since if it wasn't for him, things may have turned out much differently.

As expected, Piper dragged Rusty along to confront Laura who vehemently denied any involvement whatsoever with Gus's murder. Rusty was taken aback when Piper didn't push any further. When they walked away, she whispered in his ear that she'd allow Captain Morgan the pleasure of investigating the case without any more interference. She was tired of playing detective. Rusty couldn't help but laugh, and then assured her justice would be served.

Huddled at a corner table, Marc, Jack, and Chad beckoned for Piper and Rusty to join them. A carafe of wine and two pitchers of beer lured them to the table. Once drinks were poured, the conversation began to flow.

"Congratulations, Piper!" Chad raised his glass for a toast as the others followed suit. "Who knew one little flatiron could cause so much damage." Everyone laughed in response.

"Speaking of which," Rusty said, "how is the reconstruction going?"

Chad took a sip of his beer. "Well, Jim Wagner has been very instrumental in getting the building permits approved, so believe it or not, we're a little ahead of schedule. If we keep moving at this pace, we should be open in plenty of time for the holidays."

"Does that mean…" Piper hesitated.

"Yes," Chad replied. "If you're still interested, you may have your old job back."

Piper squealed, "Thank you!" She leaned over and gave him a hug.

Chad continued, "As long as you promise to stay clear of any electrical appliances."

"Deal!" Piper raised two fingers. "Scout's honor."

Despite being grateful for the opportunity to resume her position at Peeps & Petals, Piper still had a burning desire to find out who was behind the financial backing of the club. "Was Gus responsible for helping you skirt the political red tape in order to open your strip club?"

Rusty choked on his drink.

Chad was taken aback by her candor. "Um, I guess we'll never know. Only he can answer that question, Piper. I'm just looking forward to the reopening."

Rusty came to her aid by quickly changing the subject. "So, are both you men looking forward to duking it out in the political boxing ring?" He pretended to box with his fists. "The election will be here before you know it."

Marc was the first to speak up. "As a matter of fact, I've decided to withdraw my petition." Marc and Jack shared a private nod.

Piper was flabbergasted by the news. "Really? What made you change your mind?"

A voice from behind said, "Not what, but who." Piper turned around to find Candy standing behind her chair.

"Candy, I didn't know you were standing there. Please join us." Rusty pulled a chair over to the table to allow Candy into the circle. She elected to sit in Marc's lap instead.

Piper raised her eyebrows at Rusty. This latest development put a whole new spin on the things. Lest they forget, just days ago they both had been accusing each other of murder.

Marc draped his arms around Candy's waist. "When Jack, Candy, and I were hunkered down together in the kitchen, it gave us plenty of time to sort out our issues. Jack, here, is the best choice to fill Gus's seat, not me. He'll do a fine job as our state representative."

"Really?" Piper repeated.

Marc nodded his head.

"So, what are you going to do instead?" asked Chad. He signaled Gabe at the bar to bring another round of drinks.

Marc smiled. "For starters, I want to publically apologize for accusing Candy of being involved with Gus's murder."

Candy replied, "Apology accepted. Ditto for me." She gave him a friendly peck on the cheek.

Marc continued, "And then, I'm going to concentrate on being the best county council president Woodlawn has ever seen."

Neither Candy nor Marc addressed the future of their relationship, platonic or otherwise, leaving the others curious as to which path they would eventually follow. After a couple of drinks and some innocent banter, they left the club hand in hand. As for Jack, he excused himself from the table to head home to check for storm damage. Chad followed suit, crossing his fingers that the preliminary structure at Peeps & Petals would be safe and sound.

With a beer in his hand, Rusty said, "I want to propose..."

"No more toasts, big man. I'm too tired to raise my glass," Piper sighed. "Why don't we just head on home?" Piper leaned over and grabbed her purse from the floor. "Did you see what happened to my poor flatiron?" She held up the broken instrument. "I ought to submit a bill to Captain Morgan."

Rusty sat perfectly quiet and still.

Piper scrunched up her nose. "A bit much? I thought so." She returned her favorite styling tool to her purse.

He didn't respond.

Piper tilted her head to the side. "What's the matter? I was only kidding. I know I should send the bill to Beth and not Captain Morgan. It was her thick skull that shattered it into three pieces."

Not a word or even a comment from Rusty.

It was then that she noticed he had something hidden in his hand.

"Rusty? Why aren't you talking? Are you drunk?" Before she had a chance to question him further, Rusty got down on one knee. Now it was Piper's to remain silent.

"My original plan was to propose to you at the Member-Member party, but that didn't turn out to be the most opportune time. And, with all the chaos surrounding Gus's murder and the stress with the Carpool Chatter blogger's posts, there never seemed to be a good time," he explained.

Piper didn't answer.

Beads of perspiration gathered on Rusty's brow. "Now, I know things haven't been the best between us lately, but no relationship is ever perfect."

Piper gently placed her hands on her lap.

Rusty continued, "But if there is one thing I know for sure, it's that I couldn't imagine my life without you. Piper O'Donnell, will you marry me?" He flipped open a black velvet box. Sparkling inside was an exquisite pink diamond ring.

Piper gasped bringing her hands to her mouth in sheer disbelief.

Rusty removed the ring from the box and placed it on her neatly manicured finger.

It was at that very tender moment when Captain Morgan and Helen entered the room.

"Finally! We've found you two!" shouted Helen as Captain Morgan pushed her wheelchair over to their table. "I've been calling your cell phone for the last hour or so. I have good news! Judy called. Piper is going to be appointed to the board of trustees!"

It took but a moment for them to realize that they had interrupted an intimate moment. Now it was

Helen's turn to gasp. Captain Morgan immediately spoke up demanding to know Piper's decision.

"Well, sir, I'm still waiting for her answer." Rusty wobbled back and forth on his knee.

Captain Morgan shook his head. "Piper, don't keep the man waiting any longer. Is it a yes or no?"

They all held their breath in anticipation of her response.

Gazing at the rosy promise of a future with the man she truly loved, Piper uttered the words she never thought she'd say. "Captain Morgan. If you play your cards right, it looks like I'm going to be your daughter-in-law one day!"

ABOUT THE AUTHOR

 Jennifer Vido is best known for her nationally syndicated *Jen's Jewels* author interview column. A savvy book blogger for www.MomTrends.com, she dishes the scoop on the latest happenings in the publishing business. As a national spokesperson for the Arthritis Foundation, she has been featured by *Lifetime Television, Redbook, Health Monitor, The New York Times, The Baltimore Sun, Healthguru.com*, and *Arthritis Today*. Her first novel *Par for the Course* was published in 2010. Currently, she lives in the Baltimore area with her husband and two sons. Visit her website at www.jennifervido.com and follow her on Twitter @JenniferVido.

www.ingramcontent.com/pod-product-compliance
Lightning Source LLC
Chambersburg PA
CBHW050404260626
47156CB00003B/863